# A Week With No Labels

CALLY PHILLIPS

Published by Guerrilla Midgie Press

ISBN: 978-1-908933-00-3

This title is also available as an ebook
in both Kindle and epub formats

# DEDICATION

*'You'll laugh, you'll cry, it's better than Cats!'*

*(a recycled quote)*

For John, Larry, Marlene and all the wonderful people
I've worked with – you know who you are.

And to anyone who has ever been given a label.

Throw it off, you are so much more

# BEFORE WE BEGIN

*What you need to know*

NO LABELS is a fictional drama group. I have worked for 10 years with a 'real' drama group run 'for and by' adults labelled with learning disabilities and many of the experiences fictionalized here happened to us. Many didn't. But in this story I am a fictional character too! If there is any resemblance to real people in these fictional characters I'd say it's only the good bits which are 'real', I've made up the bad bits!

Each of the 'days' in this series represents a specific period of time (more than a day) in the life of the fictional group.

*About Boalian drama.*

**NO LABELS** owes a debt of great gratitude to Boalian Theatre of the Oppressed /Forum Theatre method which has been liberally adapted to suit the particular circumstances of a creatively anarchic bunch of people.

*Meet the team.*

Our cast of characters remains constant throughout the books so you might as well get to know them here: Here are some thumbnail sketches, developed from fictional 'hot seating' techniques employed by the group. They want you to know that while they don't have labels, they are 'real' characters. What is a 'real' character? Who knows?

**ANNIE** Is a forty six year old woman NOT a child so please don't treat her as one. She is an excellent natural actress and could give Meryl Streep a run for her money.

**BARRY** Is in his sixties and loves a good drama. He is the leader of the gang and demands the same high level of commitment from others as he puts in himself. Some may say he's a dreamer, but he certainly gets things done

**BILBO** is in his fifties and likes to dance. Oh how he loves to dance. And no, he's not a hobbit. Here's the story. He was christened William Robert. He was known as Billy-Bob by his dad. His brother misheard this and called him Bilbo. The family compromised on Bilbo. It was just a hobbit they got into and it stuck.

**DEIRDRE** Doesn't like being called 'spazzy'. Okay so she's got a 'lazy' arm but that's no reason for abuse. She suffers from tunnel vision (and when she's around it seems to be catching) She likes to read, write and organise others.

**DUNCAN** Is always happy. He loves drama. He plays games his own way and is the joker of the group. Everyone loves Duncan. A man of few words but a comic genius none the less.

**LAUREN** Is a princess. Always a princess. She lives in a world of her own and sometimes she lets us share it. If we're lucky.

**KELLY** Loves birds. And all animals really but birds most of all. She has a very good memory and likes to show it off.

**KATE** That's me. I'm the one who 'writes it down.' My label is 'facilitator.'

**MANDY** Takes everything literally. Everything. Which can get her into a lot of funny situations. And some not so funny ones.

**PAULINE** Is everyone's mum. Her label is 'volunteer.' But she's so much more than that. Often we think she's the glue that holds us all together. She thinks of the important things like biscuits and juice. Like all mums we take her for granted.

**STEVIE** Is in his twenties. He likes colours. He doesn't like talking but he's a whizz at mime. His favourite colour is brown and his favourite texture is crinkly.

# MONDAY

## *Are you sitting comfortably?*

*This is the start of our dramatic journey together. You've had a chance to glance at the cast. But this is where we'll really get acquainted. Get to know each other. Learn something from each other. And most of all – have fun*

So here we are on the Monday morning of our dramatic journey. Dealing with the thorny question of name and identity.

No Labels Drama Group was founded out of an advocacy group run for and by adults who are labelled with 'learning disabilities.' It's a funny label (unless you have it). For a start, it's not a fixed label (unless you have it – because believe me, you can't wash it off). What I mean is that no one can decide whether to call this label:

Learning disability

Learning difficulty

Intellectual disability or the OLD names (which we cannot say out loud now for fear of political incorrectness) which are

Mental retardation or

Mental Handicap.

That's a lot of labels for a 'condition' which is both hard to pin down and covers a broad range of things that can euphemistically be called 'impairments.'

And more importantly I wonder how important the specific 'label' is to the labellee (if such I can call them) because I know that if you can't see you don't give a bugger usually whether you are called blind, visually impaired or a speccy git, what you do care about is how you live your life round the problems that not being able to see gives you. And whether people make your life easier or more difficult. It's not the label that's the most pressing problem. It's the problem – you can't see.

I wonder is this the same with the many labels for those who are considered to be 'challenged' intellectually? Whatever that may mean. Because I look around the room and of the ten other people sitting there I can't really make a pattern, a connection between what each is supposed to have 'wrong' with them. Except that they are labelled. We're all labelled I guess. My label is 'normal' and theirs is 'abnormal' which I find somewhat unjust. I don't think of myself as 'normal' well, actually not until I'm in their company when I feel just 'one of the gang' and as close to being normal (in terms of accepted) as I ever do anywhere. But I digress...

We don't dodge the difficult issues in this group though. We talk about labels. More than once. Often. A lot. For example, this Monday, Barry draws pictures on flip charts and writes up things and (those of us who can read) nod sagely and agree that labels are usually A BAD THING.

We talk about what learning disability means as a label. It isn't a pretty subject. I go round the group, eager to get everyone's individual opinion because in an advocacy situation that seems to be the right and proper thing to do. Give everyone a voice. Even those like Duncan and Lauren who aren't that bothered about people hearing their voice.

To give you a flavour of things, this is what it goes like.

I say, 'so what do the words learning disability mean to you Annie?'

'My nephew has a learning disability,' she replies.

'Does he?'

'Yes, he can't read very well and he gets in trouble at school.'

2

She doesn't seem either to want to talk about whether *she* has a learning disability or not so I leave it at that. I can come back to it. No point upsetting her yet.

'What about you Deirdre,' I ask.

She rubs her glasses with her biscuit-ey fingers,

'Some people have a problem in that they are *not normal*,' she explains. 'They can't read or write and so they have a difficulty. We don't call it disability. We call it difficulty.'

'Okay,' I reply, corrected. 'A difficulty. Is it just reading and writing?'

'*They* call you spazzy,' she says.

'Sorry,' I am bemused. This is a word I've not heard since the primary school playground.

'At school,' she continues, '*They* used to call you spazzy.'

I note that she uses the word 'you' not 'I' in this context. Perhaps significant. I have a qualification in conversation analysis. I know that narrative voice is psychologically important. I decide to probe further. Deirdre can take it.

'So they call you learning disabled, sorry, say that you have a learning disability because you have a bad arm?'

'Yes,' she confirms. 'I can read and write.'

It is clear to me that as far as Deirdre is concerned her 'abnormality' is purely her 'spastic' arm.

'But I have tunnel vision,' she adds.

'But these are really physical disabilities aren't they?' I question, 'not what you'd call a learning disability?'

She looks at me out of her bottle bottom glasses and nods her head, sagely, as if to say, what can you do?

And what can you do? Indeed. Good question Deirdre. I am about to move onto Kelly but she pre-empts me.

'*They* say I have epilepsy. But I don't, she states firmly.

She does. I know she does. I also know it's a source of embarrassment and shame to her and I don't want to make her cry. She cries quite easily. And loudly.

'Is that a learning disability?' I ask. 'I'd think that's another physical condition?'

'*They* are mean,' she says. 'People are just mean. They don't like me.'

'*We* all like you Kelly,' I say and the rest of the group chime in their approval. Annie even says,

'Kelly, you are my *best* friend.'

So, today *Kelly* is Annie's best friend. I can't keep up with her. She has more best friends than... well... than I don't know what. But it is a nice gesture all the same. And shows she's still listening.

We keep on going. I keep hoping I'll find someone who will explain to me what they think the label learning disability actually means. And they probably hope I'll shut up and get on with something more interesting. A game perhaps. Or an early lunch. But I'm relentless. I'm being paid to do a job here. And after all, the group was constituted as a group run 'for and by' people with learning disabilities. It is their label. Why don't they acknowledge it in any way? Or understand what it means? Or is this the ultimate irony? Not having a clear understanding of the label is one way that *They* can suggest that you *need* that label. Except that I don't have a clear understanding of the label either.

(You'll probably hear a lot about *'Them'* and *'They'* in this little journey. We are always up against the invisible force. *They* can be all sorts of things. Watch out for them. *They* pop up at the most inconvenient moments to spoil the fun. )

As expected, there is little joy to be had out of Lauren or Duncan on the subject. When I ask Lauren she simply answers 'Don't know,' which is a good result really. Usually she just says 'sorry.' In fact today she says, 'don't know darling,' which is (according to her 'notes') indicative that she's in a good mood. No wonder, her face still bears the marks of a very messy chocolate biscuit eating frenzy. But she doesn't like wiping her face and Pauline hasn't noticed it yet. So I let it go. Surely it's her right to have a chocolate stained face if she wants. Unless there's a wasp or something around. It is November. There are no wasps.

'Duncan, what do you think a learning disability is?' I ask, determined to give him his right to voice his opinion. Even if that is likely only be 'yes,' 'no,' or 'happy,' which is the extent of his verbal repertoire with questions like this. He doesn't like talking about this sort of thing. He doesn't much like talking. I think it's because he's got a lot more interesting things going on in his head than my stupid questions. That's my theory. Yet to be proven, or disproved.

Silence.

'Does it mean anything to you?' I press. Why? I know he's not going to answer.

Silence.

Okay. It's a question he doesn't want to address. I finally get that message. Fine. I'll leave it.

'Mandy,' what about you? I ask. 'Do you know what learning disability means?'

And her reply makes me want to cry. And gets me angry at the same time.

'*They* call me a vegetable,' she says.

'Who?' I ask. She is distressed.

'Horrid people,' she says, 'Ugly sisters.'

I don't think she's talking in pantomime speak – Mandy is much too literal a person to do that.

'Oh,' I am stumped.

'*They* say I'm a vegetable. That's learning disabled. Not nice.'

I am seriously taken aback. And Mandy is upset. Time to take control.

'Mandy,' I say. 'How can you possibly be a vegetable?'

I call on the group for back up.

'Is Mandy a carrot?' I ask.

'No,' they chorus and laugh.

'She was a broad bean,' Annie says, reminding me of when we did a healthy eating project.

'And she was a red coffee bean,' Kelly says, remembering even before that, when we did a Fair Trade project.

This must be hell for literal Mandy. I explain that that's different because then we were 'pretending' to be vegetables and beans and it's not the same thing.

It does not feel like the time to talk about how calling someone a vegetable is effectively a way of saying that they are brainless and that being brainless might well be a description of a person with a learning disability. In the world that passes for normal. Here it is just exposed as the cruel jibe it is and the harmful consequences are plain to see. Damage limitation comes before explanation.

'You are NOT a vegetable,' I tell Mandy. 'And anyone who calls you that is not just wrong but very rude as well..

'She is a human bean,' laughs Bilbo. 'We are all human beans. Aren't we?'

We all laugh. Good old Bilbo managing to retrieve the situation.

Time to move on.

'It seems to me,' I say 'that most of you don't think that learning disability is a good label?'

'No,' they shout. Even Lauren. Though she shouts 'no, darling,' raucously. Definitely in a good mood today then. Until, in drawing attention to herself, she draws Pauline's attention to her messy face and Pauline, being the good mum-like figure she is to us all, wipes it clean. With a tissue. That takes the shine off Lauren's day, that does. But she withstands it manfully with just a bit of teeth grinding.

'But it also seems to me, that most of you don't seem to know what it actually means to say someone is learning disabled. Am I right? You think it's can't read and write?' I press on.

Bilbo breaks into song (an Adam Ant classic rap) *'Can't read, can't write, what can you do?'*

Which makes everyone laugh. Again.

'Can't see properly,' Annie says, remaining remarkably focussed.

'Can't move around properly,' Deirdre says. She's obviously worked out that I'm going to keep at this till I get the answers I want.

'Wait. Hold the bus, back up the truck' I say. It's part of my trying to teach Mandy not to take things literally. I avoid digressing into 'what bus?' 'what truck?' territory by adding quickly,

'Those are physical disabilities. It's different isn't it? Learning disability?'

'What does it mean then, if you don't mind my asking?' Deirdre asks. She's getting fed up and I don't blame her. This is beginning to seriously drag for all of us. But I need to press on. It's my job.

'Yeah, it's a good question, Deirdre,' I reply. And think but don't say out loud: What exactly is a comfortable definition for the many descriptors of intellectual 'abnormality.'

'Well,' I say. 'I don't know that I understand it properly either.'

What a cop out.

'But do you all know that in this group, this is a group where everyone is given the label of learning disability?'

They mostly nod their heads. Duncan shakes his head, but it is because he is tuned into the humming of the lights. More interesting by far than my wittering. I sympathise, perhaps even agree with him.

'Where's Stevie? asks Bilbo.

'Dentist,' replies Kelly. She lives with Stevie and they usually come in together.

We risk getting off track. We're good at that. I pull us back on track. (Figuratively speaking, Mandy, before you ask what track?)

'So. We are all supposed to be people with a learning disability but no one really knows what that means?'

No one sees a problem with that. Labels. Who needs them? It seems pretty much to me that the consensus of opinion is that now stated by Barry,

'*They* put labels on you,' he says. 'Nothing you can do about it.'

Except ignore it, I think. Which is the 'resistance' strategy that seems most at play here. Unless they are really confused between the physical and mental nature of disabilities.

And because I can't just let well enough alone, can I? I want to make sure that everyone 'understands.' Is this because I don't believe that 'learning disability' means that people just can't understand some things? Am I trying to empower them or just to reinforce my own belief that really they are not 'stupid,' they just need things explained in a way they understand. That it's environmental, a conversational impairment between both parties, not a cognitive impairment on the part of the 'abnormal' partner. Whatever, I keep on going.

'I think that what people mean when they say someone has a learning disability, is that they have a problem thinking,' I say. 'Does that make sense to anyone?'

They look at me, blankly. It was my best shot. But once the words are out of my mouth I realise how stupid they are.

'What I mean is,' I add, 'that if you are labelled as having a visual disability it means you can't see as well as other people. If you have a problem hearing it means you can't hear as well as most people and if you have a learning disability label it means that people think that you don't think as well as other people do.'

I pause, for us all to take in the enormity of the statement. Or even grasp the analogy. And then it hits me. How would you know? How would any of us know if we don't 'think' properly. What does it mean, to think in a 'normal' way? Okay, I know this is what lots of tests are set up to do, to reveal whether people have a 'cognitive impairment' but I also know that Duncan has taken and failed every single one of these tests and that he's actually a very intelligent person. I know that he's been the only audience member to laugh at the subtle jokes in one of my more obscure plays. He laughed, without prompting, in all the right places. He's not stupid. He defies 'labelling.' He just doesn't like tests. And no, he doesn't think like everyone else (though how can we be sure of that, or that we all think alike in any substantial way?) but does this make him learning disabled? Is he unable to 'learn'? And what does that even mean?

You could look forever for a satisfactory, all encompassing definition of Learning Disability and still come up wanting (that says something in and of itself doesn't it?) but here is what the 'general consensus' seems to encompass.

*A learning disability is a reduced intellectual ability and difficulty with everyday activities – for example household tasks, socialising or managing money – which affects someone for their whole life.* (Thank you Mencap)

It is certainly a life-long condition. There's no 'recovery' possible. Somehow, before, during or after birth, while the brain is developing, something doesn't go 'right' in the central nervous system. Or it can be genetic.

Or caused by childhood illness. Do you see that we're moving away from the specific pretty rapidly here?

But the facts are that at some point, usually fairly early on, you get diagnosed with an abnormally developed brain. Impaired cognitive function is at the base of it. According to '*Them*.' They do admit that it's hard to get a diagnosis and that some people might never get an accurate diagnosis (like Duncan) or be diagnosed at all - yes, there are people walking around as 'normal' who may well be 'learning disabled.

How would you know? How do any of us know? What is 'normal' cognitive function? How do we know we think normally? We're going round in circles here. A fact that Mencap is not afraid to state baldly (and how could they avoid it?) is that people labelled with learning disabilities are usually treated as 'different.' That means as 'abnormal.' In some particularly mean contexts (Mandy's ugly sisters for example) a 'vegetable.'

So, to summarise. A learning disability is a diagnosed abnormal development of the brain which cannot be 'put right' and means that the diagnosed (fancy word for labelled) person has difficulty acting 'normally' in a range of everyday situations as a result of impaired thought processes. Easy huh? Now... who is going to buy this one?

'Look,' I say, 'this is the best way I can think to describe it. If being blind means you can't see properly and being deaf means that you can't hear properly, then learning disability means you can't think properly. And you might need some help to do things that require thinking.'

They sit there. Unquestioning. It's what they do. It's turned into schoolroom mode and no one wants to appear stupid. Or no one really cares. What does it matter to them what the justification of the label is. They just have to deal with the consequences. And I haven't got anywhere near the consequences yet. I'm still in the realms of pointless definition.

'So,' I try my trump card to win them over. To make them understand (there's that word again) that I may not 'understand' but I can empathise with their position. (Can I ever possibly empathise with them?) Perhaps in so far as I have always felt outside the label 'normal' too. In my head at any rate. I can pass for 'normal' in everyday social situations and this is what seems to set me apart from Duncan or Stevie or Kelly or Lauren.

'Who thinks that they can't think properly?'

Of course a silence follows. It's a deeply philosophical question. I am using philosophy to show them that there is no such thing as 'normal' and therefore no such thing as 'learning disability.' What a showman. But am I right? I go round the group to prove my point to us all. Of course everyone thinks that they can think properly. How would you know? It's the whole point isn't it? The machine cannot question its construction. Perhaps I'm missing an important point here though. It's to do with 'needing help.' Because when I come down off my philosophical high horse and ask a more sensible question –with ancillary questions – who needs help? (in a range of domestic tasks) I get quite a different answer.

Everyone who ventures an opinion (that means not Duncan or Lauren and not Stevie, who has turned up but not actually joined the group yet, he's too busy going round the room touching everything that is brown) admits (quite happily actually) that they do need help with things like washing and cooking and dealing with money. Now, how many 'normal' people would admit to that? That they need help?

'But,' says Barry, 'We need to be helped how we need to be helped. Not how *They* want to help us.'

Barry does live in a world of conspiracy theories I think, but equally he has a pretty profound point. If you're going to 'help' someone you need to do it the right way. Don't just haul old ladies across the road at will.

Annie knows all about how to get people to 'help' her. And this is where I wonder about exactly what learning 'disability' actually means. 'Divergence' might seem like a better word when you hear this example. Because, as Bilbo has so eloquently put it in the past 'just because I have a learning disability doesn't mean I'm stupid.'

We laugh. Though I think to myself, sadly, Bilbo, that's exactly what it does mean. If you delve deeply enough into the label. But is he stupid, or insightful? Or just divergent?

Back to Annie. This is my best shot for why Annie is not stupid. She is manipulative, cunning and often stubborn, but never, to my mind, stupid. This is Annie's moment.

Annie doesn't have any friends. (Apart from all her 'best' friends of which, today, remember Kelly is one) She lives in independent accommodation and she is lonely a lot of the time. So she goes out to find friends. This is her plan. She stands beside the busy road, usually at traffic lights (she has been taught to cross at the lights – she can learn something then) waving her white stick around. Most of the group have white sticks which seem to function more as a weapon to bat off potential attackers, or indeed to draw attention to their perceived 'infirmity' and thus elicit 'help' from the general public or passer by. It is as such a weapon of infirmity that Annie uses the stick. She can see perfectly well. She can walk perfectly well. She knows that if she walks out into the traffic she will most likely get hit by a car and end up in hospital. She's not stupid. But she wants friends. So, she stands at the traffic lights, waving her stick, acting like she can't walk easily and when someone comes up to the lights she asks them to press the green man button for her. They do so and invariably feel compelled to 'help' her across the crossing. She latches onto their arm. A vice like limpet. And during the length of time it takes them to 'help' her across the road, she becomes their 'friend' engaging them in as much conversation as she can get away with before they finally escape. I know this is true. I've watched her do it. And watched her cross the road simply to stand at the other side and wait for someone to 'help' her back. I'd say Annie has some complex cognitive functions going on there, wouldn't you? Okay, it's not what you'd call 'normal' behaviour, but what it is, is the behaviour of an extremely lonely woman, desperate for human contact. Is this a cognitive or a social problem?

There is a darker side to Annie's antics though. I've seen it for myself. I've nearly been run over by a car trying to prevent it! Irony of ironies. Because sometimes the crossing thing just doesn't work. On those occasions, Annie is not above flinging herself onto the ground by 'tripping' off a kerb, in order to get a person to help her up. I was across the road one day (on my way, as Annie was) to the No Labels meeting, when I saw her do it. I saw her deliberately trip. I saw it. She judged it very carefully (except for not seeing me across the road) so that a passerby would not be able to avoid helping her. I wonder if Annie is familiar with the Good Samaritan Bible Story.

Of course my instinctive reaction to seeing her take a swan dive (even though I could see it was intentional) was to rush across the road to pick her up. At which point I was nearly toast myself! I got there second to the passerby and was treated to one of Annie's best dramatic performances. With my arrival she pretty much dusted herself down and held my arm across the road, none the worse for wear. She didn't need a plaster. She didn't have a graze. She was fine. She didn't want the fuss I made when we got her inside to check if she was okay. She'd just wanted someone to talk to. That is learning disability, folks.

So. On Monday morning, we all agree that we all think that we think properly (go philosophy) but that we do all need some help sometimes. Especially with that pesky thing, money. (There's a whole other story about that but I won't go into it now).

And all that leaves is how we 'feel' about the label. Because now the group largely seems to acknowledge that they do have this label. But they're not happy about it. However much I suggest that it may have benefits because it means that they can get help when (and how, Barry) they need it, they still see it as a fundamentally bad thing. A way for people to be horrid to them. And I have to say, in practical terms, I can see their point.

In a heated discussion about labels we come up with the following points (written up on the flipchart by Barry with a flourish) under the heading: What we think about labels.

They are for tins not people

They can be very hurtful

They can be used to oppress people/ to put them down

You might need them sometimes.

Barry puts the last one down only because I insist. No matter how hard I suggest to the group that a label *might* have a use (other than on a tin) they resist the idea. It's as if they were trained. In the face of this unanimity of purpose I decide the best (and easiest) thing to do is go with the majority decision. And that's why the group is called NO LABELS. It's not quite eleven thirty and we're making progress. Now, we need to look at aims.

The aim of the NO LABELS Drama Group (we have a constitution and everything) is agreed to be to use drama as a means of showing other people that labels are for tins not for people. So that we can turn the joke

Q: What are you looking at?
A: I don't know, the label's dropped off. (drum roll and beat.)

From something that might have been insulting into something that makes people think. Turning a negative perception into a positive experience. That's the point of NO LABELS. That's what we do.

So. It's eleven thirty. Time to reflect. We've all been in and said our hello's and we've all had a cup of coffee (or tea) and a biscuit. Two biscuits. Three biscuits. We've more or less worked our way (as we always do) through a barrel of assorted biscuits during our 'discussion' session. I'm left wondering who buys the biscuits? But that's one of life's imponderable questions and not one I think I should start on now. We need to get away from biscuits and back to the business of the day. Which is the thorny question of names, identities and labels.

'So,' I say. 'Put your hand up if you're happy with the name NO LABELS for the drama group?

Everyone puts their hands up. Lauren puts her hand up twice. Well, she puts both hands up at the same time, you know what I mean. If I was at a union meeting this show of hands would be fine. But with learning disability? Can I be sure this means they all agree? Or are some of them just following the others in order to act 'normal'. It's always a possibility. I decide to accept their first action. Anything else is patronising. Maybe I should ask them twice, ask them if they're happy for another name, go round the houses, or... but while I'm thinking Bilbo moves us on. He begins to chant *'Labels, huh, huh, what are they good for – absolutely nothing.'*

I have to agree with him.

He gets up and dances. We all laugh. No Labels it is then.

Annie is relieved that we have got that out of the way and are able to get back to more important matters. She asks, portentously, 'Why are there no chocolate biscuits left? Who ate them?'

It's going to turn into a murder mystery if we're not careful. I try to deflect.

'Is this the most important thing to talk about at the moment?'

Ah, sarcasm. Never a very good tool. And pretty rude really, wouldn't you say? Not funny certainly. Annie puts me in my place.

'It's important to me. I want a chocolate biscuit.'

Bilbo is on a roll, he sings, *Listen, do you want to eat a biscuit, do you promise not to sell.* He sings to the tune of *Gerry and the Pacemakers, Listen, do you want to know a secret* and Duncan joins in the chorus (singing the proper words – I'm in love with you-ou-ou..). Bilbo gets up and dances again. There's no stopping him. This is the makings of a great double act.

At this point I suppose I should let you all into a little secret. Listen up Bilbo, I'm going to tell you a secret. While we're talking about labels. I'm an anarchist. Drum roll. Explosion (of wild rapturous applause?) Or just confusion.

I'm an anarchist. No not a bomb throwing, dressed in black, kick in bank windows and never wash my hair sort of anarchist. No. I'm a 'proper' anarchist. A philosophical anarchist. I have a degree to prove it. The dissertation in my first degree (moral philosophy) debated the links between anarchy as it is evidenced in 'primitive' tribes and the international legal system. And very enlightening it was too. I managed if not to prove conclusively (it's arts not science after all) then to argue very strongly for my stated position that anarchists have to be pacifists because their most fundamental belief is the inviolability of the individual. And killing another person is pretty high on the violation stakes isn't it? For me, anarchism is about taking personal responsibility for one's actions. For not relying on rule of law set down by '*Them*' (I told you they creep in everywhere) and so I suppose it's not surprising that it's a pretty good place for the 'outsider' or should that be the 'abnormal' to reside.

Which leads me to an interesting thought about the anarchy that No Labels Drama Group exudes on a daily basis. Because, all labels aside, this is a group of people who, for whatever reason, have been positioned 'outside' the norm. So is it any surprise that for them, normal rules don't apply. Whether that be in the playing of drama games (see later) or in the modes of conversational turn taking or... you get my drift. I think this may bear some deeper exploration. They're not stupid, they are reluctant revolutionaries.

Maybe this rests on the distinction between whether they 'cannot' follow the rules of society because they don't understand them, or whether they 'don't' follow the rules of society because they've been excluded from them. My second degree (in science, or is that social science?) is in applied psychology and this equips me to analyse discourse and conversation and suggest reasons 'why' for a range of everyday odd things that happen when you talk with or to people labelled with learning disabilities. Yes, I'm a polymath.

Which is all very well, but having gone off into a reverie worthy of Duncan, I am pulled back (literally by the sleeve) by Annie. Demanding a chocolate biscuit.

'Okay,' I say, hoping to pacify her and I rummage through the biscuits till I find one that might pass for chocolate.

'I don't like chocolate biscuits,' pipes up Lauren, her face giving the lie to her comment. There's a bit Pauline missed.

'You're sitting there, your face covered in chocolate and you're trying to tell me you don't like chocolate biscuits,' I laugh.

'Yes, darling,' she replies and cackles at me.

Annie is not looking so charmed.

'That's the best I can do right now, Annie,' I say. 'Will that do?'

She gives me her best withering look.

'I suppose it'll have to,' she says.

That's me put firmly in my place. But after all, we shouldn't really still be eating biscuits this late should we? I look at my watch. It's nearly time for lunch. For goodness sake. We need to move on. Where's Stevie? Oh, over there with Pauline, touching blue things.

'Shall we get started on the drama?' I ask, generally.

There's a chorus of approval.

'Stevie,' I shout. 'D'you want to come and play a game?'

And to my amazement, he stops touching blue things and comes across to me. Where he touches my blue No Labels sweatshirt. Well, it was a partial triumph.

So what's the point of drama games? You thought this was a group of adults and now I'm telling you we waste our time playing games. Okay. Let me enlighten you. We are a drama as advocacy group at No Labels. We use dramatic performances to show people some of our problems and sometimes offer solutions - or at least another way of seeing things. The 'games' referred to are part of the armoury of a famous drama practitioner, the late, great Augusto Boal who founded the Theatre of the Oppressed movement. I'm not sure, but as far as I'm aware we are the only group labelled with learning disabilities who use TO as their primary 'method.'

We use these games as a prelude to forum theatre 'experiences.' We also use them to support our more traditional 'performances.' Because it's easy enough for an audience to miss the point of Boalian 'style' drama delivered by adults labelled with learning disabilities, and unless we teach them that we are not performing traditional mainstream theatre, they tend to think we are and that we are failing. So we need to educate them twice over. Once in what they are about to see and once by what they see. Open eyes and open minds.

The game for today that I'm keen to get Stevie interested in is called Columbian Hypnosis. Well, our variant of it which is called Magic Circles. Stevie likes Magic Circles. Here's what happens. You get into pairs and each person has a brightly coloured cardboard 'magic circle' attached to their hands via a stuck on cardboard strap. Pauline helped everyone make the magic circles and everyone coloured in their own. Pauline did the sticking for Annie because Annie doesn't like the glitter and glue and getting her hands sticky. Lauren on the other hand just dumped a pile of glue and glitter all over her magic circle and it shines and sparkles like a princesses tiara. Which pleases her. I digress.

Everyone puts on their magic circle and they stand in their pairs. One leads by making movements with their circle – sometimes small, sometimes dramatic, sometimes calm, sometimes frenetic. The aim is for their partner to 'follow' or 'copy' their movement. Then we swap over and the other one gets a shot leading. There's NO TALKING (though sometimes a lot of giggling) during this game because it's meant to help concentration. The no talking probably pleases the likes of Stevie, Duncan and Lauren who aren't big on verbal communication anyway. It is torture for Annie and Kelly and Deirdre who love talking. The louder the better.

We try to make sure that each member of the group takes responsibility for their own favourite game. Magic Circles is Stevie's favourite game so he is 'the leader.' Effectively this means that he decides the parameters of the game – such as when to stop and when to mutate. Because the beauty of these drama games is their flexibility. This means we can change the rules to suit us. And we do. Often. Sometimes too often. Then the game descends into a kind of chaos. But that's fine too. It's creative chaos.

Inevitably, because Stevie doesn't like being in one place too long, even with all the colours of Magic Circle being waved in his face; he needs to go and touch things. So, after a few minutes of stationary concentration (and a bit of giggling) we're off and running.

The first time Stevie took off during Magic Circles, Deirdre got annoyed. Deirdre often gets annoyed when people 'don't play the game properly,' and I have to explain to her that the games are for 'everyone' and everyone can choose to bend the rules. Deirdre doesn't like this. She's not quite the anarchist some of the others are. She's quite a normalist at heart is our Deirdre. And we love her for that.

'If you don't mind my saying,' she says, 'Stevie isn't playing the game properly.'

'Or maybe,' I reply, 'he's adding something to the game. Let's see.'

So what we do when Stevie abandons the game in favour of 'a wander' is everyone follows him. He got to be a regular little Pied Piper and that gave us the idea for one of our first plays. It was called Peter Pan and the Pied Piper of Hamelin. And it goes something like this.

This is just a rehearsal you understand. Anything can (and will) happen.

'Once upon a time in a land far away,' says Bilbo, who does like a good Star Wars inspired fairy tale,

'Peter Pan had killed Captain Hook and was looking for something new to do.'

Bilbo is cast as Peter Pan and he gets his band of Lost Boys together (anyone else who is paying attention) and they head off to Hamelin. Bilbo, I will admit, isn't a natural Peter Pan, he looks a lot older than his fifty odd years, and to imagine that he is a boy who hasn't or won't grow up requires the sort of suspension of disbelief rarely seen in drama. Unless you are of the belief that all those labelled with 'learning disabilities' are actually 'children' or 'innocents' in some way. But Bilbo is neither a child nor an 'innocent.' He's playing Peter Pan because he demands to wield a sword. He was Captain Hook to Mandy's Peter Pan, but it was too dangerous so we changed tack and allowed him to be Peter Pan and Mandy was promised a better role... did she get one? Hmm...

Anyway, now Bilbo Peter Pan takes hold of Annie/Wendy and leads her on a journey.

'He's my boyfriend,' says Annie. Well it's a variation on 'my best friend - or fwendy which of course is the derivation of the name Wendy- a child of J.M.Barrie's acquaintance who couldn't pronounce 'r's' being responsible.

Bilbo isn't too keen on being a boyfriend, especially if Wendy/Annie is going to stop him from charging at folk with his cardboard sword.

We switch scenes. We are now in Hamelin. Where they have a plague of rats. Which Bilbo/Peter is very keen to kill one by one with his cardboard sword. Which is brown. Which attracts Stevie. For a bit.

Basically, we develop the play out of the following improvised actions. Stevie touches the sword. He utters a kind of squeak which is as close as he gets to talking and Bilbo/Peter resists him trying to take the sword. Chaos is but moments away when I suggest that Bilbo/Peter go with Stevie, following him. I even, in a rare moment of control, manage to get him to give Stevie the sword. You can't please all the people all the time. Stevie happy, Bilbo less so. And as Bilbo follows Stevie I suggest that Stevie is like the Pied Piper and perhaps everyone should follow him and copy what he does. So they do. Everyone crocodiles behind Stevie (we learned crocodiling when we were improvising Peter Pan) and tries to copy as closely as they can how he moves, what he touches etc. It works. For a long time. Even without music. But eventually it palls. Barry has been fiddling with the karaoke machine (he's keen for us to do some singing) and he switches a dial the wrong way (intentionally?) and we get some music. Not loud enough to hear the words but loud enough to be a distraction. Except that it's not a distraction. Stevie starts to move in time with the music. It's like some kind of Tai Chi. It's amazing. Very moving. Quickly, I suggest to the others that they stand facing Stevie, and copy him. They do so. And that's how Stevie becomes the Pied Piper. It never develops into a full performance, but sometimes we do it as a warm up to an event, to show people how the group are in tune with and can work together as a group. We lost the cardboard sword though.

This gives you a flavour of what we do. This Monday though, we need to have lunch.

~~~

And after lunch we are rehearsing another game for our show.

Duncan's favourite game provides us with the material for another of our little Boalian inspired theatre pieces. It's called King John's Journey. Someone, it might have been me, trying to show off to Bilbo, might have been reciting some A.A. Milne – you know *'King John was not a good man, he had his little ways...'* which led us into a discussion about power. And it got linked with another drama game called 'Keep or Kill.' Bilbo does like it when there's a bit of 'jeopardy' in a game. It keeps him interested. And we like to oblige all our members where we can. So we develop the game Keep or Kill into a short play (with music for Duncan) called King John's Journey. This is what happens:

The set opens to Robbie Williams soundtrack 'Millennium' (and before you ask, we probably don't have the required public lending rights, but we kind of figure if we asked Robbie, he'd be quite happy for us to sing along Karaoke style to his song without giving him money we don't have. I hope so. I'd like to think Robbie was that cool.)

So – Millennium is playing and there are a bunch of peasants with brooms brushing the floor almost in time to the music. The peasants are: Deirdre, Kelly, Lauren, Annie, Mandy, Stevie and Pauline.

The advisors (played by Bilbo and Barry) and the King (played by Duncan because he's the best at shouting 'kill' really loudly, even though Bilbo likes shouting it too.) watch them. I am the jester, which means I wear a ridiculous hat with bells on and generally run around like a blue arsed fly. Pretending to keep things in order. Pretending to marshall the anarchy. Note the word 'pretending' here. It's very important.

At the point in the song where the words 'come and have a go' are sung, Bilbo and Barry stand up and square up to each other. Bilbo likes this bit of it because he's the 'bad' advisor and thinks this is more fun that sitting down under a cardboard crown being King. Luckily for us. And then, because people who come to a dramatic performance tend to like to have words, I introduce the story:

I say, 'Once upon a time there was a King called King John. He had two advisors, one was good and one was bad. He also had a lot of peasants. Singing was banned in this country. When the people worked there was music, but they were not allowed to sing and the music just dragged them down.'

At which point if we are lucky and everyone's still paying attention and no one has decided to change the rules this early, the peasants take their brooms and stand at the back of the stage. Stevie sometimes takes his broom off into the audience but that's okay too.

I say, 'One day the King decided that he had too many mouths to feed and called upon his people to see who he would keep and who he would kill.'

And the audience start to get the idea of what they're about to see. Which is organised chaos set to music. Because this is the cue for the peasants to come up one after another and offer their services to the king. And I get to introduce them.

The first one up is Deirdre. She's the King's cook.

She makes a big deal of bowing before the King, who pretty much ignores her and she gives it her best shot...

'I will cook and clean for you, your majesty,'

She rarely gets further than this (unless Duncan is humming to the lights in which case she might get a few more words out) before he breaks into her speech with his favourite line,

'Kill.'

He shouts at the top of his voice. A voice we very rarely hear. And are overjoyed when we do. Even if it is shouting Kill. When we started playing this game there was a point in time when Deirdre asked me if I would tell 'the people we live with' (because Deirdre and Duncan live in the same group home),

'Would you tell them why he shouts kill all the time, if you don't mind.'

I didn't mind at all. I didn't want them to think Duncan had suddenly lost control of his mind or was exhibiting 'challenging' behaviour. Oh no, that would never do. And we don't believe in 'challenging behaviour here now do we? No. We call it 'creative' behaviour and we applaud it. When Stevie goes on 'a wander' we don't think he's being disruptive, we think he's being creative and we all follow behind him to see where he'll lead us. Our Pied Piper remember. And the same with Duncan. He shouts 'Kill' because it's his preferred 'in character' choice. He loves the power. He is power crazed in the play. That's fine because he has little enough opportunity to exercise power in his everyday life. In all the years I've played this game with groups I find that the people who get most out of it are the ones with the least power in their everyday life. So we positively encourage it. But we do suggest to Duncan that he doesn't upset his 'carers' by yelling it too often, too randomly at them. Unless he really wants to. In which case – go for it Duncan my boy!

So. Deirdre never really gets used to the idea that the King might want to kill her and she always takes a bit of what Barry calls 'humbrage' at the scenario – so Barry (the good advisor) sympathises with her and ushers her out to where Bilbo is standing with a rather scary looking cardboard implement that he can't wait to use to chop off her head with. He glowers at her most convincingly. Poor Deirdre. Being normal amongst the anarchists can have its downside.

Next up is Kelly the King's Driver. I point out to the audience (in case they haven't got it yet) that the King is the supreme power and that this is a story developed out of a game which shows power imbalances and aims to resolve them. And – for Kelly, who is never quite sure what is acting and what isn't - remind her that this is 'only a play.' So up she comes.

'Your majesty. I'm your driver. I will drive you around...'

'To the chip shop,' Barry the good advisor butts in (he loves the comedy ad lib) 'because you've just killed your cook and you're going to be hungry.'

If this is meant to appeal to the King's better nature it fails miserably and inevitably he shouts out clear as a bell one more time,

'Kill.'

It's like Rosencrantz and Guildernstern are dead this play. In so far as however many times you like to guess which side the coin will fall, it will always be 'kill' (that's heads). It's somehow comforting to have that level of certainty in what is essentially a devised piece. Though worrying that Duncan feels the need to exert this power without ever considering if anyone else is actually worth keeping.

So that's Kelly the driver despatched.

Bilbo grins even more and usually says something like,

'It's going to be a busy day, your majesty.'

And if he's lucky the King doesn't shout 'Kill' at him because hey, if you kill the executioner what're you gonna do?

Next up is Annie, she's still clutching her broom to show that she's the King's Housekeeper. Now you know, I don't think that if he's offed a driver and a cook he's going to have much time for a housekeeper so it seems pretty inevitable what comes next, and indeed,

'Kill,' he shouts and sends Annie over to Bilbo, usually muttering under her breath, 'I never got to say anything,' as she goes.

The pace picks up as Lauren and Stevie and even Pauline are despatched the same way as the others with a shout that's turned into a bellowing roar. 'Kill, Kill, Kill.' Duncan would make a great King Lear I think (which gives me an idea for Tuesday's play). But for now I need to keep the audience up to speed so I point out to them what's happened.

'So all the peasants were doomed to death. That only left the advisors,' I say and you can hear Bilbo give it a 'da, da, dah' in the background. Which always gets a giggle if not a belly laugh from the crowd.

The advisors go up to give it their best shot. Barry can talk the hind leg off a donkey and charm a snake charmer. Surely things are about to change and the King will show mercy?

'Sire, I have been your good advisor all my life. I have known you since you were a small boy. I advised your father Good King John, before you...'

'Kill.' He's cut off in his prime.

We are all a little bit shocked. After all. Barry is the good guy here. Oh well, now for the bad advisor. He and the king have some things in common so surely...

'Your majesty,' Bilbo wheedles, 'There's a lot of killing to be done and I will kill them for you, so you have to keep me.'

The King doesn't even draw breath. Well, maybe a moment's pause for dramatic effect. Or not. Depending on his mood. But whether we get suspense or not the answer is the same one.

'Kill.'

I don't think I've got much of a chance. But I give it my best shot.

'Your majesty. You've killed all your people. Will you not be lonely?'

This line of reason isn't going to wash. The King doesn't know what being lonely means. He has no need of other people. He's above all that. He kills me too.

Which is possibly where his plan goes wrong. There is a saying that you may not be able to please all the people all the time, but if you are a monarch, even a despotic one, you've got to try and keep some of the people on your side or... revolution.

Bilbo delivers his devilish plan with much cardboard implement waving.

'I have a plan. If we all band together and rise up against the king we can kill him.'

The peasants agree. Bilbo goes off to sharpen his cardboard implement. Leaving Barry as the voice of reason

'I have a better plan,' he says.

Can there be a better plan than killing a crazed, despotic monarch who has lost all sense of reason? Oh yes, there can. But the peasants aren't convinced. They ask,

'What plan?'

And Barry fills them in. He's Gloucester to Duncan's King Lear. It is moving. If you squint and suspend quite a bit of disbelief and have a weird and strong imagination. And don't believe in learning disability.

'There has to be a better way,' he continues.

'What way?' They chorus. At least those who are still paying attention do. Stevie is probably off touching Bilbo's cardboard implement because it's brown and he likes brown and Lauren is probably jiggling about and giggling and Kelly is still a little bit worried that someone might be coming to kill her, and Deirdre and Annie are still a bit miffed that they haven't been kept. But they'll get over it. Mandy and Pauline are keeping quiet. Like good revolting peasants. I think that's everyone accounted for.

'There is a song...' Barry begins as I cue up the next track on the karaoke machine.

'We're not allowed to sing,' Annie says, importantly. No one is going to prevent her from saying her 'big' line this time.

'Yes,' agrees Deirdre, 'if you don't mind my saying so, singing's banned.'

Then Barry states the bleeding obvious.

'What more can they do to us?' he asks. 'We are going to die anyway so we may as well stand up for ourselves.'

This is the kind of logic that you would think couldn't be ignored, but they are not fully in line with the plan and they shout together,

'Kill the king!'

'No,' Barry says. The voice of reason to the ugly broom wielding mob in front of him.

'No. We don't want to kill anyone. I remember what the old King said, he had a saying *'the only thing needed for evil to triumph is that good men do nothing'* and are we good men?' (and women implied).

It's a speech worthy of Olivier and there's only one response to that of course. The peasants shout out

'Yes,' with heartfelt gusto.

'Then jester, play the song,' Barry commands.

And the song starts. It is *'No Matter What They Tell Us'* that Boyzone favourite of Mandy's and she starts the singalong. Once again, no PLR is in evidence. Once again, apologies. Desperate times. Desperate measures and all that. So sue us. And just how would you sue a bunch of people 'with mental incapacity?'

Across the stage, still sitting on his plastic throne, alone but not lonely, the tune wafts in the direction of Bad King John and he starts shaking his head in time to the music. Then... he starts to sing. It gets the audience every time. Never a dry eye in the house. Timing is one of Duncan's best theatrical attributes. And his singing voice of course. He's a big game player and here he's in his element. He sings, in tune, with feeling.

Barry points out to the peasants, in case anyone isn't paying attention, (who could not be captivated by Duncan at this point?) 'The King is singing, I think our plan will work.'

And they all go over to join the King. Bilbo lurks beside the King, not looking happy. He doesn't like Boyzone and he can see his chance for a bloodthirsty killing spree about to go a begging.

'We want to talk to you,' Barry says to the King.

'Come on, we can kill him now,' Bilbo, ever the opportunistic optimist says.

'No,' Barry says, 'We're going to sing with the King. Teach him to sing.

Okay, this is a weak point in the plot because any fool can see that Duncan is perfectly capable of singing without any help from Barry who does have a problem holding a tune that isn't quite being tone deaf but is definitely tonally 'impaired' and in need of 'appropriate help.'

But you have to suspend disbelief in drama, at least once in a play, and this is the moment. Bilbo fights a manful rear guard action saying sulkily,

'The King doesn't want to sing.'

'Oh yes he does,' retorts Barry.

And this is Bilbo's cue to leave the stage in as big a theatrical huff as he can muster. Which is usually pretty big. Often he takes Stevie with him. When Stevie is in his 'brown' phase at any rate.

'We have a new song to teach you,' Barry says to the King. 'If you keep us, we can all sing together. Do you want to...?'

And the King doesn't shout 'Kill.' Instead he shouts out just as loud, 'Yuss.' And, if I've managed to cue up the music properly without having had my ear chewed by Annie and/or Deirdre asking me if I think it's going okay, we commence our finale song. *Eternal Flame*. The Bangles. Same PLR story.

It's the go for broke finish. Where we 'engage' the audience. Moving across the stage to the King, I, the jester, start the song,

*'Close your eyes, give me your hand,'* and then the group move off into the audience to display their carefully, (but simple) choreographed moves. The simplicity is due to the fact that choreography is not my

strong point. They each pick out a member of the audience and take hands with them while singing the rest of the song. Even the most hardbitten audience member is sorely pressed not to at least let their guard down, and most fully embrace what follows.

And if they possibly can, Annie and Kelly at least manage to get some audience members up on stage with us to join in the final chorus. And then it's time for the moral. Boalian drama is about putting right wrongs and so we feel compelled to offer some kind of a moral statement. Just in case someone wasn't paying attention or goes away missing the point. Which is that sometimes you can reward evil with good and if you are good enough, you can convert even the most hard hearted round to the way of happiness and light. I wish.

Cue curtain and rapturous applause. Another performance over. Another audience exposed to our No Labels approach. No one asks for their money back. Even though we usually perform for free. They take away the message: Go home and think about how you treat people. And be careful if you are in a position of power. Chickens can come home to roost.

And that's the end of Monday.

# TUESDAY

## *The play's the thing.*

Here we are again. It's Tuesday. The gang's all here and we are ready for our greatest challenge yet. Somehow, and I'm not sure how, they have banded together to convince me that it was really important that we perform a *real* play. On a *real* stage. For a *real* audience. So that's the task.

I thought things had been going well. I mean, King John's Journey was funny, right? Peter Pan and Pied Piper of Hamelin managed to embrace the problems, or should I say, specific requirements of our group and turn them to our advantage, right? Everyone had a good time, yes? Yes. But it's not enough. They want more. They want to do something 'proper.' I'm not sure I can stall them any more that what we just did is 'proper.' They know better. They have a vision. It's a vision of theatre that most people have so I'm fighting a rear guard action from the start.

The problem/s I perceived were a) we have few members who can read –therefore few who could 'learn lines' in a conventional way. b) we have few members with really good memories or long concentration spans – again, making a 'proper' play difficult to achieve.

I guess we need to look at 'proper' here.

I suppose I can't begrudge them the desire to want to do a 'proper' play because it's a dream I spent many years of my life pursuing. Then I saw the light. I learned about the difference between traditional mainstream theatre - you know, comfortable plush velvet seats and a proscenium arch and boxes of Maltesers (other boxed chocolates are available) and a general feeling of all's right with the world and we sit back and enjoy the spectacle – and Boalian style drama where there is no such thing as a spectator. And that was where I was at when I embarked on the No Labels adventure. However, that didn't give me the right to force that on them. And when people think of drama, they generally think of 'putting on a play.'

Okay. We had to find a compromise.

I guess it's not helped that at this point No Labels actually meets weekly in a small theatre, with plush velvet seats and a proscenium arch. And we work on stage in front of the backdrops from the local am dram production. No wonder they are taken in by the smell of the grease paint and... well, you get my drift.

'If you don't mind my saying so,' Deirdre begins and I try not to pale with whatever will come next, 'We want to do a proper play.'

'What we did on Monday was a proper play,' I respond, hoping that she'll be convinced. She isn't. She doesn't like the anarchy of it all. I call it flexibility. I call it what we need to do in order to engage with this thing 'drama' and yet retain our individuality and our integrity (I don't go as far as saying 'artistic' integrity, I'm not that much of a lovey). By integrity I mean I don't want the traditional theatre going audience to encounter a No Labels production and think they've been sold short. And maybe it's mean of me, but I just can't see how we can engage in any kind of mainstream theatre production with 'this group' of people. Am I being labelist?

With Barry's 'help us how we need to be helped' ringing in my ears, I wonder what we are going to be able to do. I try to voice my concerns as positively as possible in our meeting. A quick mental audit. Real stage. We have. Or can have. Real play. I guess so. Though it fills me with terror. Real audience. Ah, if only. No one can guarantee that I tell them.

'But we can try,' says Kelly.

'Yes. We can try,' I reply.

'Music,' says Duncan.

When Duncan speaks you do well to listen. He usually uses words to deflect you, as a means of avoiding real communication. This is when he is put in the position where he has to respond to some question I (or someone else) ask him which seems very important to me but less so to him. However, when Duncan initiates a conversation such as he just has done, you listen. He never ignores my questions. He may deflect (or refuse to answer 'appropriately', but he is always courteous enough to respond – just without meaning which I take as his way of showing me that my utterance has no meaning to him, however meaningful I think it is. I learn that actually most of the time my 'meaning' is not that vital. In the spirit of reciprocity though, I feel it's important I do Duncan the respect of listening and responding to his initiations into the world of communication he so studiously tries to avoid most of the time.

'Music,' he says.

'You want music in the play?' I check. Why do I always have to check by asking him a question? He doesn't like questions. His meaning was clear. He is a minimalist in linguistic communication but surely, his meaning is clear. He wants music in the play. My heart quakes. For a moment. Then I realise actually this may be a master plan. Most of the group are not good with memorising it's true, but music, that's another thing. They may not exactly sing in tune, it's a ragged chorus that's for sure, but they do know a lot of songs. If we could pad out the play with music. I slap myself mentally. Not pad out.

Integrate. Stop trying to sell them short just because you don't believe they can do it.

*Help us how we need to be helped.* Find a way. Rise to the challenge. Just do it.

I am brought out of my reverie by Bilbo.

*'If there's something wrong, in your neighbourhood,'* he sings (to the tune of Ghostbusters) *'who're you gonna call..'*

And they all chorus out *'No Labels.'*

I laugh. 'Again,' I say.

They sing it again.

*'If there's something wrong, in your neighbourhood, who're you gonna call, NO LABELS.'*

Yes, they've got something there.

'I made that up,' Bilbo says, proudly. 'It's our theme tune.'

'We thought a musical logo would be a good idea,' Barry says, smiling.

Turns out that Bilbo and Barry had got their heads together in the taxi on the way to our session. We'd been chewing over a 'logo' for the group, which I'd explained as a visual way for us to show our identity (not a label of course an identity)

We have resolved the difference between a label and a logo or an identity. It goes something like this:

Labels, as we all know are for tins not people. But an identity is something you are proud to share. And we are proud to be members of No Labels Drama Group so we want to show the world of our allegiance.

'T-shirt,' says Mandy. 'We want t shirts.'

'Sweatshirts,' says Kelly, always keen to go one bigger.

We got money from the local Lions club to buy sweatshirts. Pauline carefully took everyone's measurements (not just carefully but very discretely making sure that the sizes were all taken down without fuss – some of our members are not exactly slim but no one likes being faced with the reality of an XXXL rating!) So. We had really nice blue sweatshirts (we picked blue because it's one of Stevie's favourite colours – apart from brown – and it means that he will generally stick around the group if everyone is dressed in that colour.)But we didn't have a 'logo.' It was one of the things we were going to discuss on Tuesday, before Deirdre hijacked me with the demand for a *real* play.

'Real characters,' she said, as I boggled at the irony.

'What's a *real* character, Deirdre?' I ask (holding back a wicked desire to finish my sentence with 'if you don't mind my saying so.')

'Like in Eastenders,' she says

'Or Dallas,' Kelly adds.

'You know, *real* characters, like on TV, but live, on the stage.'

It's a big ask, I think. I'm not sure I believe a character can be real, but I let the philosophical discourse slip in favour of understanding what was very clear to me – they just want to put on a play. Do it. Find a way.

'How about Shakespeare?' Barry helpfully chips in.

'Have you ever seen any Shakespeare?' I ask him. I'm not sure if I'm showing prejudice, or being patronising but I can't imagine that any of the group has actually seen Shakespeare on TV never mind on stage. I'm sure they didn't do it at the 'special' school all the group attended many moons ago. Even Barry, mainstream schooled, cannot, surely have developed a love of Shakespearean theatre.

It turns out that maybe no one has actually seen any live Shakespeare but they know the 'context'

'Everyone knows about Romeo and Juliet,' Barry says.

I'm not sure from the blank looks on Annie and Lauren's faces that they have a Scooby what he's talking about, but they may just be disinterested. They may be thinking of other things.

'Macbeth,' Barry says. 'There's a play.'

'Have you seen it?' I ask him.

'Oh yes,' he says.

'Where?' I ask. It's not that I don't believe him, it's just that I can't imagine Barry at the theatre.

'They came to do a show,' he states.

It turns out that some 'famous' or should we say 'real' theatre company brought a production locally some years ago and performed it at the big theatre in the town. (We are in the little theatre in the town)

'And it was great.'

'Did everyone see it?' I ask.

'No,' replies Barry. 'That was before we all met.'

'No Labels,' Stevie chants as he passes me, touching my brown hair on his way. He is leading a procession of Bilbo, Mandy, Kelly and Duncan. Duncan is doing his own version of a conga at the end of the line. It's funny. It distracts me. They pick up the chant,

*Something bad, in your neighbourhood. Who're you gonna call...'*

I can't help but laugh.

Barry sees more potential.

'Something bad,' he says 'Like Shakespeare.

' Something wicked this way comes.'

I'm impressed. He remembers a line.

'Something rotten in the state of Denmark,' I riff in response. Two can play this game.

He looks at me, bemused.

'Hamlet,' I say. 'It's my favourite .'

And before I know it, a plan is being formulated. This is creativity No Labels style. It's why I always say to our audiences that we devise our work. That everyone has an input. Because without the bizarre and ridiculous things that happen on a daily basis, we'd never come up with the truly amazing and original creative ideas that it's my privilege (once I lose the fear) to facilitate and bring to fruition. Or 'reality' as Deirdre would call it.

You'll begin to see by now that we do not progress in a linear fashion in our narrative or in our lives with No Labels. That's the way it is. You almost get into a groove of a conversation or a train of thought and then someone throws in a curve ball and you're off down another path paddling like crazy to get back to the point of departure before you forget it. It's like surfing the internet LIVE. Maybe Deirdre has a point. We may all be nothing more than real characters. We may not be people at all.

So let me try and help you recap on the things that are going on simultaneously here.

1) We are going to find a way to do a real play, possibly Shakespeare and preferably with music.

2) We are working on a logo. And a 'theme tune' or musical logo to help define our group.

3) We are not going to let the fact that most of us don't know Shakespeare from a stick deflect us from our desire

4) Inability to remember lines and lack of knowledge of the basics of traditional stagecraft are not going to dampen our spirits (I need to remember that one) or be allowed to present problems. They are challenges. Opportunities. We will adapt.

5) We (specifically Annie) want a coffee break.

That one I can deal with. Immediately.

'Okay,' I say, 'let's have coffee and we can talk about it in principle over our drinks.'

Over coffee, or tea, or juice and another barrel of biscuits – provided by Mandy's mum today thank you very much – we try to focus on the situation. Or as I term it, the problem of performing a *real* play.

Lauren sucks on a chocolate biscuit. She's not in a 'darling' mood today. Not so light hearted and mischievous. She's fully locked into the world of chocolate. She shrieks when Annie tries to point out that she's got sticky cheeks.

'No..oo..oo..' she wails.

'I'm just trying to help,' Annie says.

'Maybe she doesn't want help,' I suggest. 'Have another biscuit Annie.' Was that really a good deflection? I doubt it. But it shuts Lauren up.

'You okay?' I ask her.

'Sorry,' she replies. It's her default setting. We discourage it.

'No need to apologise,' I tell her. 'I just wanted to be sure you are happy.'

'Happy,' says Duncan. That's his default setting.

Sometimes, when I try to see myself how they must see me, I wonder what they see. This daft person constantly asking them stupid questions that don't matter... I'm not filled with confidence at this point. And I've got Mandy and Deirdre in my ear asking me about the play.

'So when can we do it?' Deirdre asks.

'Is it tomorrow? 'Mandy asks.

'No, tomorrow you go swimming,' I remind her. 'It's for the future Mandy, not right now.'

That more or less switches her off. If it's not happening now it's not happening. I try to get back to what I think the point is. The play, after all, now appears to be the thing. It's taken over from 'where are the chocolate biscuits?' We've progressed from mystery to classic drama. If we can progress at all, which I seriously doubt.

In what I hope is a gentle preamble to another deflection, I point out there will be problems.

They are not problems Barry informs me, they are challenges. Opportunities for us to show our unique abilities.

'Oh god, Barry,' I think, 'I hope you're right.'

I can almost sense him thinking back 'Oh ye of little faith.'

Barry believes in us. It's one of the most amazing things about him. One of the most amazing things he's taught me is to believe in the ragged bunch of .... assorted humanity which is No Labels. Where your average citizen sees a 'poor vulnerable' person at best and a 'spazzy moron' at worst, Barry restores the karmic balance of the world because he truly believes in each and every one of them and their potential. He even believes in me. It's a powerful magic. Complete and utter faith.

Somewhere, between coffee and lunch I am worn down. Or inspiration strikes. Or I just let go of my fears and preconceptions about what's possible and we come up with a plan. Two plans. Which will become not one but two Shakespearan plays by No Labels.

I'm most adamant that we learn Shakespeare in a practical way. I have to convince Barry that we are not going to (because we cannot) learn screeds of iambic pentameter and deliver it with costume and props to a paying audience. It will not work. But we can do something that is an adaptation. A modern take. Our unique version. He agrees that this is okay in principle. After all, many people have done this very thing. It's the point of Shakespeare isn't it, that he speaks to us all, over the centuries.

'Okay,' I say, more bravely than I feel, 'Let's see what Shakespeare says to us.

We start with King Lear. Why wouldn't you eh? Let's aim high and work on one of the seriously difficult tragedies. I'm beginning to wish I'd ever liked the comedies, because A Midsummer Night's Dream might seem like a better tack to take. But then, rude mechanicals, learning disability, prejudice, people laughing for the wrong reasons, I realise that there are many levels I'm going to have to wrestle with if this is not to end up a fiasco!

King Lear? Why? Well, if you were paying attention on Monday you'll remember that I noted before that Barry had an element of the Gloucester in him. I must have remembered it too. It's amazing what being confronted with an empty stage and ten eager (or not so eager) faces demanding that we 'do something' can do for the creative juices.

'I'm going to tell you the basic story of King Lear,' I say. 'It's a tragedy.'

'What's a tragedy?' Annie asks.

'Bad things happen, and it doesn't have a happy ending,' I reply.

Just as Annie is suggesting that she likes a story to have a happy ending, Bilbo is off again,

*'Something bad in your neighbourhood... who're you gonna call..'*

Stevie shouts out 'NO LABELS.' Which is amazing. Stevie doesn't speak. He shrieks, he squeaks, but he doesn't use words. Never. And okay, maybe it sounds a bit more like 'O..aaay...oll..' but it's said in the right slot and with a vehemence that makes it clear he's part of Bilbo's song.

'Yes, Stevie,' I say. 'That's right. No Labels.'

I add a line to the song,

*'If there's something wrong, we can make it right,'*

And laughing they respond (including Stevie at the end) *'Who're you gonna call.. No Labels.'*

Cue rapturous round of applause and Annie has forgotten she doesn't want a tragedy.

I explain there's this king and he has three daughters. And he's a bit of a mean old bugger because he sets them a test. As I'm telling the story I realise that it's awfully like Cinderella or some other fairy story and I realise that maybe we're going to be able to turn this Shakespeare thing to our advantage.

'He's decided to retire,' I say, 'and he wants to see which of his daughters loves him most and he's going to give the kingdom to her.'

Three daughters we have. Annie, Kelly and Mandy volunteer. I ask them to improvise. They like improvisation. Barry looks a bit uncertain, but I tell him this is a good way to get ourselves 'into' the story.

I tell them their names. Annie is Gonerill, Kelly is Regan and Mandy is Cordelia. Great casting though I say so myself. Bilbo is the King. (I'm saving Barry for Gloucester).

They develop a little scene which goes something like this:

Firstly we have the three sisters (now we're into Checkhov country and I'm starting to see possibilities everywhere) talking to each other, as they are convinced princesses would do.

Annie/Gonerill says to Mandy, 'what kind of a princess are you, you don't even have a good dress on?'

Mandy/Cordelia doesn't know what to say back.

'You don't look that good either,' says Kelly/Regan.

'What do you mean?' Annie/Gonerill replies.

'Your hair is all messed up and you just don't look neat,' Kelly/Regan tells it like it is.

Annie/Gonerill is not sure she likes this.

'I'm not as messy as she is,' she points at Mandy. 'She's not as good as me.'

'Think princess,' I say, 'think mean princess.'

They begin to insult each other back and forward in a stream of bickering. And who's to say that princesses Beatrice and Eugenie don't do exactly the same in the safety of their own home. You never know what goes on behind closed doors after all.

The classic line comes soon when it all appears to be getting a bit out of hand and I remonstrate with Annie/Gonerill (defending Mandy/Cordelia who seems to be getting a bit upset)

'Perhaps,' I say, 'she thinks there are more important things in life than being a princess.'

Annie/Gonerill fixes me with a stern stare and replies, '*Nothing* is more important than being a princess.'

Way to go. And I'm worried about their acting potential? I don't even laugh. She's so serious.

We move onto the next scene.

'You've got to convince your father of that,' I say. 'It's kind of like King John's Journey.

'But Bilbo is King not Duncan,' Kelly points out always one to get the detail right.

'Yes,' I add. 'And no one needs to get killed.'

'Kill,' shouts Duncan from the sidelines, just in case I thought he wasn't listening.

Back to the scene. We improvise our way through the King making his choice. We have decided we're going to show him making a bad choice and then the other way that he might do it.

Bilbo/King says, 'I want to find out which of you loves me most.'

'I love you most,' says Annie/Gonerill, which should be enough for him.

'No,' shouts Kelly/Regan (she has a very loud voice when she wants to) 'I love you most.'

Bilbo ignores them and turns to Mandy.

'Do you love me?' he asks.

Mandy/Cordelia remains quiet. She's a bit lost. Finally she says, 'I am a princess.'

'Princess,' says Lauren from the audience. 'Princess Lauren.'

I look at her.

'Sorry,' she says.

'No need to apologise,' I tell her. You'll get your turn to be a princess in a minute.

By the time I'm back to the scene Bilbo is telling Annie/Gonerill and Kelly/Regan that he's going to share the kingdom between them and Mandy/Cordelia is getting nothing.

'Is that fair?' I ask.

'No,' Bilbo replies, chuffed with himself. He's a good bad King.

In comes Barry/Gloucester to try and talk King Bilbo round to some sense.

He explains, in graphic and somewhat longwinded detail (which sends Stevie out to the toilet with Pauline in hot pursuit to make sure he doesn't just keep on going out into the street) that this is not the right way to make a choice.

'Okay,' I say, when I feel I can finally interject. 'Now, let's look at how we might do it a good way.'

This has been a trademark of our work so far, and I like it as a method. We run a scene showing the bad things that happen and then we repeat it showing a better way of doing things. It's Boalian forum theatre, of a sort and it works for us. I think. I'm looking for way to meld this with the desire to 'do' Shakespeare. I think it's working. It certainly looks good to me. And it keeps us amused till lunchtime. Except Stevie. Who has decided it's not brown or blue enough for him and he's going to take a rain check on the experience for the day. Pauline gets him a taxi.

We have rehearsed it a couple of times back and forth and I think we're onto something. I'm concerned of course that Duncan and Lauren are on the sidelines, and that Stevie has voted with his feet, and to my eternal shame I'd completely forgotten about Deirdre, but that isn't a situation that will continue.

We 'perform' the whole thing to our audience and it is rather good though I say it myself – 'nothing is more important than being a princess.' The shallow vanity. The ugly sisters arguing amongst themselves, the voice of reason telling the King not just to listen to who shouts loudest, and it all comes to an end with a screeching halt when Deirdre stands up and instead of applauding, says,

'Yes, but we want to do a *real* play, if you don't mind my saying so.'

And stomps off for lunch.

~~~

I can't pretend that I came up with what follows in the space of a lunch break, or that I'm about to show you 'one I prepared earlier.' But you must have figured by now that Tuesday is a symbolic thing. We are talking about many Tuesdays. And so, please suspend disbelief with us a bit longer and picture the scene one unspecified Tuesday, many months later, when we finally get round to the real play. Here it is. With justification.

However much I loved the line 'nothing is more important than being a princess,' I just couldn't fit it into anything. It showed me a part of Annie's character and I thought she'd make a wonderful Ophelia, she is so over dramatic. King Lear just wasn't giving us what we needed. MacBeth would be far too dark and I finally hit on Hamlet (it being my favourite) and thought I'd adapt it. A comedy adaptation, because comedy is what we do best. It took some convincing but we got on board in the end. In the end we loved it.

And I got to put in my favourite joke of all time. Look out for that one. It got them laughing in the aisles. Or us laughing in the aisles anyway.

This is how I sell the script to the gang.

'Look,' I say, 'People have expectations don't they? And I think that people don't expect that we can do Shakespeare.'

I'm not sure I think we can do Shakespeare still, but Barry's convinced me to face my fear and think bigger and not let reality get in the way of a good attempt.

'So,' I say, 'We're going to do a comedy version. The play is called Hamlet. It's about a man who can't make up his mind. It's quite a serious play, but we're going to adapt it and make it our own. If you think about it Ham comes from a pig yeah? And a Hamlet means a small place so you could turn that into a piglet... amazingly they follow me on this crazy linguistic journey. So we're going to call the play: Piglet! A little play on words.'

I am sure this is way beyond anyone's comprehension (possibly even you, dear reader) but I've learned with No Labels just to plough on regardless and hope that someone picks it up.

Duncan laughs. A deep belly laugh. He gets it. Really, I think he gets it. It gives me the confidence to continue.

'Because,' I say, 'when people think of people with learning disabilities they don't imagine that they could do Shakespeare. But if we tell them we're doing a funny play called Piglet! – complete with exclamation mark for effect of course – they will think we are doing something silly and funny and they'll come to see it. Then wham.'

'Wham,' Bilbo repeats. He likes Wham.

'Yes, Wham,' I say, 'we hit them with the real story.'

Real story. Real. That's good Deirdre will like that.

'And the point of it is,' Barry picks up, 'that we'll be showing them that there's more to us than they expect. We can tell them all about making choices and how difficult it is for everyone.'

'Yes,' I say. 'Does everyone want to do this?'

'Yes,' they chorus.

'Music,' Duncan asks. Well, it's a statement really. Remember Duncan doesn't do questions.

'Yes, Duncan,' I say, 'we'll have music, and dancing too. It'll be all singing, all dancing comedy version of Shakespeare.'

Hey, if you're going to break the rules you may as well smash them to oblivion, right?

'And,' I say, 'We have a script.'

Now we have to deal with the thorny question of people who can't read.

'But,' I say, 'It's not a problem, because it's a flexible script.'

Barry looks pleased, Deirdre looks a bit less so. Deirdre can read. She loves to read. Unfortunately she has the kind of monotone voice that makes you want to slit your wrists after a paragraph. She cannot put emotion into her reading. But she CAN READ.

'I know that we don't all read and write,' I say, not wanting to single people out. There are members of the group who pretend they can read because they think they will appear stupid if they can't. But when Annie holds her songsheet upside down on a regular basis I kind of know that the written word is not something she's comfortable with.

'And who can't see so clearly,' I add, hoping to deflect the stigma even more. 'So what we'll do is we'll record the script and people can play the CD back so that they can learn their bit. And we'll do a lot of rehearsing too. Okay?'

Because I know that those who don't read too easily have largely managed to compensate for their deficiency either by having good memories or by being able to repeat things the same way time and again once they have learned it fully. It's never going to be word perfect and it's never going to be without an element of randomness, but hey, how many real actors get the

words right every night (you'd be surprised, believe me...
it's a very very rare occasion. )It's one of the joys and
fears of live theatre for the acting fraternity believe me - I
once acted in a play where the lead character missed out
two whole scenes and delivered a speech which gave
away most of the intervening plot – and I had to bring it
back from there. So I've experienced the fear. I know
what I'm talking about in this respect. Lucky, because it
prepared me for finding ways to get No Labels rehearsed
and doing a real play but without having a heart attack. I
know the secret which is – unless it's obvious to the
audience that something has gone wrong, they'll think it's
part of the play. In this way I think mainstream theatre is
more or less the same as Barry's life. He just gets on with
it, convincing you that he meant it to be that way all along
and it's only if you delve deep and reflect that you realise
it was all smoke and mirrors. Good old Barry. But then
maybe all of us are like this to an extent. Maybe this is
what 'confidence' means.

So what I've done, and I'm quite proud of this actually,
because it wouldn't have happened without Barry's belief
and yes, Deirdre's relentless demands and a sense that I
shouldn't let them down, is create a flexible script with
each part tailor made for the real character. Result.
Although of course, the audience will be the ones to pass
judgement. But it's funny. It rocks. And it will certainly
surprise. I'm sure there are moments that will surprise
all of us, every time we do it.

After many months of Tuesdays working on this, here
we are Tuesday night. Opening night. It's six thirty and
we start at seven. We have used the set left up by the am
drams which seems to be some sort of a castle type thing.
We have got someone in (from the am drams) to run the
lights and someone else (a parent) to help with costume
and the whole play will run for a good thirty minutes if
nothing goes wrong. If something major goes wrong it'll

run for ten minutes or maybe an hour. We have the theatre till eight. We're planning to run a raffle to raise funds once the curtain has come down, followed by a 'meet the cast' where we can talk about the work we do and why we wanted to do this play. I can't even contemplate thinking that far in advance as I look out from behind the purple velvet curtains. The little theatre seats eighty people. I can see at least sixty already. Where did they all come from? I feel the fear. I'm alone in that respect it seems. If I was to digress into the label of learning disability I'd say that one of the great things about the people I know with this label is that since they tend to live in the moment, they don't get themselves wound up about what might happen. Most of them don't anyway. But still we have to deal with Mandy who is up to ninety about something I can't work out and Kelly who is refusing to take off her own clothes and so puts her costume on over them which means she's going to be stewing hot under the lights and this runs the grave risk of bringing on an epileptic fit. And Deirdre who *will not shut up* and give me time to think. And Barry, who never says or does things the same way twice. Oh yes, you can see, I'm carrying the stress for us all. And I'm just the narrator. My job is somehow to make sure that there's enough of a through line for the audience to understand what we think we are doing.

If you look in your programme you'll see the following casting. (It will help here if you know the play Hamlet just a bit – I'll put the Shakespearean character names beside ours for ease of comprehension!)

Piglet! A Little play on words. Abridged, adapted and updated from Shakespeare's original work Hamlet. With a cast featuring: (Hamlet) Piglet played by Bilbo, Ophelia (Pig) [his girlfriend] played by Annie, (Polonius) Polony Pig [her father] played by Barry, (Horatio) Nelson played by Deirdre, (King) The Big Boar [stepfather] played by

Kelly, (Queen) [Hamlet/Piglets mother] played by Mandy, (Rosencrantz) Rosie Pig played by Pauline, (Guildenstern) Gillie Pig played by Laurn, (Ghost – Hamlet's Dad) Ghosty pig, played by Duncan, with Kate as Narrator and Stevie as the lead dancing pig.

So, sit back, open up your box of Maltesers, suspend disbelief bigtime and get ready for the show.

Lights down. Curtains back.

~~~

Piglet! Scene one. It's true. The Play's the thing. Bilbo enters first and stand centre stage. He is wearing a pig mask. Others join him. They wear pig masks too and the costuming is a base layer of pink with an assortment of 'costume' over it. The pig masks are worn high on the head giving the impression of a double head – this is because some of the players (Lauren and Mandy) don't like wearing masks and others find it hard to speak out clearly from within their confines. But the atmosphere is there. I enter and take my seat as narrator in an exposed prompt corner.

'Welcome to our play,' says Nelson/Deirdre. Consummate professional.

'Our play is called Hamlet,' says Rosie/Pauline.

Bilbo throws the mask at the prompt corner. I catch it. Fortunately.

There are gasps from the wings. All the others crowd onto the stage as if they have exposed a mistake at this early stage. Pig confusion abounds. Nelson rises above it. There are titters from the crowd already. I forgot to say, by this time it is standing room only. Barry has done some kind of promotion and we are packed to the gunnels!

'Abridged,' says Nelson/Deirdre

'Adapted,' adds the Big Boar/Kelly

'Updated,' says Queenie/Mandy, not to be outdone. They join hands and go and sit on thrones upstage centre. They look pleased as punch.

Piglet/ Bilbo looks around, feigning uncertainty. The others shove him to the front of the stage (a bit too enthusiastically in my opinion) to deliver his lines.

'All Denmark's a... a...' he falters (this is intentional of course, it's setting us up to fail and then turn it round on the audience.)

Milking it, Piglet/ Bilbo looks to the prompt corner for help. A pantomime ensues where I mime at him and he makes a big deal of not being able to hear properly and finally says, 'A pigsty.'

Audience erupts.

The group react with shock and not a little joy since they never really expected the audience response. It's long ago stopped being funny to us. This is a real play after all, it's a serious business comedy.

So with lots of mock (and dare one say ham) overacting the group display shock and horror and chant to a man, 'A pigsty?'

Much shaking of heads.

'Sorry,' says Lauren. Unscripted. But it's always funny whenever she puts it in and she is bound to put it in somewhere or other during the play.

We pull back to a tone of seriousness. Nelson/Deirdre waves the audience to stop laughing. They obey. She continues.

'Hamlet had a girlfriend,' she says,

'His name was Ophelia, Rosie/Pauline adds.

The audience thinks we're back on track. We toy with their expectations a little bit more.

Piglet/Bilbo and Ophelia/Annie meet together and mime a silent argument. This involves a lot of finger wagging from Ophelia/Annie – she is a good enough actress to convince you she's shouting even when she's totally silent. It's a skill.

But for anyone who might be confused, we have 'lines' as back up.

'They had an argument,' Boar/Kelly shouts,

'She called him... called him...' Mandy says (she's worked hard to learn her lines and it hasn't been easy.' They both mock strain to hear the silent argument.

Eventually Ophelia/Annie shouts out, 'You're a pig.'

Piglet/Bilbo replies, shocked, 'A pig?'

'A pig,' restates Ophelia/Annie and stomps off the stage convincingly. The rest of the acting pigs follow, leaving Piglet/Bilbo alone in a centre spotlight. I throw the pig mask back at him saying, 'A pig.' It lands at his feet. He acts sadness and shrugs. Then he picks up the mask.

'Hamlet?' he says in his best quizzical tone and eyeballs the audience. He puts the mask on, 'Piglet?' he says. Then takes it off. He repeats the charade – Hamlet – Piglet – no mask –mask [oh yes, audience we are deep into what is an identity here – am I a pig dreaming I'm a man or a man dreaming... ]

He stands, his choice made. Mask on. I say, 'Who is Piglet?' ( in case the audience are struggling with the whole weird concept!)

Piglet/Bilbo puts his hand up. Juxtaposing simplicity with philosophical depth. Nice eh?

'Correct,' I say, and we are back into comedy.

Rosie/Pauline and Gillie/Lauren pigs enter.

'Special delivery,' I say.

They are carrying a knife. Don't worry, it's a cardboard one painted with silver spray paint. It does glint in the light but no one will be harmed. As the audience are getting their heads round the complete oddness of what they are viewing (we need them to accept early on that their expectations are going to be played with) I move the story on and address the audience (who we now hold in the palm of our communal hand of course.)

'Piglet is someone who can't make up his mind. Someone who has been lied to by the very people he thought he could trust.

At this point one can generally trust Gillie/Lauren (as long as she's paying attention and it turns out she's a big game player, she likes an audience) to interject with the line,

'That's bad.'

She obliges us on this occasion. I engage her in witty badinage. Hoping she'll pull through as we've rehearsed.

'You're right that's bad,' I reply.

'What's the story?' she asks.

This is a minor triumph the audience cannot imagine. Lauren has instigated a conversation, taken responsibility for 'a line' in the play. You probably haven't thought about it, but in plays (as in conversations) there are two kinds of 'lines.' There are the ones which instigate action and move things on and ones which respond to the previous cue. It's sheer madness to give an instigating line to a person such as Lauren who never instigates. But sometimes you have to live dangerously. We have a secret safety net actually, in that Rosie/Pauline would have delivered the line had there been a long enough pause to make it clear that Gillie/Lauren was not going to play ball.

'The story?' I question, keeping this fictional ball in the air.

'Yes, the story,' Rosie/Pauline adds, setting up Gillie/Lauren for her other big moment (best to get them out the way early before she loses interest) She comes up trumps doing a little dance and shrieking,

'Piglet, Hamlet, Piglet, Hamlet,' though it actually comes across as 'Piglet, Hamalet' because she does love to give everything its full weight when she's in this kind of a mood. Anyway, she makes a really big deal of it, wiggling her stuck on piggy tail and shimmying and everything. The more they laugh, the more she performs.

I bring it to a halt by saying,' Whaur's yer Wullie Shakespeare noo?'

Those who wanted to run analysis on the play might see that at this point we have made it very clear to the audience that we are toying with their expectations and from now on they should just expect the unexpected. Sit back and go on the journey with us. That's what No Labels is like. Out of the ordinary. Extra ordinary. And if you embrace it you'll enjoy it.

While this deep reflection is or isn't going on, Piglet/Bilbo leaves the stage and puts on more costume. The music to 'Staying Alive' by the BeeGees starts (of course we don't have PLR, we explained that on Monday to you) and the rest of the pigs enter in party mode.

I stand to usher them in, as at all the best parties. I announce them.

'Here are the pigs. Here they come. Finest Danish bacon. We have Polony Pig and his daughter Ophelia Pig. Horatio Pig (call him Nelson) he's Piglet's best friend. Queenie Pig – that's Piglet's mum. And the Big Boar he's... well... he's the King. And you know Rosie Pig and Gillie Pig.'

While I'm doing this the pigs are dancing around. No one dances with as much gusto as No Labels. Believe me. This bunch know how to party.

Time to confound audience expectations.

'The pigs are sad,' I say. They ignore me. I shout out loud, 'I said the pigs are sad.'

They turn, most keep dancing even though the music dips. I have to shout above them to be heard,

'Someone has, well, you know, gone for bacon. And it's Piglet's dad.'

The pigs keep dancing. It's like Watership Down. Or Chicken Run. No one wants to hear the unpleasant truth. Just keep dancing.

Piglet/Bilbo enters. Disconsolate in manner he says, 'I miss him. I'm sad.'

The other pigs just keep on dancing.

Piglet/Bilbo is annoyed. He expresses this, 'What's going on?' he asks in general, 'I said I'm SAD.'

No one seems to be listening. Then Polony/Barry pig pipes up.

'Get over it. We're having a party.'

Piglet/Bilbo is rightly shocked. A party. And his dad's corpse barely still in the ground.

'Who said?' he asks.

'Your mum,' Polony/Barry replies pointing at Queenie/Mandy who has stopped dancing and is sitting on her throne holding hands with the Big Boar/Kelly. Is this the time to tell you that Big Boar is dressed as Elvis? I think it might be. Big Boar is dressed in white as Elvis.

Piglet/Bilbo can't believe his ears.

'My mum?' he says, incredulous.

'Yeah, your mum, right. Stop repeating everything everyone says. We know you can't make up your mind but this is meant to be an abridged version, not the full three hours.'

Ta-ra. Comedy and moving along the drama. Delivering, in case anyone in the audience didn't know, the crucial theme of the play.

'I'm sure it's not right,' Piglet/Bilbo says.

Polony/Barry is on a roll. He also has his lines written down on a clipboard he's carrying. Barry would never remember all these lines. Even with these lines, he's likely to vary them if he gets too much of a laugh. Live theatre, right? Barry, for a man who wanted a script, really seems to enjoy improvising best. It's always a compromise and it's not just the audience who can't be sure what will come out of his mouth next. But we love him for it. Mostly.

'Listen, young piglet,' he says, 'Let me tell you something. Neither a borrower nor a lender be... uh, oh, no... some useful pig advice? Um... just get over it okay. Life's too short. What the big boar says, goes. Okay.'

Piglet/Bilbo isn't impressed. But you've got to laugh. Never has Polonius advice to Hamlet been delivered in quite this way, but it does somehow convey the fact that Polonius can be as much of a tedious old geezer as the purveyor of the wisdom of ages – unto thine own self be true – no we don't need any of that. We are looking at the man behind the character. The 'real' character of Polonius, as exposed by No Labels. If Polonius was a pig.

'I don't think that's what my dad said,' Piglet/Bilbo conveys the standard party line. This is a serious comedy after all. Polony/Barry hits him smack between the eyes with a piece of incontrovertible logic which is central to the entity of the dilemma faced by the hero in the play.

'But your dad's not here any more is he?'

At this, waving a handkerchief, clutching his clipboard and sucking on a fake cigarette in an impossibly long holder (he's come as a dandy) Polony/Barry goes back to join the dancing. He shakes his head extravagantly. All eyes follow him. This was what he wanted when he wanted a real play. This opportunity. And I'm happy to give it to him. He is a ham actor but he's just cast perfectly for this. He shines.

Piglet/Bilbo is left standing alone on the stage. Nelson/Deirdre fights her way through the dancing pigs to take him by the arm.

'Come on Piglet, join the party,' she says.

Piglet/Bilbo is not going to be swayed that easily.

'No, I won't. I miss my dad,' he says. Sticking to his guns doggedly.

'I saw him,' Nelson/Deirdre says (without, I may add, adding if you don't mind my saying so. You see, she can act when the mood takes her.)

We are all taken aback by this piece of information. Unless, that is, we know the 'real' play Hamlet and have decided that this version will stick relatively close to the plot at least. Then we might have expected it. But Piglet/Bilbo acts his socks off and pretends he has no idea what is going on.

'What? You can't have... he's... he's...' he can't bring himself to say it. It's extreme poignancy. The audience are lapping it up.

Time for the narrator. The point of the flexible script is that you have to put in the bits that move the plot along at the appropriate moment so that despite everything that can go wrong, the audience are still able to follow the dramatic journey. Time to tell them where we are.

'Piglet knew his dad had gone for bacon. We ALL know his dad has gone for bacon. But there are some things you just don't like to talk about. Don't like to rub it in... no pun intended,' I say.

Nelson/Deirdre doesn't break character. She carries on as if I'm just not there. (Deirdre is rather good at that. Rather too good at that sometimes, I feel. Still, I never get the feeling that she *wishes* I wasn't there so that's a positive. )

'I tell you. I did see him. He spoke to me. It was kind of spooky,' she confesses.

Piglet/Bilbo seems less than convinced.

'So where is he?' he asks.

Nelson/Deirdre is in her element. In control. And she's learned her lines. Though she's not good at the instigating lines, she generally gets the response ones spot on. And this time is no exception.

'Come with me. Tonight. At midnight,' she says portentously and the lights dim, the party fades and we go to blackout. End of scene one.

The lights come back up a moment later to scene two which is later that night. Led by Stevie in a cape, we have Michael Jackson's Thriller pounding out and a line of Ghost Pigs behind Stevie do a passable job of the song and dance routine we've practiced for so long. They all have white gloves and capes and it is as atmospheric as you can be when you don't have a Lloyd Webber type of budget. Or any budget. It's Stevie's big moment. And he doesn't let us down. He gives Michael Jackson a run for his money at any rate. The audience clap along.

As the dance dies down and the pigs disperse into the wings (for another quick costume change) Piglet/Bilbo and Nelson/Deirdre enter arm in arm at the front of the stage.

'Ill met by moonlight,' Nelson/Deirdre says.

(No, it's not a mistake, it's what the writer thought was funny!)

And in order that the audience 'get' the joke the writer, now playing the narrator, has a second bite at the cherry.

'I think that's another play,' I say, dryly.

It's the point. If we put in deliberate errors and build audience expectation that we will be making errors for comedic effect, when the wheels fall off and we do make a serious mistake, they might just miss it. Is this cheating or is it the work of a genius? It's for you to decide.

'Yeah?' Nelson/Deirdre says, unconvinced.

'Yeah,' I repeat. Another nice little interchange. Another subtle moment of acting genius.

She carries on, remembering an instigating line for which I'm eternally grateful.

'Well, I'm scared. So I'm off. Hope your dad comes, Piglet.'

Piglet/Bilbo is now left onstage alone again. Since repetition usually works for both emphasis and comedy he takes the mask on and off a few times as if he's really not sure who he is or what he's doing there.

Meanwhile, Duncan, shoved on by Barry and encased in a mask and a ghosty cloak, enters silently, comes right up behind Piglet/Bilbo and hugs him from behind. The hug was Duncan's own interpretation. We just wanted him to stand behind Piglet/Bilbo who jumps as a disembodied and very 'doctored' recorded version of Duncan shouting is played.

'PIG-LET.....'

That and the hug are enough to make Piglet/Bilbo jump. And I swear Ghostypig/Duncan will be smiling behind his mask.

Ghosty pig does something (again unscripted) which might be either a kiss of the neck or a vampire bite from behind. Enough to remind Piglet/ Bilbo of his line

'Dad, is it you?'

There is silence. Piglet/Bilbo turns round to return the hug. There is no response this time. He says, 'Dad...dad...what happened to you? I thought you'd...' he can't bring himself to say it. And Ghosty pig/Duncan predictably enough doesn't reply.

'Had his bacon,' I say. Someone has to deliver the unpalatable truths. That's the role of the narrator isn't it? To stand outside the action and deliver the truths the *real* characters are unable to see or stomach.

Ghosty pig/Duncan sniffs Piglet. Sniffs him up and down. Duncan may not say much be he's quite an actor.

Piglet/Bilbo is phased by this (despite the many times we've rehearsed it... ah, you see, he's an actor too, he can carry of surprise in the face of the familiar.)

'What is it dad? What's wrong?' he asks.

'Something's rotten in the state of Denmark,' I say. Most of the audience catch up with the smelly pig gag and laugh.

Piglet/Bilbo looks at me in his best mock anger.

'Leave us alone. Rotten? Pigs are very clean you know. I don't smell.'

The audience erupts. Ghosty pig begins to leave the stage. Once again his voice is carried in a distorted recorded form saying, 'Murder most foul,' as he begins his long walk to the wings.

'What do you mean, dad? Murder?'

Ghosty pig/Duncan turns back and comes close to Piglet/Bilbo. He is joined by the other pigs in their ghosty capes. It wasn't such a quick change after all, they've just been cooling their heels in the wings. The quick change must be next. I hope someone is co-ordinating it, I never had time to arrange it. I just see what comes onto the stage and hope for the best in the backstage environment. No one, not even me, can control everything, everywhere, all the time.

The next song is cued up. The pigs sing and it's all Piglet/Bilbo can do to not join in, because it's one of his favourite songs, adapted for the cause.

*'Piglet. do you want to know a secret, do you promise not to tell.(woowh woowh whooh)*

*closer (woowh woowh wooh) let me whisper in your ear (woowh woowh wooh) say the words you need to hear, It was the big boar (woowh woowh wooh).'*

Having finished their song, the pigs leave, taking Ghostypig/Duncan with them. He appears reluctant to leave. Well, you would, wouldn't you... you know, murder most foul and then the chance to catch up with your beloved son... or even if you were just a guy who seldom gets the limelight. Every one likes a moment in the spotlight once in a while. Even if they can't shout KILL.

Once again Piglet/Bilbo is left alone on stage with no one to talk to but the narrator. Breaking the boundaries of traditional theatre here but fortunately Barry and Deirdre don't know the conventions of traditional theatre well enough to be able to complain. One can shift more towards Brecht than they are ever going to be aware of.

'What was that?' Piglet/Bilbo asks me and slightly later than cued three cock crows ring out.

'The cock crowed,' I say, 'three times. He had to go.'

The crowd laugh. Got away with that one then.

Piglet/Bilbo is standing looking stunned when Nelson/Deirdre re-enters. She's remembered her line again.

'What's wrong Piglet? You look like you saw a ghost,' she declaims.

'It was... my dad... a ghost... he said...' Piglet/Bilbo burbles.

I wave at him to be quiet. We are building for more comedy.

'Ah well, I always say...' Nelson/Deirdre begins, then to me, 'What do I always say?'

This is funny on a number of levels. Funny to the audience as they can see the interaction between actor/narrator and thus enjoy the breaking down of the traditional conventions , dispensing with the fourth wall and inviolability of the 'world' of the play... for us it's funny because half the time Deirdre has to ask me this because she just can't remember. So it kills many birds with one stone and is funny to boot (believe me). That's great drama, right?

I put her out of her misery, 'There are more things on heaven and earth.'

Now if you've ever been exposed to Hamlet the play you'll know that line, yeah? It's up there with to be or not to be... so people have to recognise it don't they?

While we ponder this, we keep the comedy rolling as Nelson/Deirdre responds with,

'No, that's his line,' (pointing at Piglet). 'Pay attention will you. You're meant to be keeping *us* straight.'

A little reflection there on who is in charge. On whether 'normal' actually does keep 'labels' straight. Ah, a small thought gem. But we press on regardless. Only you, reading this after the event are lucky enough to get the reflective analysis. To see the reality behind the fiction. Maybe.

Nelson/Deirdre must push the play on now though, the live audience lives in the moment as our actors do. As we all do, in real life.

'Now Piglet,' she says. 'Tell me about your dad.' And they exit, talking. It's the end of scene two.

Things seem to be going reasonably well as the lights rise for scene three. Everyone somehow has got back into their appropriate costume and we are set for the palace. Big Boar/Kelly and Queenie/Mandy are in their thrones, though if you look carefully you'll see they've changed sides. Ushered in are Rosie/Pauline and Gillie/Lauren pig.

Now this is probably the time to offer a confession. If you were paying attention on Monday you might have noticed that Lauren tends to repeat things. The technical term is echolalia. I make no apology for the fact that we use this in the play. It turns what can be seen as a defect into a skill and adds significantly to the comedy. And after all, she only repeats when she wants to so it's not like we're making her play the performing monkey. Please accept my assurance that Lauren only ever does what she wants to do! If she wasn't happy she'd either walk away or scream. Very loudly. So her repetition in the dramatic context is taken by me as a tacit acceptance of her participation. I hope I'm right. In the particular context of this play you may also be aware of the characters of Rosencrantz and Guildenstern. They were minor characters in Shakespeare's play who rose to prominence in Tom Stoppard's absurdist drama 'Rosencrantz and Guildenstern are dead' which turns the table on the traditional Hamlet and in doing so raises, I think, some very interesting issues about the nature of drama as well as the roles played by real people in real life, not just on the stage. It's Stoppard who gave me some of the confidence to write Piglet! Because after all, he'd played around with the Bard's work and made a comedy out of it. So surely I couldn't be sued for doing similar? For Stoppard, Rosencrantz and Guildenstern show that there's no such thing as a 'small' part, only a small actor. And this, for me, resonates importantly with the notion that those with 'labels' are actually just R&G to our 'normal' main cast. And thus in Piglet we can champion them and bring them to the fore with the weight of dramatic and philosophical depth afforded them by Stoppard before me. Oh, and it's really useful because it means that Rosie pig can say something and Gillie pig inevitably will echo it and that's funny. And if she says the opposite (which sometimes happens) that's funny too. So it gives Lauren her moment in the spotlight without us having to have kittens about the random nature of her conversational interactions. Funny and clever. We think. And just a little bit profound. But mainly funny.

So, Rosie/Pauline and Gillie/Lauren enter, arm in arm. Nonchalent as anything. The Big Boar/Kelly shouts at them (Kelly doesn't have much volume control you may have noticed by now).

'Listen you two. We need your help.'

And now it begins. Rosie/Pauline replies, 'Our help?'

Closely followed by Gillie/Lauren, 'our help?

'You want us to help you?' asks Rosie/Pauline

'You want us to help you?' copies Gillie/Lauren.

This can go on indefinitely, but to draw attention to the humour I interject with, 'Come on. This isn't YOUR play. Stop hogging the limelight.' Funny on oh so many levels, depending on your understanding of Shakespeare, Stoppard, disability issues...'

Big Boar/Kelly gets in on the act.

'If there's any hogging to go on here, I'm doing it.'

You see, we even get a pig joke in as well.

Before the audience, and Big Boar/Kelly burst their sides, Queenie/Mandy says, 'Sit down, stop upsetting yourself.'

The King and Queen of the pigs sit down. But it's just a moment's relief.

'What is it?' Rosie/Pauline asks.

'What is it' Gillie/Lauren echoes. She's into this. She's really into this. She's enjoying playing the game. She likes the audience laughing.

'Oh, for heaven's sake,' I say, winding it all up that bit further, 'They haven't got all night.'

'There's something wrong with Hamlet,' Big Boar/Kelly says. She knows all her lines and she'll deliver them despite laughter, flood, fire or plague. Which somehow makes it even funnier.

'Hamlet?' Rosie/Pauline says

'Piglet?' Gillie/Lauren says

(See, I told you she was doing it for comedy effect. She remembers the Piglet- Hamalet – Piglet laugh from scene one. She's a big game player. )

'Piglet.' Rosie/Pauline says, standing corrected.

'Yes, Piglet.' I say, 'There's something wrong with Piglet. Everyone got that?' It's good to show the audience that I as narrator am completely out of control. That's our point. I may be there to 'help as they need to be helped' but if I overstep my mark...

The Big Boar/Kelly leaves the throne and comes down to my place at the prompt corner.

'That's what I said,' she shouts at me. Point made, she turns on her heel, does a bit of an Elvis impersonation and stomps back to the throne.

'His dad's dead and you've just married his mum. What do you think is wrong with him?' I say cheekily, to the audience, so that they're clear he can't hear me.

Back at the throne we stagger on.

'What can we do to help?'

'Do to help?'

Are you getting into the rhythm?

'I want you to glean what afflicts him,' Big Boar/Kelly says.

'Glean what afflicts him?'

'What afflicts him?'

Rosie and Gillie are playing a blinder.

Big Boar/Kelly acts more anger and says, 'Find out what the hell's wrong with him. He's making his mum unhappy and I'm getting really annoyed with it.'

Nothing can put a damper on our double act.

'Okay,' Rosie/Pauline says.

'Okay,' Gillie/Lauren mimics.

'Okay,' I say from prompt corner. 'Go off and find out then.'

And they leave the stage to rapturous applause. In fact they come back on and take a bow for their pains. What ever made me think we couldn't do a *real* play on a *real* stage for a *real* audience. They are eating out of the palm of our hands. We rock. Careful though, as with all live theatre, it could all come crashing down around our heads at a moment's notice. We're only in scene three after all. But for now it's going well. The audience are on our side and it's more than I dared to imagine.

'I said we should cut them out. It'll go on forever,' I say as they finally disappear and the applause finally dies down.

Nothing happens. Now I need to prompt for real. Everyone has just stopped still amazed at the audience response. Everyone's completely forgotten what comes next. So luckily I'm cued up for the oldest ad lib in the dramatic book, 'Here comes the girlfriend AND her dad.'

Enter Polony/Barry and Ophelia/Annie. They are feeling the love and they're going to want some of this for themselves. They will be overacting their socks off you can lay bets on it.

'He's being really mean to me dad. He's a pig,' Ophelia/Annie says.

'We're all pigs, dahling,' Polony/Barry says, waving his handkerchief and arranging his lavish lace cuffs to titters. 'Don't worry,'

'I don't mean pig. I mean... he's being such a MAN.'

Annie never got this right in rehearsal. But here, with the audience expecting another funny line, she manages to remember. Go Annie.

'He's lost his mind,' Polony/Barry informs her. 'Mad with grief. About his dad. Could happen to anyone. I mean. If you lost your dad... you'd go mad wouldn't you darling?'

There's another pause. This time not because she's forgotten. This time it's deliberate comic effect. She looks him up and down. Takes her time. The audience can read the subtext.

'I might,' she replies and the auditorium erupts. It's a classic. Delivered with perfect comedy timing.

Polony/Barry replies with a level of chagrin (some of which may be Barry actually getting pissed off that he's being upstaged by Annie, in which case we need to watch out. That's when he starts getting random and it tends to throw the rest of the cast off stride.)

'You'd better. If it's good enough for Piglet, it's good enough for me. Honestly. Some children are just so ungrateful...' and he makes the most of his flamboyant exit. Ophelia/Annie stomps off after him in her pink tutu. She is the most unlikely Ophelia you could imagine and yet... if Ophelia was a pig labelled with learning disabilities... she owns the role.

Having negotiated scene three we are about half way there. And I'm beginning to feel that we'll get out without a lynching or people demanding their money back. It's not till later that Barry tells me he let everyone in for free and the only money we've made is from the raffle and a number of sizeable 'donations' which probably equate to the ticket price I'd thought we were charging.

Scene four sees Polony/Barry talking to our favourite comedy duo Rosie/Pauline and Gillie/Lauren.

'Okay. Your job is to glean what afflicts him,' Polony/Barry says. 'Me. I know. He's mad with grief because his dad's dead.'

Rosie/Pauline is having none of it. She's not going to bow to pomposity whether it be Polony or Barry delivering it. Real or scripted, pomposity is pomposity to Pauline and so she delivers her line with feeling, 'Yeah, yeah, will you just get off and let us get on with our part.'

'Our part,' Gillie/Lauren repeats right on cue.

It was funny before and it's still funny now of course. The audience respond.

'Oh, here we go...' Polony/Barry mutters and begins to exit, 'Young pigs today. No respect. No respect.'

The stage is left to Rosie and Gillie pig and an audience who can hardly contain themselves. They think they know what to expect next. And they're loving it.

Rosie/Pauline starts. Of course.

'So what are we going to do?'

'What're we going to do?' Gillie/Lauren chirrups.

Rosie/Pauline steps up the game. Just what the audience didn't expect.

'Do you have to repeat everything I say?'

'Yes,' Gillie/Lauren replies. (It would actually work just as well if she said 'no.' so we win either way. The audience find new things to laugh at. Insight.

'You didn't that time,' Rosie/Pauline adds, just to ram the point home. But doesn't give them time to reflect on it all. 'Oh, here he comes. I know. We'll tell him jokes. Put him at his ease.'

Enter Piglet/Bilbo.

Rosie/Pauline starts. As you would.

'Hi.'

'Hi,' Gillie/Lauren says. This shouldn't be funny now should it? It's a standard greeting. But of course whenever one of them opens their mouth now it's going to bring the house down.

Piglet/Bilbo replies, as you would, with 'Hi.'

'How are you?' Rosie/Pauline asks and Piglet/Bilbo gets his response in quickly so that he isn't upstaged yet again.

'Who wants to know?' he asks.

'Me. Him (she points at Gillie/Lauren) Them (she points at the audience) All of us,' Rosie/Pauline says.

Piglet/Bilbo steels himself. It's time for him to be funny. A different kind of funny right enough.

'When the wind is west I can tell a hawk from a hacksaw,' he says. A line from the real play that I've convinced him is really funny. He doesn't' get a laugh. He looks at me, baffled. What's gone wrong? I smile back at him. He's forgotten he's the straight man and the best joke in the world is coming up. People may actually wet themselves in the audience at this now we've whipped them up into such a frenzy.

Rosie/Pauline replies acerbically, 'Yeah. Okay. If you say so.' She dismisses him and he acts crushed. I hope he's acting. It's rather convincing. I don't have time to worry about it, because Rosie/Pauline continues, 'Hey.

Here's a good joke. Get this one. If a baby pig's a piglet. What's a baby toy?

This just is a great joke. All the cast have loved it. Mandy especially loves it. Literal minded Mandy can't get enough of this joke. I'm giving you time to work out the answer for yourself here before we give it to you.... Got it...?

Piglet/Bilbo replies with the answer, 'A toilet.'

The place erupts. A pig joke and a toilet joke combined. Does life get any better?

Except Piglet/Bilbo just doesn't seem to think it funny. I'm still not sure if this is acting or if he's going into a decline. If he might start singing the No Labels theme tune to regain control of his situation. And it's his big moment coming up. Come on Bilbo. You can do it.

While I'm at prompt corner worrying about what's coming next, Rosie and Gillie have delivered their lines, and are on the way out. I miss the moment when Rosie explains to all her understanding of what afflicts Piglet which is – he's lost his sense of humour.

Piglet/Bilbo stands alone on the stage. All lights go down except the spotlight right on him. It's his time to shine. I give him a surreptitious thumbs up and he goes for it.

'To be. Or not to be. That is the question.' There is a long pause. This is, after all the crux of our play, of Shakespeare's play. Of life in general. Time for reflection on the enormity of the question is quite appropriate.

But remember this is comedy. And after a good long dramatic pause, he continues, calm as you like, 'I don't know what to do for the best. Really. I just don't know.'

Time for us to play the double act. I chastise him with

'I think we're going a bit off script here...' (It was all scripted this way you understand.)

He turns on me, 'Hey. What do you expect? I'm a piglet. Not even a grown pig. You can't expect me to learn a whole soliloquy.' He throws down his mask and exits. And I swear someone in the audience cheers.

With scene five we are back at the palace with Big Boar and Queenie sitting on their thrones. Big Boar/Kelly shouts,

'Well,' as Rosie/Pauline and Gillie/Lauren enter to a hum of audience anticipation. They are more raucous than a pantomime audience. I bet Shakespeare's never seen the like before. Even Stoppard's version isn't this funny.

'Well?' choruses Queenie/Mandy.

'Oh no, now *they're* at it,' I say, laying the comedy bait and reeling the audience in.

Rosie and Gillie pig deliver their verdict on the what afflicts Piglet question.

'He's gone nuts,' Rosie/Pauline says.

'Pignuts,' Gillie/Lauren says (unscripted but hilarious.)

Polony/Barry picks up on it and gets back on track, 'I agree, He's gone nuts. Pure and simple. Chestnut and apple stuffing.'

I give him a withering look, 'That was uncalled for,' I suggest. 'It's not a gore fest.'

Piglet/Bilbo enters.

'Hey, want to watch a play,'

'A play?' (Boar)

'A Play?' (Queenie)

'A Play?' (Rosie)

'A play?' (Gillie)

'A play?' (Polony)

You get the picture. Everyone's in on the act now.

Nelson breaks it. Of course. Normal Nelson/Deirdre plays her 'sensible' role to a tee.

'Yes, a play. A play. Okay. A play. Let's just get on with it.'

I think that's called raising the dramatic stakes. Still funny though.

The Big Boar/Kelly asks what the play is called and is told by Piglet/Bilbo that it's called the Mousetrap. Everyone looks at each other muttering 'nuts, told you he's gone nuts.'

Piglet/Bilbo carries on regardless, 'It's more of a dumb show than a play,'

'You can say that again,' shouts someone offstage (prompted!)

'Can we *please* get on with it,' I pretend to side with Nelson's voice of reason.

'Okay, watch this and make up your own mind,' Piglet/Bilbo says as the dumb show commences.

Stevie (dressed as Elvis) leads in Ghostypig/ Duncan and gets him to lie down. He pours something in his ear. It took us weeks to get Stevie to do this reliably, even though it was only an imaginary pour. It helped that the vessel was brown!

Music starts. Shaggy's *'It wasn't me,'* blares out and the pigs sing along with our adapted lyrics. I think you can probably guess them. It's fairly indistinct to be honest apart from the repeated *'it wasn't me's'* which everyone joins in with gusto.

At the final one, Big Boar/Kelly gets up from his/her throne and stomps off the stage, leaving us to consider as Piglet/Bilbo points out,

'Why's he so annoyed if he didn't do it?'

Pigs have fairly simple and straightforward reasoning processes it seems.

Blackout and exeunt pigs.

With scene six we are really cooking on gas. Can you believe all this has been achieved in some fifteen minutes of real time. And we're still on track and on script and no one has fallen off the stage or had a fit, real or hissy, and the audience are loving it. Here we are now, in Queenie's sty at the palace. I set the scene, 'Piglet's in trouble now. His mum is really angry with him. Showing up the big boar like that in front of everyone... watch out Piglet.'

Piglet/Bilbo enters his mum's bedroom.

'What are you playing at Piglet?' Queenie/Mandy asks him

'Nothing mum,' he replies. ]

I will admit that a prompt is needed here but as soon as I say, 'I brought...' Mandy is back on track with,

'I brought you up better than that, piglet.'

To which he replies, 'but my dad... he said...' and there is a scuffling behind the curtains accompanied by Duncan's recorded/distorted/disembodied voice shouting 'NOW PIGLET.'

Piglet/Bilbo draws his cardboard but shiny dagger and stabs furiously behind the curtain. Out staggers Polony. The script calls for him to 'fall down dead,' but I swear Barry takes a full two minutes of writhing and staggering around before he finally carks it. He's got his money's worth. This was the moment he'd been living for it seems. This is drama for Barry.

Finally we assume he's twitched his last and Queenie/Mandy gets the nod from me to continue,

'Look what you've done now!' she says.

Piglet/Bilbo acts all innocent.

'What was he doing behind there?' he asks.

'I've told you not to play with knives,' Queenie/Mandy replies. I mean, it's important we get the odd easy moral in there isn't it? Even in comedy. Never miss an opportunity I say. I may be the writing equivalent of Barry, it occurs to me just at that moment. Maybe less is more. Too late to worry about that now. You can't stop the wilderbeast in full flight.

'I thought it was... the big boar... oh, no... what have I done?' says Piglet/Bilbo with as much remorse in his voice as he can muster. Though it's clear he really, really enjoyed the stabbing!

I stand up. I move to centre stage. I break more conventions. It's time. I address the audience directly.

'So you're asking yourself,' I say, 'How did that happen? Did we miss something? What was *he* doing there? Well, let me tell you this. If you hide behind curtains you get what's coming to you in my opinion...'

Polony/Barry stops me in my tracks. Despite being dead he just stands clean up and flicks me in the face with this handkerchief.

'When we want your opinion we'll ask for it,' he says and exits reprising his great mutter sequence, 'No respect. No one shows me any respect...' as the lights go down.

We're nearly there. It's the final scene. Time to tie it all up and get to our ending, tragic though that might be. Lights come up on Ophelia/Annie. In her tutu. A vision in pink. Enter Nelson/Deirdre who with characteristic bluntness states, 'Bad luck Ophelia, your dad's dead.'

Ophelia/Annie responds in time honoured fashion, 'My dad? Dead?'

Nelson/Deirdre, never one to sweeten the pill confirms, 'yes, Dead. Sorry,' and looks at the audience. 'No point pretending. Look what happened to Piglet when they didn't tell him the truth.'

I interject, 'She'll go mad now. You could have been a bit more... a bit less...'

While I'm still stumbling through the horror which is unfolding before us, Ophelia/Annie makes her moves.

'That's it. I'm going to drown myself,' and turns on her heel. She tries a little pirouette but it doesn't really come off. Baby elephant is what springs to mind, never mind pig in a tutu.

'That's a bit extreme,' Nelson/Deirdre states. 'Ridiculous.'

And as if we needed anything more ridiculous we get a chorus line of pigs with linked arms dancing across the back of the stage singing *'madness, madness they call it madness. madness. madness they call it madness I try to explain what goes on in my brain but madness madness they call it madness.'*

And they exit the other side of the stage.

Ophelia/Annie turns on her heels and addresses the audience with, 'It's what he would have expected,' before she finally exits leaving Nelson/Deidre standing alone on the stage. She turns to me. Expectation. Resolution.

'What now?' she asks.

Enter Piglet/Bilbo.

Someone to talk to.

'Piglet,' she says, 'Your girlfriend's gone mad and drowned herself.'

I bash my head with my hand and cry out, 'He'll never learn.'

Time for the grand finale. The rest of the pigs enter.

Piglet shows great emotion at the news of another death, 'What?' he asks of all and sundry.

'Drowned,' says Rosie/Pauline.

'Drowned,' chimes in Gillie/Lauren.

'Drowned?' repeats Piglet/Bilbo sadly.

Nelson/Deirdre regains control.

'Yeah. Drowned okay. This is getting out of control. Can we please get on with the story before there's no one left alive to tell it.'

I interject again stating the bleeding obvious, 'That is the point of a tragedy.'

Fed up with me, Nelson/Deirdre turns to the audience and directly addresses them. We have thrown convention to the wind by now you'll see. (But Deirdre and Barry both like audience attention and they don't really care if they've broken the fourth wall, they are pretty keen for the whole thing to be over and get their rightful acclaim by this point if we're honest.) She says,

'What would you do?'

I close in for the final run of humour, 'That's it,' I say, pulling proceedings to a halt and they all feign confusion. 'Sorry times up. We said it was abridged, adapted, updated and we couldn't afford the theatre for the whole play... so you'll have to go away and ask yourself what you would do?'

It's everyone's last chance to shine.

Piglet/Bilbo goes first as is only fair.

'If someone killed your dad,' he says.

'If a ghost told you someone killed your dad,' Nelson/Deirdre corrects him.

'And married your mother,' Queenie/Mandy says.

'And you killed the wrong man,' Big Boar/Kelly shouts.

'In an act of haste,' Polony/Barry can't help himself but take an early, unscheduled bow.

'Misplaced revenge,' I add.

'And you went mad and drowned yourself,' Ophelia/Annie says. Her best delivered line in the play.

'What would you do?' Rosie/Pauline says and it should be no surprise that the next line is,

'What would you do?' delivered by Gillie/Lauren.

Followed by everyone joining in with the grand finale of 'What would *you* do?'

And as they are about to give us a standing ovation I deliver the final line, after which everyone will go into an orgy of bowing and clapping themselves.

'No wonder a piglet found it so hard. Could you do any better?'

The curtain comes down, and up, and down. And they get the standing ovation they deserved and the clapping goes on for what seems like forever but is certainly long enough for me to realise that Barry and Deirdre were right and I just had to learn how to help them how they needed to be helped and believe in the magic and try that little bit harder and not let a label dictate to me what someone's capabilities are. Lesson learned. And that Tuesday night we had a raffle and an after show party and still everyone was home in their beds by ten o'clock and I think a sense of pride all round was achieved. And I think a lot of people who hadn't quite known what to expect when they left their homes at six o'clock went home much wiser and a lot happier but probably with their sides still aching from all the laughter. Which has to be a good thing for a Tuesday doesn't it?

# WEDNESDAY

### *Politics is rubbish.*

It's Wednesday. Half way through the journey of our week. Ten o'clock in the morning and the gang's all here. Drinking tea, coffee or juice (or if you're Mandy you're drinking tea *and* coffee *and* juice, just because you can and I predict you're going to be telling me you've got a stomach ache by ten twenty. ) And talking about politics. What? Back the truck up? We're talking politics in a group of adults labelled with learning disabilities? Are we crazy?

Ah, you see, you've fallen into the trap. We all do it. However much we think that the label doesn't mean much, it's still so very, very easy to see a group of people wearing this label as people who are intellectually 'subnormal' and therefore unable to have an opinion about politics. If I had a pound for every time I've had an interaction with a 'carer' or 'service provider' who tells me that really 'these people' (or this specific person) is childlike, unable to understand – basically suggesting that they a) need to wrapped in cotton wool from the realities of life and/or b) are just a waste of time to talk to about anything important. It happens no matter what the topic of discussion is. In dramatic terms it usually ends in the suggestion that we do 'fairy stories' or some children's level drama. We resist. At No Labels, that's what we do. Resist.

If the members of No Labels 'resist' on their own, individually, on their own time and in their own environments it tends to be seen as 'challenging behaviour' but if we all do it together it's a lot easier to put across the line that we are 'resisting' not just the label but the preconceptions of how you have to deal with someone who is labelled. Speak. Very. Slowly. Don't. Say. Anything. Complicated. Never. Talk. Politics.

Who are they trying to kid? When I started working with No Labels (before they were No Labels of course... I suppose when they were just an amorphous labelling group) I had never personally encountered people labelled with learning disabilities. I didn't know how to treat them. I didn't know what the 'rules' of how to treat someone as 'special' (for which read like an idiot) were. So I just treated them the same as I would any other group of people. It worked for us. Of course each member has their idiosyncracies and we've had to work hard to get to know each other and to learn to communicate beyond the basic. But that's the case for any group of people. Certainly for any group of actors. We muddled along. And we talk about things. Things that matter. Things that affect our lives. And believe me, politics affects the life of a person with a learning disability label as much, if not more, than the rest of us.

Maybe there's something wrong with me, but my attitude is, if someone doesn't understand what I'm trying to say to them, it's my job to work at it till I get to a point where I can explain myself clearly, where we reach a mutual understanding. Certainly if they're paying me (as No Labels do) and even in daily life. Communication is the way we move outside our own individual worlds into a shared environment. The social milieu if you like. And most of us want to do that some of the time at least. Some people who show no interest in moving outside of their heads and communicating with others actually just don't find that the 'others' are communicating anything meaningful to them. Duncan is a case in point. Some people think that Duncan is near brain dead. That he's got nothing to say, nothing to offer and is basically what one might colloquially call 'a moron.' All because he has a very limited range of vocabulary which he uses in standard conversational situations. But there are others of us – dare I say those he now calls his friends – who can have great conversations with Duncan (as long as we obey *his* rules – he doesn't like a questioning format) and we have found him to be funny, witty and highly intelligent. He has an extensive knowledge which spans 50's music right through to politics. His favourite television programmes are *Mastermind* and *Newsnight*. Go figure.

So yes, the key point here is that some people (with labels) are like Duncan, and indeed Lauren is another example, and what's different about them is that they invent the rules of their interaction with others. They invent the social and linguistic rules by which you have to interact. I think that's a sign of intelligence not stupidity. Most of us just go with the flow of what we think we have to do to interact. Duncan and Lauren have developed their own system. And once you crack it... Let me put it this way. With Duncan and Lauren you have to approach communication as if you were trying to get to know someone who speaks another language (and not one based on European Romance patterns) and you have to learn the rules as you go. If you try to get them to play by your rules you'll probably have a rough ride, but when you let go and try to come to them 'where they are' and engage using their rules, it's a lot more fun.

For example. Lauren is drinking juice. I'm drinking coffee. (Fairtrade. We are most insistent that we use fair trade produce where possible. We know what it's like to be an oppressed mass here at No Labels) We generally think that people being paid a fair and living wage for their bananas, sugar, coffee and tea is a good thing. Is that too political for learning disability? I digress.

'So, Lauren,' I say. 'What did you have for breakfast this morning?'

'Sorry,' she says.

'No need to apologise,' I say. 'Did you have cereal?'

She looks at me. It's game on.

'I did,' she says.

*I did* is good. *I did* means she's throwing the gauntlet down. *I did* means – okay, I'll talk to you, I know this game, now we're going through a range of stupid options and I get to play around till I'm ready to tell you what I think you need to know. The options for her at this point would have been a simple no (at which point I'd start asking if she had toast etc) or a yes (at which point she knows I'll start asking what kind of cereal) So she knows that with any of these 'appropriate' answers I'll just keep asking her questions. I did is her way of saying, okay, lets skip all that line of questioning and move onto something more interesting. It means. Stop asking me about my breakfast and engage with me on a more interesting level. Believe me, I've spent three years with Lauren and I'm beginning to know her language games. They are complex. They keep me on my toes. And I need to come up with something better than 'did you have cereal?' Of course, if you were here on Monday you'll know that if she says 'yes, darling,' I know we're having a good day and I go up the ladder to the next level. Because I do sometimes think that conversation with Lauren is pretty much like a snakes and ladders game. I may throw the dice, but she's the one who says what number is on the face.

Usually with Lauren you have to work your way into a conversation. She tests you to see if you are willing to really engage. Only then will she start something meaningful. It's a game. I know it's a game to her. So I play her game.

'Do you like apple juice?' I ask her.

'No,' she replies.

'Do you like Coke?' I ask.

'No,' she replies, laughing because she's drinking Coke at that very minute.

'Do you like orange?' I ask. I know she likes orange.

'Nooo...' she says, raucously.

'Would you like a biscuit?' I ask (note that I've changed subtly here. I'm not asking her in an abstract way what she does or doesn't like, I'm asking her if she wants something, a concrete something that I may give her.)

'No,' she says.

'A chocolate biscuit?' I suggest

'No,' she says but again, smiling at me as I offer her the tin for her to look into.

'Is that a no no or a yes no?' I ask her. (It took me a year to learn this construction but when I did it opened a load of conversational doors between us)

'Yes no,' she says and takes a biscuit.

So what is going on there? Does Lauren have no concept of the abstract? Can she only make a choice when a chocolate biscuit is waved in her face? There are those who would have you believe that. Or, if you take the time, and learn as I did, you may see another set of patterns emerging. This is what I believe is happening.

I ask Lauren if she wants to talk with me. To chat. She doesn't really. She doesn't see the point. She's drinking her drink and why is it important to talk about other drinks she may or may not like (yes, Lauren, why indeed? It just shows how little I have to talk about doesn't it?) She resists me with her 'no's.' Each of them is a sign to me saying 'try harder,' 'try harder and I might let you in,' So I keep on trying. But because she's built up the pattern which is 'no,' she doesn't want to let go of the pattern and I've got to do something different (modulate the tune) before she will change. That's the value of the 'no no or yes no?' question. That is me saying, 'I know that you are using the word no in a way particular to you, as a test for me to see if I'll just give up and either give you something you don't want or give you something I want you to have or just go away. But what I'm doing isn't that pattern. What I'm doing is actually asking you what you think. Really. I want to know. I want to play your game. I want us to use the words in the same way – but you are in control. If you want to change your no to yes you can do that. It's only a word. And the action is more important.'

That may seem complex and convoluted to you, and I'm probably not using the best example, but believe me, Lauren has some very complex linguistic games up her sleeve and I have to keep all my wits about me to keep up with them. Of course most people don't bother. If she says no once they take her at her word and do what they were going to do anyway. Because sad but true, most people with the learning disability *have* learned that they have little choice in the matter. They can say yes, they can say no, they can express preference or choice or desire but they end up with whatever was coming their way anyway. So they learn not to bother to make choices and then they get out of the habit of it and then they just don't make them. Or don't want to make them. They don't like the constant disappointment.

As a general rule I don't think you should promise people things you can't deliver and that is a hundred times more the case when someone is shouldering a learning disability label, because their life is so riven through with disappointment and broken promises that you have a responsibility not to add to that. It matters to them. Keep your word. Don't offer them the world and then deliver nothing. Lauren is used to this kind of conversation.

'Lauren, do you want apple or orange to drink?'

And if she said

'Orange please,' like a nice conventional person, they say, 'oh, sorry, we don't have any orange, so you'll have to have apple.'

And to add insult to injury they usually follow it up with, 'you like apple, don't you?' without waiting for any reply. They just plonk the apple there and that's it.

Now don't you think that after a lifetime of people doing that with you (on every level of communication/decision making) you'd get fed up with it and either become 'challenging' in your behaviour or just check out and play your own game?

Politics it is. Politics is in everything you see. All decisions impact on real people. At every level. For people with the learning disability label the impact is on service provision. They can't work because they are deemed incompetent (or it's too difficult to find a job they could do – Annie for example would love to sort litter all day – cans from bottles would suit her great) and so they are reliant on benefits. But they aren't able to handle money or make choices about how that money is spent (they haven't been taught to any degree to do this and they may have conceptual problems which reinforce this) and so they just have to rely on other people and do as they are told. They are victims of politics and policy. And everyone then forgets that there are plenty of vital choices they can make about their lives and should be allowed to make. The failure is not with the labelled people. The failure is with the system which imposes the label and fails to 'help them how they need to be helped.'

You can see I'm getting on my high horse here and I've been bending the groups ear for a while during coffee about this very thing. Barry loves it. Barry and I have a sort of tacit understanding that we are political radicals (in a non party political sort of way.) Call us social reformers if it makes you happier.

Here's a flavour of a conversation we're having this coffee time, (once I've abandoned my linguistic jazz improvisation with Lauren. If only I could think of more intelligent things to say to her!)

'Annie,' I say, 'what do you think about money?'

What kind of a question is this? Do I imagine Annie actually thinks about money at all? Unsurprisingly she just blanks me.

'I mean,' I say, 'do you think you should get to choose what you spend your money on?

'Yes,' she says. Am I an idiot? What kind of question is that? Who is going to say no to that question? I of course have secret information here. I've been told that Annie would spend all her benefit money on sweets if she was given it. That's the justification for why she has her money doled out by her 'carers' from a jar. I'm about to go further into this conversation when Annie gets there first.

'I won at the bingo on Monday night,' she tells me.

'How much?' I ask.

'Twenty pounds,' she says, slapping her hands together and cackling with delight.

'Yah beauty,' Bilbo says.

'Lend us a tenner,' Barry says. (Annie has a reputation for being mean with money. I'm not surprised really if she has to rely on hand outs from the tin or the bingo wins. It's not exactly like she's rolling in it.)

She laughs at him, guessing he's joking, 'Away with you Barry,' she says. 'You're not getting your hands on my money.'

'Tight,' Barry says. 'Short arms and deep pockets,' he laughs. 'You owe me more drinks that...'

He never gets to finish because Annie is getting on her high horse.

'It's my money...' she starts.

'Yes,' I say, 'and what happens to it? Do you have to put it in the jar?'

She looks at me in horror. How stupid am I? Do I really think she's confessing her winnings to her carers? No. She runs a dual economy does Annie. She works to the Cuban model.

I have often thought that either Annie is the luckiest woman alive or that the bingo is rigged. It's bingo for people with learning disability label. Held once a week in a local pub. And Annie wins with astonishing regularity, about once a month. So I'm guessing that the people running the bingo have a fair idea that they are supplementing the meagre incomes of the participants. That they are providing Annie with 'spends' and I applaud them for that. Of course the service providers couldn't condone this. But more than this. They seem to spend a lot of time telling us all that Annie can't manage money, that she spends it all on sweeties and yet she's dealing with an extra twenty to forty pounds a month that they don't know about and she doesn't spend all that on sweeties does she? I know she likes sweeties (but if you lived Annie's life I'm guessing you would comfort eat too) but she doesn't buy that many. She uses them for comfort eating. She also uses them to prove that she's not as tight as Barry says. She loves to slip you a sweetie. She loves to be a friend. She thinks she needs money to do that. Having been denied any prospect of earning money to give her a sense of worth, she still sees that money is a way by which people measure success, normality and worth. I decide to try and explore Annie and the money situation further.

'Hey Annie,' I say. 'How about if you and me went up town with your winnings. What could we buy?'

'Jumper,' she says. She wants a new jumper.

'Okay,' I say. 'This is a game then. A pretend. Let's pretend, you and I are going up town with your twenty pounds and we have a look in the shops.'

She is batting an imaginary person off with her white stick as we go – because we are acting this out for those who are still slurping and chomping.

'What are you doing Annie?' I ask.

'He's in my way,' she says. 'He's pushing me, he always does it.'

There's a chorus of approval from the table. She's not the only one who is jostled and jeered at when she goes out in the street.

'Okay,' I say, and take her arm. 'Now we're going into the shop to look at the jumpers.'

We look round quite a few imaginary shops and discuss quite a few imaginary jumpers costing from between five pounds and forty pounds. I suggest we look in a charity shop so that she might get a cheap jumper and have money left for other things. She looks at me in horror. She used to do volunteer 'work' in a charity shop but they reckoned she couldn't be trusted to handle the till on her own (and they wouldn't commit not to leave her on her own with the till) so the placement was terminated. Unfair I think. Anyway, she's not keen to get a jumper from a charity shop. End of. So we fix on a nice jumper, a pale blue cable knit I think it is, from a reputable shop and they pack it up for us and we take it home. She's not too keen to take it home for some reason. I want to know what her carers will say when she turns up with something new for them to wash. They hold the purse strings after all. They do the washing. Will they not notice?

I ask her and I am totally unprepared for her response.

'Annie?' I ask. 'What will your carers say when they say your new jumper?'

Without a beat of a pause she replies, 'They'll say it doesn't suit me and I should take it back.'

I choke. While Annie has a great imagination, this smacks of something that has been drummed into her.

'But,' I say, 'It does suit you. We picked it out together. It was your choice. There's nothing wrong with it. It fits fine and it's...'

'That's what *they* say,' she says and shrugs.

And I fear that *is* what they say. That way *they* keep control.

'Do they ask you where you got the money from?' I ask.

'Maybe,' she says.

'Do you tell them?' I ask.

She smiles at me, poor benighted fool that I am. Think about it. Would you?

'No,' she says. 'I tell them it was a present from my sister.'

Do you see why I think that there are all kinds of subtle games going on between the labelled and the non labelled? Are you beginning to see beneath the surface? It's all politics. Domestic politics maybe, but politics all the same.

But we must move on. We have a play to produce. If you were here with us on Tuesday you'll remember that we have so far tackled Shakespeare to great applause and now we are spreading our wings a bit further. We are moving into political drama. We have a commission. A gig. We are going to perform at the Scottish Parliament no less. We are devising a whole new play for the event – which is Disability Day- and it's called 'Politics is rubbish.'

Yes, it's another play on words. We are using the phrase literally. Because that's how people say that the learning disability fraternity see the world. Literally. So we're going to subvert it and throw it back at them. Make them think for a change.

We all get it. Politics is rubbish. It's about recycling and waste. About not wasting resources. We care about that at No Labels. Believe me, we know all about rubbish and about being treated as rubbish. We play a game called 'I went to the tip.' You have two people and they sit in a chair and pretend to be something that's been dumped on the tip. Like a bottle or an old shoe. And they chat to each other about all the uses they could have been put to and then they make a plan for 'escape.' It's a good way to develop improvisational skills and use the imagination. (Which learning disabled people are not supposed to have. Let's scotch that myth right away. They have as much imagination as the rest of us. They just may not express it the same way but it's there.) I truly, truly believe this is a communication issue not an intelligence issue.

Here's how it goes. We're going to do a quick round of the game (oh yes, it's long past ten twenty, it's nearly eleven and Mandy is settling down after having had her stomach ache at the allotted time) before we start rehearsing for the play.

Kelly and Annie take the seats.

'Hello,' Kelly says, 'What are you doing here?'

'I'm an old jumper,' Annie says (not a new one you note) 'and I've been thrown away.'

'I'm a bottle,' Kelly says. 'They chucked me when they'd drunk me.'

'That's ridiculous,' Annie says, 'They could have recycled you.'

'Of course they could,' agrees Kelly.

'They make fleeces out of plastic bottles,' Bilbo pipes up. He remembers that gem from last time.

'Yes, they could use you and me together and mix us up and make a whole new jumper,' Annie says.

'What's wrong with you?' Kelly says. 'Worn out?' (I think we can assume she's still in character here and asking the question of the jumper, not of Annie.)

'Just a little hole in my elbow,' Annie says. 'But they just got bored with me.'

Put like that it seems so ludicrous. So wrong. The rest of us are on the edge of our seats.

Then things turn a bit less practical and a bit more magic realism. But that's all good. That's imagination.

'I know,' says Kelly, 'If we wrap you round me and tie it up tight then when a kid comes along he can kick us over the fence and we can escape.'

That's it and the end and they stand for their applause. We don't need to interrogate what they will 'do' when they escape and whether it wouldn't be better to go to their allotted bins and be reincarnated as something more useful to society. We let it be. You get the picture. Maybe you even get the subtext if you think really hard!

So this is the sort of thing that we do when we work to devise a play. We play around imaginatively. We learn a lot about the topic we are going to present. We think of ways to make it funny and to get the points we think are important across. It's not just me telling them we are going to be worthy and do a recycling play. It's me giving them the opportunity to engage with politics. With the world around them. I can tell you, Bilbo, Duncan and Mandy are experts at litter picking. It's one of the 'activities' they are given to do on a regular basis when they attend Activity centres on days they aren't at No Labels. They're good enough to go on the streets picking up your litter (unpaid) but you don't think they could understand the implications of a world where things that aren't in brand new condition or things that are slightly out of shape or deemed past their best are just dumped. They know all about being thrown away. They know all about rubbish. And it's for me to show them a bit more about how politics relates to their lives. To help them how they need to be helped. Not by playing kids games and fairy stories. By engaging as a group of adults with a purpose. That's what we do.

But we'll do it after lunch.

~~~

After lunch we get down to the business of rehearsal. While I'm not that comfortable about us performing on Disability Day, we have all agreed to take a pragmatic approach to things. We know the power of 'hungry and homeless please help.' We know that sometimes to get funding we have to tick the 'vulnerable' box. Actually, some of the group, far from finding this an offensive concept, find it quite amusing. We've talked about it a lot. And in conclusion we've agreed that despite us not recognising the label, in order to educate other people, sometimes we have to go in to a situation wearing the label and in the process of the event showing them how we (and they) can throw the label off. And that's what this play is about. About showing *them* in this case the politicians, that we may be different from them but we have something to teach them too. Let's face it, to social policy makers, real people (never mind real characters – that's joke from yesterday) with learning disabilities are possibly little more than labels until they meet them in all their unique and individual glory.

We resist. But we also provoke. The title is provocative don't you think? Politics is rubbish? But we'll show a positive outcome and at the end of the performance we hope very much that we'll have shown that people with the learning disability label have opinions and thoughts about recycling, the environment and other issues and yes, that they have imaginations and a good sense of humour too. That's not bad for a day's work is it? We plan to run the play, which will last about thirty minutes and then Barry will lead a workshop which will include 'games' such as 'I went to the tip,' and the impressive 1-20 game, which when it works is the best way I know of showing that the label of 'learning disability' is futile in many important contexts. More of that another time.

Since yesterday you got to see a performance in all its glory, today we'll not go into the actual trip to Parliament and all the excitement that went with it, but we'll focus on the afternoon rehearsal. Process is as important as performance after all. So, sit back and enjoy. You are an audience of one. We may still be a bit rough around the edges but we hope we'll get the message across.

The play is called Politics is Rubbish. The story has been devised from an original idea Barry had but all members have put in their ten pence worth and I've developed one of our legendary flexible scripts to keep things going along.

There are several settings: Petrol Station, Spaceship, Forest, Factory and Iceberg. Each member plays multiple characters. And this time, wait for it, we *have* got permission to use the music. One song is key to the play and it's called *The End of the Age of Oil* by David Rovics. He's an American who writes social conscience songs and I saw him perform once then I emailed him and asked if it was okay for us to use his song in our play and he said yes.

We open to a petrol forecourt. You can tell it is because there are a line of three petrol pumps, played by Duncan, Mandy and Kelly. They are dressed in bin bags with stickers of BP/Shell/Esso on their fronts and they each have a finger in their ear (to represent the nozzle of the pump) Very impressive it is too.

The music starts. The song begins. Even though he's a petrol pump, Duncan sings along because he knows all the words and he likes the song (and its sentiment?)

*It was as if there was a contest*
*To see how many holes could be dug*
*To see how much of it could be sucked from the ground*
*To kill off every beetle and bug*
*To kill off every woman and child*
*To kill off every man*
*And they put it all in barrels*
*Then they put the barrels into cans*
*That's how it was at the end of the age of oil*

While this is going on, three cars fill up with petrol from the pumps. You can tell they are cars because each driver holds a cardboard steering wheel. First is Pauline, then Lauren, then Stevie and Deirdre in a car together. Stevie is driving. The steering wheel is brown after all.

Each of them fills the car up with fuel.

We have used recorded narration for this play. We got this really cool software that distorts your voice and makes you sound like an automaton. To be honest, having Deirdre reading it out loud would have much the same effect but we like the tinny quality this gives and it does give us one more useful actor (if you don't mind my saying so.)

At this point it's Barry's voice, distorted which tell you: *The modern world is built with oil. Oil keeps our cars on the road and planes in the air. Our transport system is almost entirely dependent on oil and our global economy is almost entirely dependent on transport.*

*We live in a world where food is carried from one hemisphere to another, where we think nothing of roses plucked in the morning in Kenya, arriving on the shelves of Marks and Spencers by the afternoon. Of apples from Canada and potatoes from France and cheap clothes from*

*Indonesia. But with the price of oil sky rocketing how does that effect our everyday lives?*

*Imagine if you were an alien, watching our world...*

And we switch scene to a spaceship. It's remarkably like the Starship Enterprise actually and we've robbed a bit of the theme tune, in case anyone hasn't got that. In the spaceship are Captain Barry, Science officer Bilbo and Drone Annie. They are on the deck, preparing for landing. Wooh, oo, woooh.. oooo....oooo (etc)

But in this spaceship the 'aliens' are dressed in white anti-radiation suits and you should know that they are protected by a veil of invisibility when threatened.

Science officer Bilbo speaks first. It's important to set the scene clearly.

'Captain. This is planet Earth. We haven't been here for thousands of years, since the age of the dinosaur.'

Captain Barry has a clipboard (to help him remember his lines and prompt other aliens who might need it).

He gives the command, 'Prepare the shuttle and send out our drone.'

Annie the drone is a metallic looking creature (in a cardboard box covered with tin foil) with hosepipe arms. She stumps her way across the stage towards the petrol pumps. She addresses them,

'Stand to attention. Take me to your leader and take your finger out of your ear when you are being addressed by an officer.'

There is silence. Though we anticipate a titter from an audience at the very least. It is so ridiculous. But Annie is an incredibly convincing drone. She has many talents. Not just Shakespearean heroines!

Mandy (Esso) takes her finger out of her ear because the drone told her to. Then remembers she's a petrol pump and doesn't have cognitive function so cannot obey commands and puts it back in. The others stand firm against the onslaught of Drone Annie.

Drone Annie stomps back to the spaceship and as she goes, those who had formerly been cars have been transformed into oil slicks (they are also wearing bin bags now) and they remove the hoses from the petrol pumps and generally spread oil all over the place. Obviously we're not using real oil. We represent all this will big rolls of black plastic.

The recorded narration continues for those who may be missing the point, *What happens when the oil flow dries up? Imagine turning on the light switch and the room stays dark.* (Duncan mimes this action – he likes light switches, it's his job to turn them on and off at the beginning and end of our sessions.) *Or trying to light the gas hob and there's no flicker of a flame.* (Mandy and Deirdre mime this action) *Or turning the ignition and the car doesn't start.*(Pauline and Stevie mime this.) *Doesn't bear thinking about does it? That's life at the end of the age of oil.*

The cast look stunned. To a man. Desolate. Disconsolate. Depressed. Then under the silent instruction of Pauline, they set to clearing up the oil slick.

We shift focus back to the spaceship. The alien spacemen (they were Bilbo's idea) observe.

'Is this Earth's new life force?' Science officer Bilbo asks.

Captain Barry shakes his head, sucks his teeth (which I suspect may be false) and tugs at his beard (grown specially for this occasion) and says with gravitas, 'This is the end of a civilisation.'

Science officer Bilbo replies, 'They are wasting precious resources. Can we help them?'

Another shake of the head. Tug of the beard. It's not that easy is it?

'We cannot take sides. Our laws are strict about this. We cannot interfere. We can only observe,' says Captain Barry.

Drone Annie wakes up (following some surreptitious waving from me in the sidelines) and stomps towards Science Officer Bilbo. She sticks out her arm and points at her box. He puts his head towards the box as if listening. It's a crude gimmick but we can't ever get Annie to remember to bring the prop mobile phone which is what he really needs. So we adapt to the circumstances we find ourselves in. Science Officer Bilbo makes a big deal of listening, because he knows it would be much better if he just had a phone, but he's learned to live with it and reports in a loud, clear voice, 'Captain, our sister ship has a message for you.'

Captain Barry must have some supernatural power because he already knows the message it seems.

'Yes, rain forests of the Amazon. Set out course.'

And with much twiddling of knobs they are on their way. Now follows some music. Sort of jangly synthesised stuff. Not very pleasing to the ear.

When this starts the cast move in pairs to form two opposing sides which pull back and forth on an imaginary rope like a tug of war contest. Believe me, this took a lot of choreographing, during which time I learned that Mandy has a real fear of stepping backwards. But after a few months and a bit of adaptation we got over it. They recite lines from a poem, which was written by Barry. Barry is generally an ideas man, but he decided that this play was important enough to commit something to paper. I'm no poet so I can't comment on the quality of the work, but it fit into our play so we used it. Juxtaposed against the music there's a strange, unearthly quality to it. Each 'team' speaks as one voice. Almost. Usually. The poem is called: The Conflict.

Team one starts with *'Blood spills out as land is cracked'* and they heave backwards. Team two responds with, *'Wails of men turned against one another,'* and they heave forwards.

'*You don't see the holes in the ground where we were put,*' team one pull back

'*We are the unfound,*' team one pull forward (you get the picture)

'*We are the uncounted,*' say team one.

'*We're not even the small print,*' reply team two.

'*Or the bit in brackets,*' team one say.

'*Because we were somewhere else,*' team two respond.

'*Because we lived far from you,*' team one again.

'*Because our minutes, hours, days and years did not last as long as yours,*' team two. Are you getting this? I think it's a fantastic poem on diversity, disability, and 'otherness.' It goes on with team one chanting, '*Because your cameras point the other way.*'

'*Because you talk about other people,*' respond team two.

'*Or that moment when we went,*' team one again. It's like a Greek chorus. Honestly. Euripides, eat your heart out. And this was written by a man with a learning disability label.

Both teams speak together for the final line,

'*You can't even say you missed it.*'

Seriously. You think people with learning disabilities are stupid? I don't think so.

The tug of war ends, and the combatants are exhausted (acting and really.) Mandy is relieved she's survived all those times moving back and forward. She still hates it but she's learned how to do it without the fear of falling. A lesson we all need to learn I think.

We shift to the tinny, recorded version of Kelly telling us, *Around the world there are at least thirty armed conflicts going on. In today's wars, most of the casualties are civilians and almost half of those are children.*

Yeah, think about that folks. Think. Really think. We have thought about it. We care. Label or no label we don't think war is good.

Back onstage the spaceship lands with a good old Star Trek judder and some carefully times music. (You'll note that I'm not a participant in this play. That's because I'm working the sound. With variable success.)

Space officer Bilbo is concerned for the tired mass of bodies which litter the stage. He asks his captain, 'Surely we can help them?'

But Captain Barry is firm, 'We cannot interfere,' he says, statesmanlike.

Space officer Bilbo is made of sterner stuff. He's not giving up.

'But we can help the wounded,' he says and Captain Barry doesn't have a problem with that it seems. The command is given, 'Put on your invisibility gloves,' and the two spacemen, accompanied by Drone Annie, walk amongst the wounded, touching them gently, helping them to their feet and generally 'reviving' them before going back to the space ship. The 'wounded' are amazed because of course to them, the spacemen are invisible.

And we move onto the next scene. It's called Man and Animal. We developed it out of a range of movement games and we had great fun being 'monkeys.' There's some suitable jungle music playing in the background. The group, led by Stevie, our king of the silent action, begin to 'monkey' around (though Pauline is somewhat embarrassed by this but most of the others get into it very quickly). They pick up prop 'branches' and generally hang around scratching, jumping, picking fleas off each other and hooting and hollering. Even Stevie breaks radio silence to deliver a few well places 'ooohh ... ooh... oohh's'

Kelly's distorted voice comes across as recorded narration as the monkeys quiet down.

*'From steamy rainforest, to Britain's hedgerows, from the oceans to the skies, the animal kingdom is under threat. The orang-utan is the closest animal to man – and*

*we are killing it. Orang-utan is the Malaysian for Man of the Forest. They used to range throughout South East Asia and into China but today they are restricted to two islands, Borneo and Sumatra. Orang-utans spend most of their lives in trees. Logging is destroying their habitat.'*

And as if by magic (which of course theatre is) the monkeys have transformed themselves into trees. The branches they swung off (cardboard of course) have now become a part of their body and they move fluidly (well that's the stage direction, you have to put some imagination into it as well to see that sometimes!) with the changed music which is now much more pan pipe sort of floaty eco-system stuff. It's a lovely peaceful scene until the air is cracked with the sound of a cranking chainsaw (recorded of course.) On come Lauren and Stevie holding cardboard blades out in front of them. They generally run amok, swiping down the trees. Space officer Bilbo looks on in extreme jealousy. He really wanted to be a chainsaw, but eventually was convinced that he couldn't be a space alien *and* a chainsaw. He couldn't be both good and evil in the same play. It would be too confusing for the audience. Stevie and Lauren enjoy this role fully. Nothing like a bit of imaginative destruction eh?

Once the chainsaws have done their worst, there is only one tree left standing. It's Pauline. She speaks (for all trees), 'The trees stoop with mourning at their loss, One by one the leaves now wrinkled and old fade slowly to the ground.'

And the trees which have been chopped down by the rampant chainsaws sink one after another into the ground each declaiming,

'The breath of life no more,' that's Deirdre,

'The breath of life no more,' Duncan (yes, Duncan said that all by himself. On a stage. Every time.

'The breath of life no more,' Kelly intones

'The breath of life no more,' Mandy says and then they all repeat, as one forest together, almost, though Stevie and Lauren are less vocal than the rest.

'The breath of life no more.'

Silence.

The next verse of the David Rovics song kicks in in case you haven't got the point.

*It was like a competition*
*To see how big everything could get*
*From the highways to the strip malls*
*To the giant TV sets*
*From the MOABs to the draglines*
*Monster trucks and SUVs*
*And the massive roaring chainsaws*
*That cut down all the trees*
*That's how it was at the end of the age of oil*

While the audience are chewing on them apples, the cast move themselves into the next scene. It is a Factory. The spacemen have changed into a production line and the trees have become the materials for cardboard boxes. They form a line waiting to be 'processed'. Mechanised music kicks off, lots of bells, jangles, whistles, bumps and cracking, grinding noises. Industrial hell.

The recorded voice tells us, '*In Borneo, traders cut down an area the size of Wales every month to meet the demand for Palm Oil which is used in soaps and ice cream. It is all about money.*'

Kelly, Mandy, Duncan, Deirdre and Pauline are shoved through the logging machine by Stevie and Lauren, stripped of their branches (Stevie enjoys collecting the branches and especially stripping the green paper leaves off the brown cardboard stems) and pushed forward to the factory production line where, in goggles, hard hats and hi vis vests, Barry and Bilbo first demonstrate their prototype box – which is Drone Annie, tin foil removed from her box, and then begin to process them, which involves miming much stapling and sealing tape.

Each cast member leaves the production line clutching a large piece of cardboard box.

The narration explains the mime for those who need words, *'Trees are cut down for wood, for paper, for oil, to burn, and to make boxes with. Everything comes in boxes. The forests are turned into packaging materials. Beautiful trees become waste materials thrown into landfill.'*

As they leave the production line they make their way centre stage (we have chalked the outline of a box on the floor) and they arrange themselves as pieces of one big cardboard box. We have to make sure Mandy is at the back because then she can walk round, not have to back into place. There's usually a bit of undignified jostling for position at the front, facing the audience because of course they forget that they are going to have to hold up their cardboard which will hide their face. No one is too keen on that move but I finally convince them it's important that we do it. A big box they become. After quite a bit of jostling and shoving. Nothing worth doing comes easily eh? And I know they are all real actors at this point because I don't know a real actor who doesn't love being centre stage!

Box in position the spacemen remove their factory clothes and go back to the spaceship.

Where they offer their 'alien' commentary on what they've just seen. Ah, as Rabbie Burns said – tae see ourselves as others see us –

They put their invisibility gloves on. For safety!

Science officer Bilbo opines, 'I can't believe what I see.'

'What is it?' Captain Barry asks (once he's found the place on his clipboard. He had to put it down to run the factory and he forgot to turn the page over.)

'They're destroying the lifeblood of the planet. Do they realise the consequences of their actions?' Science officer Bilbo says, portentously.

Yes, Bilbo. Actions. Consequences. The link between the two. We all need to consider this. Seriously.

Captain Barry knows about the spacetime continuum though and the rules of inter-species non intervention. He replies, 'We can't interfere. They will learn, like the dinosaurs before them.'

There's nothing left but to reflect on the waste of human kind. Science Officer Bilbo does so and says, 'The trees were beautiful. Why have they turned them into boxes?'

Giving Captain Barry the last word is always a good idea. As long as he's managed to find the right page in time. Luckily for us he has and he concludes, 'They have no respect for the riches of their planet.'

Think about that, folks. David Rovics kicks in for his next verse for those who still need a bit of a prompt to think about actions and consequences. While he does so, the box breaks down to reveal loads of poly bags all filled with other poly bags and bits of paper waste. The cast begin to throw these around, litter everywhere, the aim being to cover the entire stage area before the song ends.

*It was like they were trying to see*
*How many garbage dumps they could fill*
*How many flagpoles they could squeeze*
*Onto a single windowsill*
*How many countries could be bombed*
*How much black gold they could drill*
*How much coal could they extract*
*If they just blew up the hills*
*That's how it was at the end of the age of oil.*

Yes. The place is a total mess. They love doing this. Even knowing that they are going to have to pick it all up again, they love throwing the litter around. It's primal.

It's like confetti. It's just pure FUN. But so that the audience doesn't get carried along on the jubilant atmosphere of anarchic destruction we have Deirdre's distorted recorded tinny voice telling us that, '*Each year the UK produces more than 434 million tonnes of waste, with every one of us throwing away seven times our own bodyweight. Packaging waste alone constitutes 4.6 million tonnes of rubbish a year. The average British family throws away six trees worth of paper every year. Litter not lifted or cleaned up can take hundreds of years to break down and disappear. A cigarette butt can take from one to five years to degrade. Plastic bags and ring pulls from cans can take more than twenty years to biodegrade.*'

Back at the spaceship the 'aliens' shake their heads solemnly. Science officer Bilbo is still looking for solutions. Still wondering how he can 'help us how we need to be helped. He says, 'Surely we can teach them the value of recycling?'

Captain Barry shakes his head, 'We cannot teach them to respect their planet,' he opines.

'We must help them somehow... they are intelligent life forms...' Science officer Bilbo says. 'If they understood what they were doing...'

Captain Barry shakes his head and tugs his beard again, oh, and a bit of tooth sucking for good measure as he has the final word on the fate of humanity.

'They will end up like the trees they have killed.'

The spacemen put on their invisibility gloves once again and walk amongst the people, picking up the rubbish and putting it into piles. To begin with the people don't notice, then they look surprised, then some of them also help to clear the rubbish. Then they all do.

The recorded Deirdre continues, '*Our own way of life is causing mass destruction to planet earth. Climate change is a present reality and we can't afford to think this is a problem for governments. If that's the way you think –*

*think again. We all live on the planet and it's everyone's problem.'*

As they have finished the tidying up an alarm sounds and Science officer Bilbo points it out, 'Captain, the drone has sent an alarm.'

'Back to the spaceship,' Captain Barry commands.

The spacemen go back to the spaceship. Meanwhile, more music, of a calming nature, begins and the rest of the cast form themselves into one circular body, hand in hand, then each taking a part of a large white sheet Pauline has picked up and they wave it up and down over their heads. This is the iceberg. It 'floats' around the stage, billowing up and down while the final David Rovics verse is played,

*It was as if there was some kind of test*
*And the only way to pass*
*Was to turn the planet's atmosphere*
*Into a cloud of poison gas*
*It was like the only thing that mattered*
*Was the death of life on Earth*
*That seemed to be the proof*
*That you had made your money's worth*
*That's how it was at the end of the age of oil.*

You are doubtless, as an audience, captivated by the floating iceberg. It's a good image. And while you are thus captivated you have failed to notice that the spaceship has transformed itself into a TV newsdesk with two newsreaders (Annie and Barry). There is a BBC style news bulletin ident played, recognizable enough to shift audience focus and Annie starts the item with, 'We interrupt this programme...'

Barry continues, reading from his clipboard of course, 'Reports are coming in from NASA space agency. Satellites have identified a huge landmass of ice estimated at twelve hundred kilometres long by eight hundred kilometres wide has parted from the Barents Bridge and is heading for the Gulf of Alaska.'

It's Annie's big moment. She can't read, though she'll not admit to that. So she's had to learn this lot off by heart. Good on you Annie, I say.

'If these reports are confirmed the consequences for humanity could be catastrophic. Stay tuned for our next update...' She gets it word perfect.

Pumped by her success, but kind of wishing that she'd got a round of applause for her efforts, because I've been unable to convince her that while this is a massive achievement, to the audience it's just another line in the play, the newsreaders go to observe the circle. Bilbo has picked up a crude shoulder mounted TV camera (made of cardboard) and records the events.

Barry reports, 'We are live at the scene of the action. The UN has decided to meet to try to save the planet... we will hear the voice of everyone in the world...'

The 'circle' begins to speak. Each of the group has a word which they say. It's not, to be honest, always the same person or the same order, but basically it goes something like this:

Deirdre says, 'LIFE'

Pauline says, 'HOPE'

Lauren (usually) says, 'LOVE'

Duncan (always) says 'JUSTICE'

Mandy says, 'PEACE'

Kelly says, 'TRUST'

Stevie just waves the iceberg. Unless he decides to go and look at the cardboard camera.

Deirdre says, 'HARMONY,'

Pauline says, 'COMPASSION'

Lauren (usually) says 'JOY'

Duncan (always) says 'BEAUTY' Okay once he said 'Happy' instead. But usually he goes with Beauty.

Mandy says, 'SIMILARITY,'

And Kelly says, 'DIFFERENCE.'

And the group become a semi circle, facing the audience. This little word game was developed out of the 1-20 game we play in the workshop to impress the crowds later. That game basically requires that we all stand in a circle so that everyone can see everyone else. One person at a time can speak. The first person says 'one,' then the next says 'two' and you see how far you can go. If two people speak at the same time you have to go back to the beginning. It's a very hard game. You have to watch each other very carefully. You can cheat it a bit by planning a rota in advance, but that sort of defeats the purpose. Done properly and when you get up to twenty it's a really, really good example of people working co-operatively and focussing attention. It's not a game for labels. It's a game for people. Individuals working together as a team.

It's time now for the moral. We do all appreciate that you have to teach people something in a play and give a decent moral at the end so they go away thinking is always a good idea. This ending is called: **THE THREE R'S.**

Barry starts. He tells the audience, 'We are all throwing away far too much rubbish.'

Bilbo follows, 'Most of it ends up being buried or piled up in big heaps, or incinerated.'

Annie proudly points out that, 'It doesn't look nice and it isn't good for the planet.'

Deirdre says, 'If more people were eco friendly and used the 3R's the world would be in a better shape.'

Kelly buttonholes the audience, demanding their attention, 'The good news is everyone can play their part – including you.'

She hands out a card to an audience member, asks them to hold it up and read it out. It reads **REDUCE**. Kelly explains, 'This means making less rubbish and not using as much energy.'

Annie hands out a second card to a carefully selected victim (I mean audience member) and asks them to hold it up and read it out. It reads **RE-USE.**

She explains, 'This means we have to find other uses for things instead of throwing them away.'

Deirdre hands out the third card, same routine. It reads **RECYCLE.** She explains, 'This means turning the rubbish into something else rather than just throwing it away.'

The whole cast join together to chant: 'Remember the 3 R's. Reduce, Re-use and Recycle.

Then they take their bows during which time there is a final recorded narration. This time it is not distorted. It's just Barry in all his glory saying, '*We do not own the world and its riches are not ours to dispose of at will. We should seek to preserve its beauty and resources for the other species with which we share it, and for generations to come. No Labels Drama Group leaves you with the challenge – How can you simplify your needs and recognise the boundary between need and greed in your own life.*

So politics is rubbish yeah? Well, we performed that play at the Scottish Parliament. We had our say. We told them what we think. We showed them that putting a label on a person doesn't mean that person can't engage with the most pressing social and political issues of our day. That beyond that label we have something to say. Something worth listening to. And if you're really, really smart you'll understand that you can't treat people with learning disability labels like so much rubbish either. Because the world needs us all.

# THURSDAY

## *Cup cakes or fairy cakes?*

It's Thursday. We are cracking on through the week aren't we? Today it's all about choices. About those impenetrable life questions such as: when did fairy cakes become cup cakes? Is there a difference and if so which do you prefer?

Here at No Labels we are pretty much aficionados of all things sweet and as such the search for the perfect fairy/cup cake is high on our agenda of things to discuss. Which is lucky as it presents a great way for us to get into today's work. We have been given funding (sorry that makes it sound like something that came easy, fell into our lap –far from it. We fought tooth and nail until our brains bled for over a year to get funding for a project which is to do with choices and how to make them.) We finally got the money. And we can start the project.

As is our whim we shall run workshops and from them use improvisation to devise short theatre pieces which we will deliver to an unsuspecting public (this time, along with free fairy cakes and fair trade beverages) We like to tick as many 'good' boxes as we can at a time you see. Our trademark is humour. We like to use comedy to show people that if you throw away the labels we all wear you can actually learn something about how other people see the world.

The dark stuff here is the background of the funding. Social policy. (Cue pantomime boos) Now I'm sure that people who make social policy are really trying to do a jolly good job so I'm not in the business of slating any of them personally but sometimes, just sometimes, I wonder what part of 'real world' they don't get. There is this blinding *new idea* called Self Directed Support which claims it will give choices back to the people. Setting aside the small matter of making a choice a 'real' choice – unless there is the money to back up the choices then it's kind of pointless (a situation No Labels members are all too familiar with), there is also the larger issue that in effect what this policy may do is make people who are labelled learning disabled have to become employers of their 'personal assistants'. The irony of making people who you deem incapable of being employees because they are 'with incapacity' into employers, responsible for PAYE and the like, seems to have escaped the policy makers. They just do a little sleight of hand and suggest that if someone is 'with incapacity' (which you have to agree sounds so, so much better and inclusive than calling them 'without capacity') then instead of them making their own choices they can nominate ANOTHER PERSON to make their choices for them. In short, they can choose (how?) to let someone make their choices for them. End of.

I suppose this is a bit like our parliamentary democracy and many folk don't have a problem with that, but surely, surely people you can see this is a stupid system – the social policy not the democracy I mean. Or both if you're that way inclined. I don't want to offend. I'd just ask you to think it through.

You're beginning to see why we need fairy/cup cakes instead of chocolate biscuits when we sit down to start discussing 'choices, the making thereof.'

We are interested in looking at what is an 'informed' choice and what is a 'real' choice. If it is going to be the case that our members (most of whom are considered 'with incapacity' by the way) are going to have to make some important choices (or have them made for them) I think it's quite important that we learn HOW to make choices. More specifically how we learn to make choices well. Or make good choices. I appreciate the value laden nature of this diatribe but seriously, one of the big problems as I perceive it of the whole 'learning disability' label is that once you have this label it's carte blanche for the people 'in charge' never to bother to either a) ask you your preference or b) and more importantly, teach you how to make it and express it. That's why so often people are labelled with 'challenging behaviour.' Often what they are doing is trying to express their preference (god help us, sometimes it may be a 'no') in the best way they know. And if no one listened to you repeatedly when you said you didn't want to go swimming, bowling, to a horror film but took you anyway, or when you asked to go to a movie and they took you to McDonalds, wouldn't you start exhibiting 'challenging' behaviour?

Here's an example from real life. Fictional real life okay, but believe me, this is real.

Annie wants to go out to her friend's party. It's on Friday night. She wants to buy a present for her friend (well you would, wouldn't you?) So she needs money. She asks her carer for money. Her money. They won't give it to her. They say they'll come with her to buy the present, 'to make sure she doesn't spend it on sweeties instead.' [Strike ONE] But she'll have to wait because there's no one available to go shopping with her that day. Annie sits around the house because there's no point going to the shops without money now is there?

The next day, when they *do* go to the shops with Annie and make sure that she buys an 'appropriate' gift to the value of no more than a fiver (in this case a new bath towel from a cheap shop), Annie suggests that they have a quick bite to eat in a local sandwich shop. She asks if she has enough money in her weekly budget to do this? The 'carer' hums and ha'ahs and eventually says yes, they can stretch to it. As long as she's careful what she orders.

Oh, and because the carer is with her she'll have to buy the carer lunch as well. [Strike TWO] So Annie chooses a large sub with meatballs. The carer tells her this is unhealthy and too expensive so she should have a salad sandwich instead. Annie doesn't want a salad sandwich. But as she begins her 'I'm a forty six year old woman' routine the carer fixes her with a stare and suggests that 'if she's not going to behave they'll go home right now,' so Annie backs down and orders a salad sandwich. And a coke. Oh. No. She can't have a coke. She has to have apple juice. It's healthier. Annie doesn't actually like apple juice so she negotiates a cup of tea. Which, when it arrives and she's about to put a spoonful of sugar in (well, okay probably two) the carer creates a fuss and tells her she's not 'allowed' sugar in tea. Never mind that when Annie is on her own (as she is for the best part of 16 hours a day in her 'independent living') she can make her own tea and put as much sugar in it as she likes – unless they don't let her buy any on the weekly supermarket shop.

The carer orders pastrami on rye and a fizzy drink by the way. And Annie pays. (I'd like to think the carer has Vimto, because I don't like that and I don't want the damned woman to have a nice time on Annie's money. Even fictionally!) [Strike THREE and out I say.]

Now, let me just ask you. If you weren't allowed to spend your own money on what you wanted. If you couldn't go to the shops to buy the present you'd had your eye on (a teddy bear which is what Mandy wanted because it's her birthday) but instead had to buy a towel (you compromise here because it's soft and fluffy which is what Mandy likes) and if you then had to have a debate over whether you had enough money to have a quick bite to eat –AND you had to buy lunch for your companion (oppressor, jailor?) the very person who was making this whole experience so unpleasant in the first place, and if you then couldn't choose what you had to eat or drink but still had to pay for it, don't you think YOU might feel just a tiny bit pissed off. Don't you think that you might feel that no one listened to your choices?

Oh, and to cap it all off. It comes to Friday night. Annie is all dressed up and ready to go to the party, but she can't go. The rotas have been changed and there's no care worker detailed to go out with her. They don't let her go on her own and so she misses the party. Where are the 'real' and 'informed' choices here? And please remember that Annie is, as she will forcefully tell you if you ask, a forty six year old woman who does not need to be treated like a child. I'll admit that sometimes Annie acts like a child. But I think I would if I was given her life to live. That label is so very firmly tied round her neck it's strangling her.

But today, we are eating fairy cakes. Or cup cakes. I think we are calling these cheap fairy cakes cup cakes because we want to 'live the dream.' As I understand it a cup cake basically costs five times as much and has shitloads of icing on it. A fairy cake has a discrete amount of icing and is more about the cake than the topping. Cup cakes are 'in yer face' and sell themselves on the huge amount of sugar in the most amazing variety of designs possible to fit onto what is basically a wee sponge cake in a paper case. Though I also suspect that 'real' (expensive) cup cakes actually come in these plastic cases (cups?) While I am trying to work out the in's and out's of when is a cup cake not a cup cake, as is my philosophical whim, the rest of the gang are just doing the 'locust' thing that No Labels are really, really good at. They are hoovering their way through a huge box of cakes brought by Mandy's mum because it's Mandy's birthday. (Remember, she had a party. Friday night. A real party. Not a fictional one. And Annie bought a real present. But couldn't go.) Ah, the confusion between reality and fiction is every bit as strange as the demarcation line between fairy and cup cakes.

Do you think I'm getting away from the point here somewhat? Maybe so. Bilbo agrees with you,

'It's all cake,' he says, stuffing another one in his mouth.

You are right, Bilbo. Let them eat cake.

I ask Pauline. She knows about food fashion.

'Are these cup cakes or fairy cakes?' I ask, and, because I just have to get an ancillary question in there, 'and what's the difference.'

Pauline isn't sure. She's more worried about how many chocolate cup cakes Lauren has put away and more to the point how many cup cakes Mandy is putting in her mouth at the same time. We can't see how many but I bet it's some kind of record. And I bet she'll have a stomach ache before lunch!

'You can choose whether to call it a fairy cake or a cup cake,' Barry says.

And he's probably right. It probably doesn't matter. It's just a label.

We take a vote on whether we'd rather call them fairy cakes or cup cakes. Consensus is that we like the idea of fairies and so we'll call them fairy cakes. But, as Kelly points out, cup cakes are more 'posh,' and so maybe we should tell other people we ate 'cup' cakes because they'll think better of us.

'Fairies are for children,' Bilbo states. He does not go with consensus. He wants to eat a cup cake.

'Interesting point,' I say. I think of J.M.Barrie and Peter Pan and Tinkerbell. I think of how many adults with learning disabilities are labelled as 'child-like' and condemned to live lives where everyone thinks they have the 'mental' age of a child. According to some developmental tests which have been invented by people trying to prove that one can 'grow up.'

And a subversive plan comes to mind.

'Right,' I say. We have to do this thing about choices yeah? And we have to discuss what choices are. And we have to make it funny.'

They nod. No one speaks but that's probably because they are all still chomping on the cupcakes/fairy cakes. How many people did Mandy's mum think were coming today?

I take the opportunity to continue while silence prevails.

'And while Bilbo says that fairies are for children and yes, we all know fairy stories from when we were children, how about if we use the fairy stories – which people expect are the only stories you know – and we update them, change them around a bit and use them to show how sometimes we don't get to make choices. '

'And make them laugh?' Bilbo asks.

'Yes, make them laugh,' I say. 'But make them think too.'

'Yes, we've got to make them think,' Barry says.

'What's good for you,' Lauren pipes up. It might seem randomly. But think a bit and you might see that actually it's not so random. It's a comment on the world she lives in.

So that's how it begins.

We do a few weeks worth of workshops looking at the nature of 'choice.' Of what is a real choice. Of what 'informed' choice means and of what you can do when you aren't given either. The tales I hear would curl your hair. Annie and the party is the least horrific one I can assure you. And from these real stories we develop two short plays based on fairy stories but right slap bang up to date with the issues that are bothering us at this particular point in time.

~~~

Several months later, on a Thursday afternoon, we are ready to show our plays. We invite an audience of carers, service providers, local dignitaries and other 'labelled' people as well as anyone from the 'general public' who happens to be passing and fancies an hour and a half of entertainment. And we provide them with free cupcakes. Or fairy cakes. Fairy cakes and fairy stories. But of course, nothing is as it seems with No Labels and the cakes and the stories have other significances beyond their 'fairy' label.

We open with a new version of the Goldilocks story. This one is called Goldilocks, the Three Bears and the Shower. The cast is as follows: Deirdre is the narrator. Pauline plays a sort of Brechtian role titled 'Prompt' and wears go faster stripes to show that she's a real speedy Gonzalez. Goldilocks is played by Mandy. This is because the 'shower' problem is her real story and it took us weeks to get to the bottom of the problem, so we wanted to give her her chance to work through this problem – it's our adapted Boalian method at play again.

The Bear family comprises Barry as Daddy Bear, Kelly as Mummy Bear and Lauren as Baby Bear. Duncan has the vital dramatic and comedic role of The Shower and Annie plays the Fairy Godmother, fully equipped with a wicker basket of fairy cakes to give out. Bilbo plays the Plumber. Eat your heart out Bob the Builder. Stevie and I are sitting this one out. His big moment will come in the next play. And I am in sole charge of costume changes and general 'wrangling' of cast. No mean feat.

It will come as no surprise to you that we start at the house of the Bears. Scene One. Deirdre sets the scene, 'Okay, you all know the story. Once upon a time Goldilocks goes to the house of the Three bears when they are out. It's not for us to ask what she was doing there, or why, when she rang the bell and got no reply, she didn't just go on her way. But she didn't. She goes into the house and wants to sit down.'

In the process of devising this play we discovered that Mandy has some very good mime skills. Not the same as Stevie's because she moves quite clumsily whereas he is a natural dancer, but she can express emotion without saying a word. Which is lucky because she's not good at remembering her words. But give her instructions and she can act it out slowly, methodically but with great feeling. As she does now. Following Pauline's instruction.

'The first chair is TOO BIG the second chair is TOO SMALL and the third chair is JUST RIGHT. She's hungry, she sees there's some porridge, so she tastes it. The first plate is TOO HOT the second plate is TOO COLD and the third plate? (Pauline delivers and aside to the audience) come on, you know the answer.'

There is a stunned silence. The audience weren't expecting to join in. Panic. Silence.

Pauline carries on regardless, 'Yes, it's, come on, everyone together.'

And led by the cast they join in shouting, 'Just right!'

Mandy acts it out as Pauline continues.

'She's tired so she goes to bed. You know the way the story goes. The first bed is TOO HARD the second bed is TOO SOFT and the third bed is...'

She cups her hand to her ear waiting for the reply which comes, a bit less reticently this time,

'Just right.' They are getting into it. Or maybe they've just clocked the cup/fairy cakes which will be their prize in the interval. And want to get through the preliminaries to get to the FREE FOOD.

Deirdre continues,' Well here's where the story gets interesting. It's not quite the version you might be familiar with so pay attention please.'

You know, Deirdre would have made a very good headmistress had she not been labelled with a learning disability at an early age!

'Goldilocks wakes up the following morning. The bears are on holiday you see, and she decides she's feeling a bit grungy so she goes to have a shower. She goes into the shower,' Deirdre continues and jumps as Pauline interjects. This is acting. Despite it happening every time in rehearsal, Deirdre still jumps when Pauline interrupts her. She can't quite bring herself to accept it's part of the play, not just someone being rude. All good comedy needs a straight man. All good groups of anarchists need a normalising influence. Deirdre is our normalising influence. I think I've told you that before.

'Hang on, Goldilocks... put a towel on,' Pauline says, handing Mandy a towel.

Oh, at this point I should try to describe what Goldilocks/Mandy is wearing. For some reason (probably the same reason that some of us are petrified of clowns and others of us – myself included – baulk at balloons) Mandy has a phobia of wigs. This is a real phobia. In this context of course it's a real fictional phobia but my point is, she's scared of wigs. It's not like her supposed phobia of dogs. We were told that Mandy didn't like dogs. And it's true, Mandy thinks she doesn't like dogs. I have a collie dog who has to come to work with me. It presented a possible impasse. But we got round it. Before giving Mandy the chance to do what Mandy does when fear strikes: -stock still and shaking - impervious to movement or reason – and then runs without thought of consequence- before this I explained to her that my dog had to come to work with me, that I would keep him away from her in the back room but that if she wanted to try to get to know him he was very friendly. From this start point she stood in the room and watched me walk him through to the back. Not happy, but not running

(Mandy, not the dog) Throughout the day she kept suggesting that he was not a dog, more a teddy bear. I went along with this, encouraging and persuading that he *was* fluffy like a teddy bear and she could stroke him if she wanted. She likes to stroke fluffy things (remember the birthday towel Annie thoughtfully bought for her.) And at the end of the day she couldn't help herself. She stroked my dog. He was fluffy. He was also well behaved. Because, as with many people worried by dogs she stuck her hand right out in his face (a gesture quite guaranteed to upset a dog) but fortunately his placid nature meant that he didn't respond by chomping on the outstretched hand. From that day on, Mandy and Jasper (my dog) were best of friends. She positively looked out for him coming. She stroked him endlessly. Okay we labelled him a 'panda' rather than a dog, but we ripped up the 'Mandy doesn't like dogs' instruction manual.

But wigs. No. There's no way Mandy is going to inhabit the same space as wigs. She's not that keen on hats but we can negotiate on that one (see tomorrow's story) but wigs are a big fat no no. So there was no way she was going to wear a blonde wig. And she has short dark hair. Not the ideal casting for Golidlocks then. So we did what we do best at No Labels. We adapted to suit purpose. We made a chain of cardboard locks (like padlocks) and linked them together like Christmas paperchains. And painted them gold. And hung them round her neck. Served the purpose and got a laugh. And more importantly didn't distress Mandy for this, her big title role. My suggestion is: stop worrying about labels. Start thinking outside the box and treat everyone as an individual accepting their quirks as a vital and valuable part of their personality, to be respected at all times.

Back to the play. Mandy is miming to Pauline's speech. I should point out here that Duncan is now revealed from behind a shower curtain in all his glory, holding up a shower head. He is, as you recall, the shower.

'So Goldilocks goes into the shower. She takes off her towel... SHUT YOUR EYES, SHE'S NAKED NOW...'

This never fails to raise a laugh. Of course Goldilocks/Mandy is still fully dressed, she's just taken the towel off, but we all like to have a laugh about nakedness, even when it's fictional, right?

Pauline continues, 'and she tries to work the shower. First she turns the tap one way,'

She prepares the audience for their participatory role to come by shouting out the next bit, 'IT'S TOO HOT, then she turns it the other way,'

They are ready for this and some join in with 'IT'S TOO COLD' becoming less inhibited by the minute.

Pauline ploughs on, 'and then she turns it again... what do you think happens?'

She eyeballs the audience. They're not getting away with it. So they have to reply and of course they say, as we've set them up to do, 'It's just right.'

Pauline shakes her head and wags her finger at them.

'No. You're wrong,' she says. 'It's too HOT.'

Ah... a joke. Funny. Laugh. (When are the cup cakes coming out, they said there'd be fairy cakes?)

Pauline keeps on with the story and Mandy keeps on miming.

'She turns it again IT'S TOO COLD. Whatever she does, she can't get the shower to be JUST RIGHT. Because Goldilocks can't work the mixer tap. I bet you're asking, So what happens next?' (well those of you who aren't still wondering about the cakes.)

Deirdre, sensing that the crowd may become ugly at any minute, (an intelligent observation, we have an audience without great powers of concentration and a fierce desire for cakes) gets her own back on Pauline and interrupts (scripted of course.)

'Okay. Well what happens next is that the bears come back and find Goldilocks in the shower. She tells them she can't get the mixer tap to work,' Deirdre says.

In come the bears, right on cue.

Now for this play we had a bit of a scripting problem. Or a bit of a memory problem. Or a bit of a timing problem. But we used it to our advantage. We used the prompt and the concept of repetition (aka echolalia) taught us by Lauren as part of the comedy of the piece. Echolalia and Brecht combine into a powerfully comedic 'routine' where basically Pauline as 'the prompt' tells people what to say and they then say it. This is in some way an example of alienating the audience (Brechtian style) without actually alienating them in fictional reality (by them thinking we don't know the lines and the interval with cakes is never going to come.) Ah the magic of theatre! And remember, Barry doesn't have a clipboard in this play. Pauline is his live clipboard. This is flexible scripting folks. Don't say 'they can't do it,' just find a way that works and make it work.

So Pauline says, 'Daddy bear says 'that's your problem.'

Daddy Barry repeats, 'That's your problem.'

Pauline says, 'Mummy bear says you shouldn't be in our shower anyway.'

And Mummy Kelly repeats, 'You shouldn't be in our shower anyway.' Normally Kelly would remember this without any prompting but she's been having a lot of epileptic fits recently and it's seriously affecting her memory. We're all sad about that but we don't want to draw attention to it and upset her more, so we use our 'device' to save her shame.

Pauline says, 'and Baby Bear says you need an advocate because no one is listening to you. I have the same problem.'

There is a pause. Because Baby Lauren says nothing. Which we quite expected. And turned to our advantage. We have a strategy for every situation now.

Pauline continues by cocking her head and cupping her hand to her ear as she continues, 'But because Baby bear has a very small voice, no one hears him except Goldilocks.'

There you go. Seamless. If you were in the audience you'd never know it was a mistake. Indeed our flexible script means that 'mistakes' can't happen. It's the same principle as our 'there's no such thing as challenging behaviour, only creative behaviour' rule. Just change the name. Lose the label. Make the words mean something different and focus on the action not the words. Focus on how we *can* communicate, don't stress on all the ways our communication is less than perfect.

Next, Goldilocks/Mandy asks baby bear if he has cold showers as well.

'Do you have cold showers as well?' Mandy asks Baby Bear Lauren.

Pauline responds, 'And Baby bear nods and says yes.'

And fortunately for us Lauren doesn't say, 'No,' loudly. Though she well might. But equally she might shout out 'yes, darling' and that would be fine as well.

Goldilocks doesn't know what to do at this point. She doesn't know what an advocate is. But she thinks maybe she should help Baby Bear. Pauline instructs her to tell the bears in a louder voice than Baby Bear can muster that the shower is broken and they need an advocate to fix it.

'The shower doesn't work properly. Baby Bear says we need an advocate to fix it.'

Just as the audience are laughing at the idea of an advocate to fix a shower (unless they are still consumed with the cake dilemma) we hit them with the finest line in the play. The line that Duncan has been waiting to say and will say at each appropriate moment possible. It's quite a progression from 'Kill' on Monday, isn't it?

'There's nothing wrong with me,' he shouts.

Everyone falls about laughing. A talking shower. Who ever heard of such a thing?

Pauline lets the laughter subside, then continues, 'Mr and Mrs Bear don't know what to say. They can't decide to laugh or be angry. First Mummy Bear laughs,'

'This is a fairy story. Fairy stories have fairy godmothers but NOT advocates,' Kelly is back on track.

Pauline confirms, 'You're right there Mummy bear, fairy stories do traditionally have fairy godmothers rather than advocates.'

She continues, giving Bilbo his cue to act, 'Daddy bear gets angry. After all, who does Goldilocks think she is, coming uninvited into his house and messing with his shower.'

'If the shower isn't working you don't need a fairy godmother, you need a plumber,' says Barry.

I should come clean here and say that Barry really wanted to play the plumber and we started off that way, but his plumber was so random that we had to recast and Bilbo stepped out of being Daddy Bear quite happily to become a fully certified plumber (fictional.)

Pauline moves the story along, 'So Daddy bear rings the plumber, and Mummy bear calls for the fairy godmother. Goldilocks goes on her way home.'

Time for scene two. Except something terrible happens. Mandy freezes. No one knows why. It's not stage fright, she's impervious to that. I need to find out. And quickly, without it interfering with the play. To cut a long story very short, I find out that there is someone in the audience Mandy is scared of. A man. Looking at her. It turns out to be a care worker. I don't have time to worry about why Mandy is frightened of this man (and he looks pretty dodgy to me I must admit.) I only have time to ascertain that she's not going to continue unless he's out of the place. Which presents me with quite some problem. I mean, you can't pick your audience can you? But the show must go on. So while the following shower scene is being played out, I'm up in the audience and manage somehow, (I'm still not sure how) to convince the man to move to the back of the auditorium, well out of Mandy's sight level. He protests that 'she knows him,' and 'she likes him,' just a little too much and I shudder when I think about the various shower 'issues' that lie behind this little play of ours. I leave the worst thoughts up to your imagination. We'll debate the 'point' of the play once the audience are all eating their cup/fairy cakes in the interval if you don't mind.

On with the play. Mandy stands rigid at the side of the stage. I'm negotiating with 'the man' … no, I'm sorry, in reality or fiction I'm going to label him 'the odd man' and Pauline and the gang carry on regardless. Thank goodness. The rest of the audience are barely aware of any fuss and bother. My blood pressure may take a week to recover though.

Deirdre calls Bilbo to the stage.

'The Plumber comes to fix the shower,' she says. Her tunnel vision is coming in useful right now. She's oblivious to Mandy.

Bilbo doesn't want to miss his chance to shine so he strides past Mandy to centre stage and replies,

'Now what seems to be the trouble?'

Daddy Barry remembers his line (a first) and says, 'There's nothing wrong with the shower.'

Cue our comedy shower,

'There's nothing wrong with me,' calls out Duncan, clear as a bell.

Pauline reminds Kelly of her line, 'Mummy bear sticks her 10p's worth in and says it's the mixer tap.'

And Mummy Kelly chimes out, 'Baby bear says it's not working.'

Pauline describes the actions being carried out by Bilbo and Duncan.

'The plumber turns the tap one way and the other and it seems to be working right. He tells Daddy Bear there's nothing wrong with the shower.'

'There's nothing wrong with the shower,' Plumber Bilbo says confidently.

And Pauline, to keep it real, adds, 'And sticks him with a bill for sixty pounds for a call out charge. Daddy bear is very angry!'

'Well you would be,' Deirdre adds, unscripted. She's sure she could have played Pauline's part better.

Daddy Barry remembers another line, remarkably, and jumps in with it, 'I said there was nothing wrong with the shower,'

'There's nothing wrong with me,' shouts Duncan.

'It's that girl causing trouble. Who invited her anyway?' Daddy Barry asks.

Moving right along to the next scene Pauline informs us that the next morning Baby Bear goes into the shower,

'And says good morning most politely,' Deirdre points out.

'Good morning,' says Duncan, because Lauren isn't saying anything. Lauren isn't that bothered at the moment. I suspect she's thinking about fairy/cup cakes covered in chocolate. I don't blame her. I'm a wreck having just managed to convince Mandy that 'the odd man' is no longer any kind of a threat. I'm wishing I could have ejected him from the audience because if she doesn't feel comfortable with him in the room I'm sure there's a good reason, and I feel I've cheated her somewhat, but this isn't the time to go into abuse allegations so I have to live with what we've got.

Pauline tries to get Lauren to focus and tells her what to mime. Lauren obliges, thankfully (mainly because she likes the shiver jiggle and the hot jump that she's developed over the rehearsal period.)

'But he still can't get the mixer tap to work. He shivers TOO COLD (nice work Lauren),

He jumps TOO HOT (again, nice work. Duncan the shower also jumps because he likes jumping. Well, why not. If showers can talk they can jump can't they? The only barriers here are your imagination, right?)

Pauline carries on not worried by the improvised additions. We are used to that after all. We are an improvisational troupe.

'He doesn't know what else to do, so he starts to cry (which Lauren doesn't do but it doesn't matter.) Mummy Bear hears him crying and comes to see what all the fuss is about,' Pauline states.

'She isn't very sympathetic. She tells him he'll have to learn to work it properly,' she continues.

'You need to learn how to work it properly, Baby Bear, you have to learn for yourself. Ask Daddy bear to teach you.' All Kelly needed was an initial prompt and she had the line nailed. Daddy Barry may need more,

'Daddy bear hears him crying and comes to see what all the fuss is about. But before baby bear can ask for his help he gets angry and tells baby bear there's nothing wrong with the shower, Pauline says, nearly drowned out with Duncan shouting once more,

'There's nothing wrong with me.'

Barry is not being upstaged by a shower and pulls it out the bag, 'The shower works perfectly. I have showers that are just right, Mummy bear has showers that are just right. Stop being such a baby. And get out of the shower, it's my turn now.'

Baby Bear Lauren is ejected from the shower. Deirdre moves the story on, 'And luckily for everyone, just at that moment, the Fairy Godmother appears – as if by magic.'

Cue Annie entering in the same pink tutu she wore as Ophelia on Monday but waving a pink cardboard wand with a big star on the top and carrying a wicker basket full of fairy cakes (we know these are fairy cakes because she's a fairy godmother right?) I hope that not too many folk get wind of this early distribution of cake or things may get ugly. Lauren is looking interested at last.

Deirdre continues, she's a born narrator.

'Daddy bear is in the shower and Mummy bear is in the kitchen making porridge.'

This sends the actors to their appropriate places.

Pauline takes over, 'So Baby Bear lets the fairy godmother in and offers her a seat.'

Annie, making the most of her role and proving there's no such thing as a small part, only a small actor, makes a big deal of knocking at the imaginary door. Bilbo, unscripted, stamps on the floor with each knock. Way to go Bilbo. Lauren must have smelled the cakes because she begins to look interested and goes to the imaginary doorway and pulls Annie in.

Pauline continues with the story, 'Baby bear tells the fairy godmother his problem and she listens most sympathetically.'

What actually happens is that Lauren drags Annie to the table and forces her to sit down and give her a fairy cake which she stuffs in her mouth. Sadly, it's not chocolate but that doesn't stop her reaching for the one Annie has now deposited on Mummy Bear's plate. Why did I have that smart idea of using real fairy cakes at this point? What was I hoping to achieve?

Pauline carries on, 'When Mummy bear brings in the porridge she gets quite a surprise to see the fairy godmother sitting there.'

'What have we told you about inviting strangers into the house Baby Bear?' Mummy Kelly says in a gruff, bearlike voice.

Daddy Barry has stopped paying attention so Pauline brings him back into the action with a fairly pointed delivery of the line, 'Daddy Bear comes out of the shower and he's annoyed about seeing another person at the breakfast table.'

'What is this place? Sauchiehall Street? 'Daddy Barry says. Great, we're in Glasgow today. We've had any number of streets in rehearsals, some funnier than others, but today this one gets a laugh. And doesn't throw the rest of the cast. It's the most we can hope for.

Deirdre intervenes, frostily. She hates it when Barry goes off script. And I think she's got Oxford Street written in her script. Or it may be Princes Street. I lost count after draft five.

'The fairy godmother speaks up,' Deirdre says, in case Barry thinks he's going to keep on going.

Annie's moment of glory. She's got an 'instigating' line. Remember I spoke of them yesterday. Or the day before. One day anyway, and how hard they are for many of the cast. I try to avoid giving them to the cast members who struggle, but sometimes I get it wrong and then we fly by the seat of our pants. And frankly, there's no one who's that good at taking the lead without prompting so it's hard to give everyone the 'follow on' lines. But Annie does us proud. She's obviously practised with her CD player (probably all those evenings she can't go out because the 'choice' is taken away with the carer's cut back rota that means evening cover is not available.)

'I hear you have a problem with the shower?' Annie the fairy godmother says. And beams at the audience. Waves her wand.

Barry's not going to be upstaged that easily. This is a combative situation.

'No. And we've already been robbed by one plumber,' he interjects.

But Annie is game for this. She's seen the audience. She knows all eyes are on her. She likes that feeling. She continues, with a flourish and a wave of her sparkly wand.

'I'm not a plumber, I'm a fairy godmother,' she declaims. In case there was any confusion.

Pauline waits for the laughter to stop and gives Annie a prompt she really doesn't need because she's already doing this, and Lauren by my count is on fairy cake number five.

'She gives them a fairy cake each to prove it.'

Deirdre enters the fray, 'The fairy cakes are very tasty.'

I think Lauren will attest to that.

Pauline gives Kelly her cue, 'Mummy bear says that's nice, the last visitor only ate our porridge,'

Which Kelly repeats word perfect, 'The last visitor only ate our porridge.'

Allowing Daddy Barry to remember his follow on line, 'And slept in our beds.'

And because it's very clear that all we're going to get from Lauren, if anything, is a stream of regurgitated fairy cake, Pauline continues,

'In a very small voice, so small no one could hear except the fairy godmother, Baby Bear asked if the fairy godmother had come to fix the shower.'

Lauren reaches for cake number six. Annie has spotted that they are now very low on cakes and she wants to keep one for herself so she pulls the basket away from Lauren which actually works very well with her next line,

'About the shower,' and motivates her to move, clinging onto the basket, towards the shower.

'There's nothing wrong with the shower. It works fine,' Daddy Barry says.

'It doesn't work for Baby Bear,' Fairy Godmother Annie declaims, pulling Lauren's hand off the basket.

'That's his problem,' Daddy Barry says.

We need a laugh so we've given Deirdre the following line which is quite funny when delivered in her dead pan monotone.

'Which seemed a bit rude and uncaring.'

And breaks the tension of the great fairy cake in a basket struggle which threatens to become all too obvious to the audience.

'I've come to fix his problem,' Fairy Godmother Annie says, pro to the last. She's not going to let anyone rob her of a precious line. Or another fairy cake.

Pauline instructs them where to go next.

'So they all go into the shower room. It's quite a squeeze.'

It is indeed. Annie makes sure that Barry is positioned between her and Lauren.

No one is really speaking to each other by this point so it's lucky that Pauline is on hand to tell the audience what they are watching.

'The Fairy Godmother asks Baby Bear to show her what the problem with the shower is,' she says. And the mime begins. Baby bear turns the tap one way JUMPS .

'Too hot' a number of people shout out.

'And the other way,' Pauline says.

'Too cold,' those who are paying attention and have lost their inhibitions shout as Lauren does a great little shiver wiggle.

'I don't see what the problem is. He's just stupid,' says Daddy Barry. The 's' word. Takes everyone aback. A moment's pause.

Deirdre pulls us back on track, 'Mummy bear says he's not stupid, he just wants attention, she says.

'He's not stupid, he just wants attention,' Mummy Kelly repeats.

'You are both wrong,' Fairy Godmother Annie says with a wave of her wand. But that's all she's got. She can't remember the rest. Pauline steps in.

'And patiently she explains to Daddy Bear and Mummy Bear that, yes, there's nothing wrong with the shower itself,'

'There's nothing wrong with me,' Duncan obliges us by getting another laugh. We need it. We are winding up to the end, but the audience don't know that now, do they?

Pauline speeds on to the inevitable conclusion. The moral.

'Baby bear doesn't have the skill to work the shower yet and needs help. Daddy bear and Mummy bear agree he needs to grow up and learn for himself. Baby bear begins to cry again. The fairy godmother steps in with a plan. She tells them that one day Baby Bear will learn to use the mixer tap but until then, perhaps they could help him.'

Annie remembers this is a play. She has lines. One of hers is now, and says, 'You can help him.' It doesn't get applause. She's disappointed. Don't the audience know the effort she's put into this damned play?

Pauline continues, 'And make sure he doesn't get a cold shower or scalded by a too hot shower.'

And Deirdre picks up the baton for the final leg, 'The Bears agree that this is probably a good idea because having a cold shower is uncomfortable, but if a shower is too hot it can burn you and that's dangerous. And the moral of the story is...'

This is Bilbo's big moment. He shouts out, 'If you can't find a fairy godmother, find an advocate.'

Because we know, don't we, that this isn't really about plumbers. It's an analogy, get it?

And Annie gets the final line because she thought it up in the devising process. So it's her due. And she does like to be the focus of the ensuing applause.

'And knock before you go into other people's houses!' she says. Good moral Annie. What was Goldilocks doing breaking into the house in the first place? That was a question we never answered in our devising and rehearsal process. Think about it.

So. We've arrived at the interval. Which affords the audience with the opportunity to drink fair trade beverages and indulge in fairy/cup cakes as they choose to label them. The cast are not allowed to stuff their faces with food at this point because I don't want mass projectile vomiting during the dance number in part two, and because I've shown them 'their' cup cakes which are for after AND promised them they can hoover up any of the cakes left over once the audience have gone at our post show pigout (sorry, party.) And this is now the time for us to consider what exactly all that Goldilocks thing was about and how we arrived at it.

Because I'm not sure the play as you've just seen does it justice.

During an improvisation one day Mandy kept going on about the shower. It wasn't easy to get out of her what the problem was, and I'm still not sure I fully get it. But the gist was that she couldn't work the shower in her shared accommodation. I think it's because she feels vulnerable in the space and has to hold onto a rail and that presents problems when she wants to wash her hair, because, she doesn't have three hands. Have you ever tried to wash your hair with one hand? Add to that her inability to work the mixer tap and you've got shower time being quite a difficult time for her. From what we could glean, her carers just got annoyed with her. They were insistent she have privacy when naked (fair enough) but they didn't understand that she needed some help in this situation. Didn't understand or didn't have the time to engage. Mandy didn't explain her problem clearly to us so I'm sure she's never managed to explain it clearly to them. We listened to her for hours on this subject. We played out a range of improvisations and it was five weeks before we realised she couldn't hold on plus wash her hair. And her 'carer's' are detailed to 'be there' for 'personal care' for something like fifteen minutes – they have four 'clients' to service in an hour I think, so they didn't have the time and just assumed she was being 'difficult.'

It took a long time for us to convince Mandy that she should explain her problem to her carers. I forgot that she probably doesn't have consistency of care so she'd have to explain the same thing to multiple people – until someone took it upon themselves to write down the problem. But do the others have the time to read the problem? Can you see here how social policy may purport anything it likes but the practical reality (even in fiction) of Mandy's personal care package is quite removed from the ideal of the policy. If you can't tell someone of your problem in ten minutes you are condemned to live with that problem indefinitely. And get scalded or frozen into the bargain.

So. We thought we'd cracked it. I asked Mandy if she had explained her problem. She said she had. She said she had no problem any more. Result, I thought. Until I probed further. It turned out she'd spent the weekend at her mum's who has a walk in shower. Problem solved. Until the next time Mandy has a shower at her own place. We debated long and hard about how and who would broach this subject with the care staff at Mandy's place and finally Pauline went round and chatted to Mandy's key worker and we hope (fingers crossed) sorted things out. The agreement is that the shower will be set to an acceptable level (agreed by Mandy and a worker) before she enters it and that someone will be on hand, just outside the shower, to help her physically with her hair if required. Yes it is less privacy than might be desirable but it means she'll get her hair washed without being burned or falling over. Help how she needs to be helped.

I admit this is not exactly the most obvious story about 'making choices' you could find, but perhaps, if you think on a bit, you'll realise that while Mandy is well able to choose many things, she needs to be taught how to communicate her problems and her choices to others – like the fact that she'd rather lose some privacy in order to feel safe in the shower. She'd rather not have a specific (and he remains nameless as the odd man) carer anywhere near her (and someone somewhere needs to take time to work out the why of that one!) and others need to have the time and take the time to listen to her. Her entitlement under social policy is one thing. The reality is somewhat different. Our second play will hopefully focus a bit more on the concept of 'real' and 'informed' choice. But it may be equally oblique to you. Depends on your opinion of the relationship between policy and practice I think.

~~~

Here we are then. Bellies full of delicious fairy/cup cakes. Ready for round two. Sorry, the Second Act of our drama. I'm happy to say that the 'odd man' had to leave in the interval, taking one of his charges (sorry) clients away with him. So a sort of calm was restored in the breasts of both Mandy and myself.

And we are about to perform The Emperor Penguin's New Pyjamas. I think I'm safe enough in assuming that everyone knows the basic story of the Emperor's New Clothes. It doesn't take a huge leap of the imagination to see some parallels with current social policy. Hey, even people with learning disabilities can devise a drama that shows it in all its technicolour glory. Don't be thrown off by the Penguins. Penguins are just a device. To stop us being sued.

The stage is set. The 'penguins' are dressed in black capes (recycled from Piglet! on Tuesday if you recall) with white t shirts underneath. And black baseball caps for beaks. Our Penguins are: Stevie, Pauline, Duncan and Lauren who are going by the combined name of 'the random penguin dance troupe' for this event. Plus, with a crown (cardboard painted gold) as well as a cap, Kelly is the Emperor Penguin. The music starts. It is the beat, beat, beat from the beginning of Chariots of Fire (PLR – forget it – we laugh in the face of danger) and I am incapable of describing to you the immensity of the skill with which Stevie leads the troupe of penguins in time to the music. It is awesome. There is no other word for it. This is Stevie's finest hour. The man was born to dance. And the others follow in a more or less randomised fashion.

We allow them a full three minutes of music to do this dance. And no one is even wiggling in their seat in the audience. Everyone is captivated. That's quality. But like all good things it has to end and as the music fades out Barry, who is being prompt to Deirdre's narrator, opens proceedings. (Deirdre was offered to be a random penguin but she preferred narration. She made a real and informed choice. She's not a keen dancer, Deirdre). Barry is not my first choice for a prompt, but hey, we are flexible here aren't we? We are also, so you can place us, in the Emperor Penguin's palace.

'Once upon a time in the land of penguins, the Emperor Penguin was a real show off,' says Barry.

Kelly makes a performance of showing off her cape and shoes as the random penguins look on. Deirdre picks up the tale.

'He always wanted the best of everything,' she says.

'I'm the Emperor, I should have the best of everything,' Kelly states and who are we to argue with her.

'And he was very, very vain,' Barry opines.

'He loved to look at himself in the mirror. But even he had to admit, when he looked at himself that very morning, that something was not quite right,' Deirdre says, straight as a die.

Which makes the audience laugh even harder as Emperor Penguin holds up a tiny babies pyjamas and says,

'I've grown out of my favourite pyjamas. What can I do?'

Lest the audience think this is a rhetorical question, Deirdre steps in, 'He asked the penguins. One penguin said 'give them to charity.'

That's the cue for Mandy to say, 'Give them to charity,' which she does.

'Go on a diet,' Lauren shouts, 'darling.' Ah. She's back with us. Fuelled by chocolate.

'Get a new pair,' Pauline chimes in. This is the important line after all. Without this we can't continue.

'That's a good idea,' Emperor Kelly says, 'I'll get a new pair. Now... Can anyone here recommend a good tailor?'

Once more, this is not a rhetorical question and we move right along to scene two to discover the answer.

We have more than one set running here, it's almost a promenade performance. We are not on a stage. We are down at the level of the audience who are seated café style at tables wiping the last remnants of fairy/cup cakes from their happy jowls. The Emperor Penguin's set is slap bang in the middle but the scene we go to now, The McGuff Tailors Emporium is situated behind many of the audience so they have to swivel in their seats to get a good view.

You don't have to swivel. That's the joy of reading it. You just need to know that there's a table, a tailors dummy, a flip chart and a LARGE pair of scissors (made of cardboard!) on show. And sat in a chair either side of the table are the McGuff brothers. They are twins. Not strictly identical because Annie and Bilbo don't look alike at all, not even if you have your eyes shut in a darkened room, but for the drama, they are twins.

Barry sets the scene, 'The McGuff Tailors were new in town. They were looking for a way to drum up new business. Usually penguins don't have much need for clothes, and they were trying to work out a cheap way to make a profit. But they couldn't agree.'

Prepare for comedy. Mostly scripted. Some not.

Deirdre winds them up and sets them going, by telling us that 'Mork McGuff (that's Bilbo) would say something like, How are we going to make a profit?'

That's all the cue Bilbo needs.

'How are we going to make a profit?'

You have to be patient when you're setting up comedy. And also sometimes our comic actors forget their lines which somehow doesn't always make it more funny, so Deirdre feeds them again with, 'and Mindy McGuff would reply...'

'How are we going to make a profit.' Nice one Annie.

In case the audience are not prepared for a comedy duo of the level of Morecombe and Wise, Laurel and Hardy, Barry helps get them in the mood.

'Getting irritated, Mork would say: Do you have to repeat everything I say?'

Quick as a flash Bilbo chips in with, 'Do you have to repeat everything I say?'

'Do you have to repeat everything I say,' Annie mimics.

The audience get it. They laugh.

Barry fixes them with a stern stare.

'It wasn't funny!' he states and continues, 'So before the brothers came to blows they agreed they'd each put their best idea up on the board.'

'Let's put our best idea up on the board,' Mork/Bilbo says.

'Let's put our best idea up on the board, Mindy/Annie says.

The audience laugh.

Deirdre intervenes.

'Mork tried to be polite and said 'you go first' to his brother.'

'You go first,' Mork/Bilbo parrots.

'No, you go first,' Mindy/Annie says. She's in her element. She loves it when she gets a laugh.

Barry helps them out. Milk it Barry, milk it.

'Mork insisted, he was determined to be the most polite brother and said, through gritted teeth – no YOU go first.'

Now comes the competition of speaking through gritted teeth. First Mork/Barry.

'No, you go first,' he says.

'No, you go first,' Mindy/Annie responds.

I think she wins. Her teeth were not just gritted, I'm sure I detect a bit of grinding too.

Barry steps in, mock serious, 'Okay, okay, Mork, would you just put your idea up on the board.'

Mork/Bilbo puts his *idea* on the board. The idea is a bit of card with the word *invisible* on it.

Deirdre reminds Mindy/Annie who is still gritting her teeth that the joke must go on.

'Not to be outdone, Mindy put *his* idea on the board. ' (sorry the emphasis is mine there. Deirdre doesn't do emphasising words. She just repeats them, if you don't mind my saying so. Sorry, Deirdre.)

The comedy at this point is not me making a cheap shot at Deirdre, no, it's that Mindy/Annie puts her cardboard *idea* which says *cloth* on the board, but upside down. That raises a laugh from those who can read in the audience. Luckily for Annie her embarrassment is spared and the comedy reclaimed because the idea then falls off completely and Barry is able to help her stick it up again the right way up. Deirdre is looking perplexed. She doesn't see the humour in this. This isn't one of the funny bits is it? She has a line to deliver and she's going to do it.

'This is called brainstorming, But penguin's prefer to call it 'blue sky' thinking,' she says.

People laugh. She isn't impressed. Why do they laugh at that? It's not funny. I fear Deirdre shares a sense of humour with many people I've tried to amuse over the years. And who's to say she's wrong and I'm right. Not me. I have no confidence in myself as a comic writer. I'm just telling it as it is. Annie is the comedy genius.

Barry now joins in the fray.

'The brothers were pleased with themselves. They were more clever than Jedward!'

The McGuff brothers raise their bowler hats (I forgot to tell you they were wearing bowler hats and I suppose I shouldn't have taken that as read.) Their hair is sticking up (not as much as Jedward's obviously)

'And more handsome,' Barry continues.

'Genius idea,' says Mork/Bilbo.

'Genius idea, repeats Mindy/Annie, wishing she hadn't clocked her nose with the bowler when she went to put it back on.

Deirdre tells them what to do next. Just as well.

'And they sat back to look at their handiwork. They read out the idea,' she instructs.

'Invisible,' says Mork/Bilbo.

'Cloth,' says Mindy/Annie. And who would know if she read it or remembered it?

Deirdre doesn't leave you with time to think about that. She carries on, 'They were impressed with themselves. After all, as Mork said, it would be so cheap.'

'It'll be so cheap,' Mork/Bilbo says.

'So cheap,' Mindy/Annie repeats.

'And so easy to make,' Barry opines.

'So easy to make,' Mork/Bilbo says.

'So easy to make,' Mindy/Annie adds as loud as she can because the audience are still laughing. It's not just Lauren experiencing the sugar rush then. Careful folks. We're about to change pace.

'There was just one problem,' Deirdre says.

Everyone looks at Deirdre.

'A problem?' Mork/Bilbo says.

'A problem?' Mindy/Annie repeats.

'A problem?' Barry add. He can't help himself. He's enjoying the laughs.

Deirdre is *not* amused.

'Yes, who's going to be stupid enough to fall for it?'

The 's' word again. Silence. That stops the laughter. The word you do not want to use in a group of people labelled with learning disabilities is stupid. Believe me. You don't. Want. To. Do. It. Ever.

But we do it from time to time, just to remind people that labels are for tins, not for people. So, while the audience is getting their heads round the 's' word and the McGuff brothers are still scratching their heads wondering who might be stupid enough to fall for it, the random penguin dance troupe make their way, accompanied by music, to the McGuff's Tailor's Emporium. They waddle/dance their way there and hand Mindy/Annie a rolled up scroll of paper. Luckily Stevie isn't carrying it and it isn't brown so we don't have a struggle to get it off him (we have done in the past, in rehearsal. Sometimes cardboard *isn't* the answer, believe me.)

'What is it?' Mork/Bilbo asks. Like he doesn't know.

'A summons. It's a letter from the Emperor,' Deirdre enlightens him.

Ah, it seems that things are looking up for the McGuff brothers. They make a meal of handing it back and forth between themselves. And it looks like this might go on indefinitely so Barry snatches it from them. The penguins after all, are getting restless and threatening to steal the show. They are off on a random waddle/dance, this time not accompanied by music.

'Boys, boys,' Deirdre says, fearing the random penguin dance anarchy which may engulf the entire production at any minute.

'Ah, I understand your problem,' says Barry, having a good peruse of the scroll. He's impervious to Deirdre's flashing glances telling him to hurry it up before things get out of control.

'His handwriting is appalling,' Barry continues, immune to Deirdre's evil eye. 'But I think the gist of it is that the Emperor wants a new pair of pyjamas. The summons asks you to come and measure him up. What do you think about that?'

The random penguins are now dancing amongst the tables and the McGuffs have to work hard to hold onto the audience. They give each other a high five.

Barry says, to anyone who is still listening, not captivated by the random penguin dance troupe, 'The McGuffs were very happy.'

Deirdre is determined to get things back on track so she steals Barry's line, sure that she can give it the gravitas it requires and she says, 'If they could just invisibly iron out the problem of getting the Emperor to buy the invisible pyjamas, they would be rich beyond their wildest dreams.'

Barry's back. 'What'll you be boys?' he says.

'Rich beyond our wildest dreams,' they chant.

Luckily for us the penguins have gone back to their starting positions. I think they've more or less worn themselves out. It gives the audience the chance to focus on the McGuffs again for a moment.

'Mork thought for a moment then he asked his brother what his wildest dream was,' Barry says, determined to reclaim comedy for words not dance.

'What is your wildest dream?' asks Mork/Bilbo.

'What is *your* wildest dream?' parrots Mindy/Annie.

Yes folks. Remember the scripted comedy. That's what you're supposed to be laughing at, right?

'Mork thought for a moment, wondering if his brother was playing a trick on him? To be safe, he threw the question back – what is YOUR wildest dream?' Barry is going to milk this one more time.

'What is your wildest dream,' Mindy/Annie is up for one more bout of laughter.

Deirdre intervenes, 'Oh my goodness, not this again,' and mistakenly pauses while the audience laughs before she finishes her line, 'I think it's time to move on to the next scene.'

Which indeed it is.

Scene Three finds us back at the Emperor's Palace. It seems so long ago, doesn't it? You've got to feel sorry for Barry and Deirdre. They are working hard for their cake aren't they?

Barry tells it like it is. Or should be.

'A short time later the McGuff's were ushered into the Emperor Penguin's dressing room.'

Pauline the least random of the penguins goes to fetch the McGuffs and present them to the Emperor. There is much bowing, scraping and general regal like behaviour.

'The Emperor wasted no time in telling them of his problem,' explains Deirdre.

He shows them his tiny pyjamas. Cue another laugh. It's a good thing. Once you get an audience laughing they'll just keep on going. Even when the jokes aren't that funny. Once you hit critical mass they will just keep splitting their sides.

'I think they must have shrunk in the wash,' Emperor Kelly says amidst more laughter.

Barry continues, 'The McGuffs agreed with him. Mork told him this happens with cheap fabric.'

'This happens with cheap fabric,' he says.

Annie holds herself in with difficulty. It would be so easy to go for the laugh. But she's a job to do. She's not supposed to speak now. She doesn't.

'I don't want cheap fabric. I want EXPENSIVE fabric,' shouts Emperor Kelly. 'Only the best. I want the finest pyjamas in the land.'

The McGuff's look at each other and smile. Well, more a smirk than a smile. They know what's coming next.

'Get out the special fabric,' Mork/Bilbo says.

'The fabric fit for an Emperor,' Mindy/Annie says.

So they get out the invisible fabric (clingfilm in this case so that people can see it is invisible but also cloth. I always said clingfilm was a marvellous invention and it saves our bacon here.)

'It suits you sir,' Mork/Bilbo says.

'It suits you sir,' Mindy/Annie repeats.

Because we're not above giving away where we get some of our comedy ideas from. Even if we don't generally like that show.

Deirdre explains, 'The Emperor looked worried. He couldn't see anything. He felt the fabric they held up before him. He wasn't sure he could feel anything. '

'I'm not sure...it's very light... it gets cold here in winter,' Emperor Kelly says.

The McGuffs look at each other. It's obvious to us all that this is their big chance. And they are going to take it.

'The fabric has a special property,' Mork/Bilbo says.

'Which is?' Emperor Kelly replies, suspiciously.

Barry notes the air of suspicion.

'Mindy McGuff panicked and started to say it was cool in summer and warm in winter.'

'It's cool in summer and warm in winter,' Mindy/Annie says.

'The Emperor doesn't look too impressed,' Deirdre ventures, scripted. 'So Mork shut his brother up. He told the Emperor that the fabric had one very very special property. It was INVISIBLE to stupid people.'

'It's invisible to stupid people, your majesty.' Mork/Bilbo says.

The 's' word again. No. It can't be true. But yes, it is. The 's 'word is obviously a key part of this play. It's important. Believe me.

'The Emperor drew a deep breath,' says Barry.

And he wasn't the only one. A lot of the audience are not laughing any more. The 's' word has that magic power.

'He couldn't see a thing. But now he didn't dare say,' Deirdre picks up and runs with the line. 'He turned to one of his attendants and asked him if he could see the material.'

'Can you see the material?' asks Emperor Kelly.

'Of course your Highness,' says Penguin Pauline.

'And you?' the Emperor asks Mandy.

'Your majesty, it's beautiful,' she replies. It may be one of the few lines she has in this play but she's remembered it on cue.

'And you?' the Emperor asks penguins Duncan, Lauren and Stevie.

And at least one of them says 'yes,' in response.

'It seemed that everyone but the Emperor could see the material and he didn't want to appear stupid so he said,' Deirdre says.

'Yes. I'll have it. Make me up a pair of pyjamas as quick as you can,' Emperor Kelly has spoken.

The McGuff brothers look very happy. Indeed they may exchange an unscripted high five at this point.

Deirdre is having no unscripted activity if she can help it so she rapidly carries on with her line, 'The McGuff brothers were very happy. And just a bit too greedy for their own good, so they tried to get more and more money out of the Emperor.'

'Would you like tassles?' Mork/Bilbo asks.

'Of course tassles.' Emperor Kelly replies.

'Would you like braiding?' Mindy/Annie asks though Deirdre did have to mouth the word 'braiding' to her before she picked up on the line.

'Of course, braiding. Tassles, braiding, every extra you can think of,' says Emperor Kelly. There's no problem making choices if you're an Emperor it seems. You just pick everything.

Barry is going for the laugh.

'One of the penguins, thinking he was being funny asked if the Emperor could have go faster stripes.'

And with a bit of a nudge Mandy remembers she has another line and says, 'Go faster stripes, your majesty?'

'Yes. Go faster stripes,' Emperor Kelly demands.

At which the McGuff brothers nod their heads solemnly and so vigorously that their bowler hats nearly fall off and they tell the Emperor that his wish is their command.

'Your wish is our command,' says Mork/Bilbo McGuff.

'Our wish is your command,' says Mindy/Annie getting it the wrong way round by mistake but the audience find it even more hilarious. They are primed for the repetition remember.

Deirdre is having no truck with unauthorised frivolous laughter and ploughs on.

'So, the silly vain Emperor penguin ordered a pair of invisible pyjamas with tassles, braiding and go faster stripes,' she says.

'And I want them by Wednesday,' Emperor Kelly shouts out after the retreating bodies of the McGuff brothers, who fortunately remembered to hold onto their hats when they bowed low on departure.

Without more ado we are at scene four. Next Wednesday. Time flies when you're having fun eh? Barry picks up where Deirdre left off.

'The very next Wednesday the McGuff Tailors returned to the Palace to fit the Emperor's new pyjamas. They were a little bit worried but it was too late now, they'd made their pyjamas and they would have to sell them.'

The McGuffs enter and help the Emperor into his 'new' invisible pyjamas. Which of course are NOTHING.

'They are very comfy,' Emperor Kelly says and turns to one of his attendant penguins.

'What do you think of the tassles? He asks.

Deirdre is determined we'll not miss the point of the drama and delivers the line with as much gravitas as you can when you have no modulating range.

'The penguin had forgotten that the material was invisible and that only clever people could see it. He couldn't see any tassles so he said he couldn't see any tassles,' she says.

This is Lauren's big moment. Though if she chooses not to say it, we have Pauline primed as back up. But today, she says it.

'Can't see tassles,' she says.

Barry continues with the story, 'The Emperor didn't look too happy and Mindy panicked and told him the tassles weren't ready yet.

'The tassles aren't ready yet your highness,' Mindy/Annie says, thankful that Barry reminded her.

'The Emperor shrugged,' Deirdre says. 'He looked at the pyjamas more closely. He couldn't see any braiding.'

'What about the braiding?' asks Emperor Kelly.

'It's a work in progress,' smiles Mork/Bilbo.

The Emperor looks a bit angry.

'And the go faster stripes,' he says, voice raising noticeably.

Barry reminds the McGuffs what to do.

'The McGuffs stood their ground. Mork said the go faster stripes look wonderful.'

'The go faster stripes look wonderful,' says Mork/Bilbo.

'The go faster stripes look wonderful,' repeats Mindy/Annie back on familiar ground.

Barry keeps on going. 'And because the Emperor looked like he was getting angry, and he wasn't very nice when he was angry, the rest of the penguins agreed that the Go faster stripes really made the outfit what it was, which was WONDERFUL.'

Everyone joins in making the right kind of noises. I think Duncan and Stevie might have spoken a bit louder but they were busy developing a new bit of the penguin dance. Something to use for the parade which is about to happen – now.

'And then the Emperor made a big mistake,' says Deirdre. 'He was so vain that he decided to show off the pyjamas, as they were, to all the penguins out in the street.'

'Can you pay us now please?' asks Mork/Bilbo wanting to be on his way.

And the Emperor is so keen to get out and show off that he pays them in full. In full. And they beat a hasty retreat as the random penguin dance troupe amass themselves for a full penguin parade.

Which is scene five. Out in the street. Or in this case weaving in and out of the tables.

Deirdre, appropriately enough, is the voice of reason.

'Yes, we know it was silly of the Emperor Penguin to go out in public in his new pyjamas because real or invisible, pyjamas are really for wearing at home, not out in the town. But he was so proud of himself,' she says, 'and he was the Emperor after all.'

'I am the Emperor after all,' Emperor Kelly says regally. Or should that be empirically?

Deirdre comments on the Penguin parade, in case the audience forget that there is a point to all this random movement activity.

'As he walked down the streets, the word had got out that he was wearing a new, expensive pair of pyjamas which could only be seen by clever people. So everyone pretended they saw them.'

She's losing the battle a bit. The dancing is just so funny.

Barry comes to her rescue. Lining up Lauren for one more line. Talk about random. Here we just have to cross our fingers and hope she's playing our game for once.

'Except for one little penguin who hadn't heard all the fuss. As the Emperor passed by he shouted out - The Emperor's got no clothes on.'

Thanks to echolalia, or comic timing or the multiple fairy/cup cakes consumed, Lauren does as bidden if not as always expected and shouts out,

'The Emperor's got no clothes on.'

The random penguins keep dancing. No one said the 's' word after all did they? Keep partying.

Barry isn't letting it go. 'At first the other penguins didn't hear him,' he says. 'Then the word spread and they all started saying - the Emperor's got no pyjamas on... It spread like wildfire.

And a few more of the penguins pick up that it's their turn and start shouting, 'The Emperor's naked. He's got no clothes on.' Some of the audience even join in too. Anarchy is contagious you see. In a dramatic context anyway.

148

Deirdre speaks, 'The Emperor tried to ignore them. They were just stupid after all.' She said the 's' word but I think she got away with it. She carries on undaunted, 'But then he looked down at himself and realised he WAS naked.'

We had to give Barry the next line. Deirdre just wouldn't do it justice. You have to agree.

Barry says, 'He went black and white and red all over' (some people get it and laugh) 'and he rushed back to the palace in shame.'

Deirdre picks up the story again, 'He sent a penguin out to find the McGuff brothers, but they had long since left town.'

Sure enough when the penguin parade goes past the McGuff Tailor's Emporium there's no sight of them. (They are hiding just outside the room, not that happy, and listening to hear the end so that they can come in and get their rightful applause.

Deirdre says, 'So the Emperor was out of pocket. And he didn't even have a pocket to be out of, invisible or not. The only thing he was left with was a moral.'

That's the cue for Annie and Bilbo to come back in. And they do. They never miss that cue. Even though Bilbo often bows with his back to the audience he never misses a curtain call.

Deirdre asks all and sundry, 'What do you think the moral of the story is?'

'Don't go out in your pyjamas,' Mandy says. Well remembered. And so very true.

'Don't let anyone tell you you are stupid,' Pauline says. Only she is authorised to use the 's' word in this company.

And Barry, because he's Barry and the leader of the group has the final line.

'And I think the moral also is, if something looks too good to be true it probably is.'

We don't have a curtain, and there's no cup/fairy cakes left to throw but believe me there is a standing ovation and much bowing and cheering ensues.

And once that's all died down and you think about it a bit, I'm sure you'll see there's more to this story than meets the eye. And it has more than a little to do with 'real' and 'informed' choices and the relationship between well intentioned social policy and the reality of life for people who wear the label of learning disability. And that's the end of Thursday.

# FRIDAY

### *The Recycled Musical.*

Here we are at the end of the week at last. And it's been quite a journey, I'm sure you'll agree. But all good things must come to an end, and our big finale, the final act if you will, is going to be another recycled affair. This time it's a recycled musical.

'What do you mean by that?' Deirdre asks me at coffee time. 'How do you recycle a musical?'

I'm glad someone's listening. I thought that I was coming a poor second to a rather excellent box of biscuits which had been thoughtfully donated by someone who is obviously aware that without biscuits nothing can happen at No Labels Drama Group. Good ideas are secondary to good biscuits. Everyone should know that.

'Are we doing Politics is Rubbish again?' asks Bilbo.

'No,' I say, aiming to build a bit of suspense. 'It's much better than that.'

'Piglet, Ham-a-let,' says Lauren. 'Good, darling.'

And I know that I'll have her on side.

'Music,' says Duncan.

'Yes, Duncan,' I say, 'lots of music this time. A real musical.'

'Like Cats?' Kelly asks.

Kelly has seen Cats in London. Don't ask me when or how. But she can recount the entire experience verbatim. I've never seen Cats. I never need to. Kelly has it down pat.

Mandy is confused. She takes things literally. She's wondering how you recycle cats.

'Recycle cats?' she asks.

'No,' I say, squashing that one quickly.

'Here's what it is. We are going to write our own musical.'

Pause for effect.

No effect obvious.

I really should learn how to present ideas to them better. They don't see things my way, that's for sure. They don't see the hard work, or the fun, or really anything. They are used to being spoon-fed things they don't want and they don't really care about some notional, fictional future event. If we're doing a musical just tell us about it.

This is pretty much what Annie suggests to me next.

'Tell us about it, properly,' she says. That's me put in my place.

'Yes,' Deirdre adds, 'I don't think Duncan understands if you don't mind my saying so.'

I do mind her saying so actually. I don't think Duncan needs Deirdre to speak for him. I'm tired of pointing this out. I'm tired really. It's been a long week. And this isn't going down how I expected.

'Who knows the story of Aiken Drum?' I ask.

There are several nods and Duncan shouts out, 'Ladle,' which I take it to mean he knows the song version of this folk tale.

'Never heard of it,' says Pauline.

'You're joking,' I say. 'I thought everyone knew about Aiken Drum?'

'Not me,' she says. 'Is it a Scottish story perhaps?'

Ah, yes, it is.

'Well then,' she says, 'I'm English, aren't I?'

'Yeah, but you've lived here for forty odd years Pauline,' I say. 'You've got eight kids. Surely somewhere along the line one or other of them brought home the story or the song of Aiken Drum?'

'Ladle,' shouts Duncan and claps his hands excitedly.

'*He played up on a ladle, a ladle, a ladle,*' starts Bilbo.

Duncan and Lauren join in with '*he played upon a ladle and his name was Aiken Drum.*'

'Yeah, that's it,' I say.

'We did it at school, didn't we Duncan?' Kelly says. This must be all of thirty years ago but she remembers it.

'Yuss,' he says contentedly.

I'm beginning to think I might be onto a winner here.

'It's not a *real* musical though,' Deirdre says suspiciously.

'That's it,' I say. 'We're going to make it a real musical. By recycling songs and ideas from other musicals.'

'Sounds like hard work,' says Barry.

'It will be,' I admit. 'But fun too, I hope.'

'It will take commitment,' he says, turning to the group.

'What will it take?'

'Commitment, Barry,' they chorus. Well trained you see.

Coffee, tea, juice and biscuits reluctantly put aside I begin to explain things and work through the basic story and idea.

For Pauline, I have to go back through the basic story of Aiken Drum. Annie helps me.

'He's this trampy guy,' she says, 'who wears weird clothes. And he comes to town and no one likes him and everyone is scared of him.'

'Then some people do like him,' Kelly adds.

'He asks for work, remember,' I say.

'Yes,' says Annie, but I'm not sure she does.

'He says he'll work for no pay.'

'No pay?' Mandy is surprised. Her thought process clear: Why would anyone work for no money?

'Yes, he just wants to help out,' I say.

'That's why people like him,' Kelly says.

'Yes, I guess it is,' I say.

'And then a woman is sorry for him and makes him new clothes and he doesn't want the new clothes and so he goes away and he's sad,' Kelly says. Story told.

'That's pretty much it,' I say. 'But we need to think about what the story tells us. The subtext if you like.

'The what?' Bilbo asks.

'Subtext,' I say. 'It's like the story underneath the story, what it's really all about. The bit that makes you think about it later on. '

'Ah, like mean old King Lear?' Bilbo says.

'Exactly,' I say. 'Makes you realise you have to make choices based on sensible things not just on...'

'On being a mean old man,' Bilbo adds.

'So what is the subtext?' Barry asks.

'Yes, I don't know what it is, if you don't mind my saying,' Deirdre chips in.

'Of course we don't know it quite yet,' I say, 'we're only just starting. But think of this. Aiken Drum is different from other people yes? He looks different and wears ragged clothes. People are afraid of people who are different.'

'Like disabilities,' Annie pipes up. Sometimes she has great insight. Sometimes she exhibits no insight at all. I suppose that just makes her like the rest of us doesn't it?

'Yes,' I say, 'I'm not saying Aiken *has* a disability. But he's different and that's a label.'

'*Who're you gonna call... No Labels...*' sings Bilbo to the Ghostbusters tune. He takes any opportunity to get that in. We'll have to put it in the show.

'Yes,' I continue, 'and we want to show that labels...'

'Are for tins not people,' they (mostly) chorus. Not Stevie of course and not Duncan. But everyone else in on the page with me on this one.

'Yes. We're going to use the musical to show that you shouldn't judge people by their appearances or their labels and you should help them how they need to be helped.'

There is a cheer. We like this concept.

'Because,' I say 'the woman makes Aiken clothes and so he has to leave because his deal is that he works for no pay and clothes is pay in this instance. So he has to leave.'

I'm beginning to wonder if I'm overcomplicating it, starting with the subtext, but I like to try and give everyone an idea of what we're at from the very beginning, as then they can connect with the process and we often come up with really good ideas. My policy (such as it is) is to work on the basis that everyone understands what I'm talking about rather than that they don't have a clue. I'm not sure I'm always right, but often I am. And I've built enough trust (I hope) that people are happy to tell me when they don't understand what I'm going on about. It kind of works for us.

'We'll set it in the Victorian age,' I say.

'Like Bleak House,' Barry says.

'Yes, have you read Dickens?' I ask him, amazed.

'Seen it on TV,' he says. 'Like it.'

'Okay,' I say.

'We'll set it in the olden days because we want to show that money isn't the most important thing.

'Ah, anti capitalist,' Barry says.

He and I could break into a verse of The Red Flag then and there but we don't. He gets the point. The subtext.

'What about the recycling?' Annie asks.

'And the cats?' Mandy asks. Still worried about the cats.

'There's no cats,' I say.

'Any Budgies?' Kelly asks. Kelly likes Budgies.

'No, I don't think so,' I say. 'Though maybe we can work one into the story.' I'm not convinced. But I've said it now. And Kelly will remember. I'm going to have to find a way to integrate a budgie in there somehow. Not a real one, obviously.

'The recycling is the songs,' I say. 'We're going to take songs you know and change the words but keep the tunes so that they work for our story.'

'Brilliant idea,' says Bilbo. He likes to do that already so he's my firmest ally on this path.

'Thanks,' I say.

'Can Aiken make recycled things?' Pauline asks.

'Great idea, Pauline,' I say. 'Yes, he can. That way he's making things without money and they can be things people have thrown away turned into things they really want.'

'Commodities,' Barry nods sagely.

Now we're starting to get somewhere. And you're getting an idea of how we start our devising process. Brainstorming. Yes, believe me, even people labelled with learning disability are capable of brainstorming. In fact, I have to tell you they are very good at it. We've been at workshop days run by charities and service providers and when it gets to the 'breakout' group stage (where they inevitably make us go into a group on our own – lest we taint the 'real' people dare I suggest) I've always been amazed how with Barry at the flipchart the group manages to cut through the flim flam and come up with good answers long before the 'normal' people have talked their way in and out of policy, common sense, marketing speak and the like.

'It's because we're trained in advocacy,' Barry explains to me when I tell him how impressed I am.

And because what are 'issues' in social care to the organisers are real life to the group, I think.

So. The creative process, while never progressing in a straight line, and requiring multiple pit-stops for biscuits along the way, is a very fruitful time for No Labels and the work we end up with really does represent everyones input to a substantial degree. It's not just me imposing on them. They have ownership. Let's face it, without a sense of ownership a number of the group just wouldn't engage. Full stop.

But because this is drama and we want you to enjoy the show and not for a minute think of the blood, sweat, tears and biscuits that go into the making of it, we'll break for lunch now and when you come back, we'll have magically whisked our way through two months of devising workshops and four months of rehearsals (one day a week you understand) and be ready to perform THE RECYCLED MUSICAL for you. Enjoy.

~~~

Are you sitting comfortably? Then we'll begin. (You see, you can recycle all kinds of things quite happily. And some people get it and others don't, and it doesn't really matter because everyone will get some of it at the very least.)

We open to the scene of the inhabitants of a small town going about their business. It's clear from the backdrop (several white sheets stuck together with a Rolf Harris-esque painted drawing of a town skyline in black) that we are in the industrial North in the nineteenth century. In the fair north east, where we set our scene...

We start, as all good musicals, with a song. This one is not really recycled or even adapted, but just stolen from a band called Del Amitri. A Scottish band at least. And I'm sure they would love our version. We've spent months performing dance moves that suit the lines. I'm not sure I can render this effectively to you on the page, but I'll try.

*Post office clerks put up signs saying position closed* (Deirdre is the clerk and mimes closing the post office right in the face of a disgruntled Annie and Stevie. Annie is holding onto Stevie hard, which may explain why he's disgruntled.)

*And secretaries turn off typewriters and put on their coats* (Pauline and Lauren finish their mime typing and dress to leave)

*Janitors padlock the gates* (Duncan padlocks the gates)

*For security guards to patrol* (Mandy patrols. She is very officious though she won't wear the hat.)

*And bachelors phone up their friends for a drink* (Pauline, Duncan, Lauren and Mandy mime drinking.)

*While the married ones turn on a chat show* (Annie and Deirdre settle down at opposite sides of the stage to watch pretend TV.)

*And they'll all be lonely tonight and lonely tomorrow.* (Everyone stands still facing the front and does choreographed hand movements in time with the chorus.)

*Nothing ever happens, nothing happens at all. The needle returns to the start of the song. And we all sing along like before. And we'll all be lonely tonight and lonely tomorrow.* (This bit is inevitably sung with great feeling.)

*Bill hoardings advertise products that nobody needs* (Mandy and Lauren point at imaginary signs)

*Angry from Manchester complains about all the repeats on TV.* (Annie waves her fist furiously in the air)

*And computer terminals report some gains* (Barry waves his arms around like a demented trader at the Stock exchange.) He's wearing a morning suit and a top hat and is flanked by Duncan and Bilbo, similarly dressed.

*On the values of copper and tin. While American businessmen snap up van Goghs, for the price of a hospital wing* (Once again, everyone stands still and does the moves.)

*Nothing ever happens, nothing happens at all. The needle returns to the start of the song. And we all sing along like before. Nothing ever happens, nothing happens at all And we'll all be lonely tonight and lonely tomorrow.*

There is a moment's pause, then they go about their business. Pauline, cast as Elsie, begins to tell the story.

'Can I tell you the story of this town,' she says. 'This is Trade Town and every day people go to the market place to sell their goods – they trade and exchange.'

The group mime out her instructions.

'Let me introduce you to some of the people in Trade Town,' she says.

Everyone comes up and takes their bow as appropriate. Annie was particularly keen on taking a bow at the beginning of the show because that's her favourite part of a play.

Elsie/Pauline continues, 'The most important people are the Trades. Thomas, (Barry) Terence, (Duncan) and Timothy (Bilbo)Trade.'

They are all dressed in morning suits and top hats. They stand behind a table in front of the backdrop and they look every inch the men of substance they are aiming to be.

'The Trade triplets really run the town because they decide what things are worth,' says Elsie/Pauline. 'You can't have a transaction in Trade Town without the approval of the Trades.'

Thomas/Barry pulls himself up to his full height and sticks his fingers under the lapels of his jacket. He's in his element. Not since Polonius has he been able to give so much to a part.

'And not surprisingly, they are the richest men in the Town,' Elsie/Pauline explains.

'Who else do we have?' she says, turning from the Trades. 'Let's see. Oh, here are the Sunshine Sisters, Meryl (Deirdre) and Beryl (Annie) They are twins.'

They take their bow. They are dressed in matching long skirts and straw bonnets.

'Then we have the Favour twins,' Elsie/Pauline says, introducing Stevie and Lauren who don't look too happy to be there.

'That's Manny (Stevie) and Fanny (Lauren) to you. We're all on first name terms here,' she continues.

'And Ethel Parker (Mandy)' says Elsie/Pauline, waiting for the laugh. It doesn't come. The audience are still not quite sure what they are in for yet. Elsie/Pauline helps them along.

'Don't call her nosey,' she says and because Mandy reacts so well, the audience realise it's okay to laugh. Mandy wouldn't wear a bonnet so she's just got a ribbon in her hair.

Elsie/Pauline has a job to do and she gets on with it while the rest of the cast make a big deal about lining up to sell their wares to the Trades. Who are not that keen to buy. Thomas keeps rejecting things and Timothy even throws something away, occasioning the silent wrath of Beryl/Annie Sunshine.

'I suppose,' Elsie/Pauline continues, (the consummate professional, she's learned to keep going whatever chaos is happening in the background,) 'this is a town like many others, people old and young coming and going, living and dying. Most of them are lonely and most of them can't see the point.

I wonder whether we are drawing it out too long, and the audience are missing the point as well because they seem pretty stuffed shirt about it. But I bury my head in my music stand (I'm playing guitar accompaniment to the musical numbers) and hope for the best. Should I have put this much exposition in? It's not exactly Half a Sixpence now is it?

Elsie/Pauline keeps on going, 'But today, something different happened,' she says.

I swear I hear someone in the audience shout 'about time.' Then I realise it's Bilbo. Trying, no doubt, to inject some humour. This is all we need. I've finally capitulated and worked on a fairly fixed script and now everyone wants to improvise. I think I may be beginning to sweat. Which won't help my guitar playing.

'Something new,' says Elsie/Pauline, fixing Bilbo with a stare.

'There's someone new come to town. Someone strange. Someone we don't know. And the people of Trade Town aren't used to strangers.'

Our attention is drawn away from the Trades and Bilbo the comedy Trader, and towards Mandy who stands in the aisle. She's dressed in some ragged old clothes. In fact some weird kind of green fluffy jacket which makes her look a bit like a budgie (we negotiated away from having a live budgie into her wearing a jacket that made her feel like a budgie!) and a battered old straw hat with holes in it. Her trousers are ripped and held up with string. Her shoes have the toes out of them. She's a sorry state. But she wears it well. She knows she's the star of the show.

In case anyone hasn't seen Kelly. (Believe me, you couldn't miss her) Elsie/Pauline informs us, 'While Meryl and Beryl are bargaining with the Trades, the stranger observes them from a distance.' And indeed this is more of a cue line for Annie and Deirdre than anything else. They begin the task.

'It must be worth more than that,' Meryl/Deirdre says.

'What?' Thomas/Barry says, in his best shocked voice.

'This isn't enough money,' states Beryl/Annie.

Pathos? It's like Oliver. Believe me.

'I decide what something's worth. That's my job. And you didn't work a full day at it,' Thomas/Barry says, sternly.

'I was at the doctors,' Beryl/Annie states, hoping for sympathy.

'If you don't put in a full day's work, you can't expect a full day's pay,' Thomas/Barry responds, giving her none.

'But my family still need to eat, and with the cost of medicine for Meryl...' Annie is pulling a blinder here, she's worked so hard with her CD to learn her lines and she's really nailed it. I'm proud of her.

'You need to learn to budget my friend,' the rude Thomas/Barry states. He's not impressed by her sob story.

And still giving Oliver a run for his money in the pathos stakes (and remember he was a blond haired little cherub and Annie is forty six year old woman with a penchant for sweeties, so she starts at a disadvantage here) Beryl/Annie begs him plaintively, 'Please help me... I'll give you two for the price of one tomorrow,'

'We can't give you any money,' Timothy/Bilbo says gravely.

'But I can give you a piece of advice,' Thomas/Barry says. He's referring to his stock sheet – yes, the clipboard again.

And I begin to strum. Which is the cue for them to all get into position. The song is a recycled version of that classic from Cabaret – Money Makes the World go Round. (Well, it had to be, didn't it?)

Despite the fact that he has no confidence (and little timing and a rough sense of tune) we think it only fitting that Thomas/Barry Trade opens the song so he gets his solo off and running. I try to keep up.

*'Money makes the world go around, the world go around, the world go around,*

*Money makes the world go around, it makes the world go round,'* he sings.

The rest of the group then join in lustily, while moving round in a sort of cartwheel circle. If our choreography is simple it's as much because I am *not* a choreographer as much as the group are not dancers. And Stevie's 'wandering' style of choreography was not deemed appropriate here for a song about going round in circles. We do our best. It looks better than it sounds here anyway. And mostly everyone gets the words right.

'*A mark, a yen, a buck or a pound, a buck or a pound, a buck or a pound, Is all that makes the world go around, that clinking clanking sound, Can make the world go round,*' they sing.

Now we are going for hitherto unanticipated complexity. But hey, it's the end of the week, we are hardened and experienced professionals here. We can do it. Like the *real* musicals. Prepare to be amazed. Watch out now, because Bilbo and I have changed the words a bit.

'*If you happen to be rich, then you'll find that your life is quite perfect, you can buy all the things that you need,*' sings Terence/Duncan. Yes, that's right, the man who doesn't talk. But sings like an angel.

'*But if you happen to be rich, you still can be lonely, Cause your friends live on primetime TV,*' the group chorus back at him.

'*If you think there might be more to your life but you don't know what it is, just stop thinking what you need... cause,*' he throws it right back to the group who pick up with an enthusiastic chorus,

'*Money makes the world go around, the world go around, the world go around, Money makes the world go around, of that we all are sure. No fun being poor.*'

Okay. One verse down. Now we're onto a duet. Terence/Duncan and Meryl/Deirdre. We have no fear! We have ripped up those labels and squished them in the dust. They do not exist.

'*But when you haven't any coal in the stove and you freeze in the winter and you curse to the wind at your fate,*' Meryl/Deirdre sings.

'*My advice is work harder, my advice is work longer, and you'll see what a difference it makes,*' Terence/Duncan replies.

'*But when you haven't any shoes on your feet and your coat's thin as paper and you look thirty pounds underweight,*' she continues.

And the next line is my favourite in the whole play, entirely because of the feeling Duncan invests in it.

'*My advice is get a job, get a mortgage, pay with credit, have all the luxuries you need...*'

I don't care about the audience, that is pure musical theatre at its very best. We shall not see its like again!

The group all pick up on the line with, '*and see that money makes the world go around, the world go around,the world go around. Money makes the world go around, the clinking, clanking sound. It makes the world go round.*'

At the end of this song, I think we all know that we have achieved something remarkable here. Only two songs into the show and we *are* musical theatre. We *own* the space. Even the hardest hearted audience couldn't fail to be impressed. I can tell you, I've seen many many worse am-dram productions. And the odd professional musical turkey which doesn't have the guts of this one or the commitment of the performers. I won't pretend we are all always in tune, but I like to think of it as if you were in a *real* world situation where people just burst into song. They wouldn't all be in tune always now would they? But they are giving it their all. And it's great.

Elsie/Pauline pulls us back to the play from the musical number. The show must go on.

'The people go back to their houses for a cup of tea, leaving the Sunshine Sisters standing alone,' she says.

Then as a cue to Kelly, 'The stranger, Aiken Drum, approaches them. They are scared.'

'Please don't hurt us,' Meryl/Deirdre says. Not looking that scared to be honest. Or sounding it. Should have given that line to Annie. But Kelly looks odd enough and is good enough to redeem the situation.

'Why would I hurt you?' she asks. 'I just want to know the name of this place.'

(Ah, I stole that idea from Godspell, where John the Baptist wanders on stage 'just looking for a place to get washed.' Maybe I shouldn't be giving away my trade secrets, but hey, why not, it works.) While I'm patting myself on the back silently, the cast continue with the play. As they should.

'This Is Trade Town. Everyone knows that,' Beryl/Annie says.

'Yes, everyone knows that,' repeats Meryl/Deirdre. (Familiar territory? See Piglet! on Tuesday and Fairy/Cup cakes on Thursday if you aren't getting the joke here)

Beryl/Annie fixes Aiken/Kelly with a hard stare that wouldn't go amiss if Paddington proffered it and says, 'You're not from round here are you?'

'No, I'm not,' replies Aiken/Kelly.

Now it would be nice to think that Mandy could initiate her line herself without a cue here, but that's never going to happen, so in the spirit of helping her how she needs to be helped, we gave Elsie/Pauline the cue line.

'Ethel Parker has been listening in,' says Elsie/Pauline to get her attention, 'and she tells Aiken to get lost.'

'We don't like strangers here. Get lost,' says Ethel/Mandy. And adds an unscripted, 'please.' She refuses to be impolite even when it's scripted. She knows she's being rude and she doesn't want to get into trouble for it somehow from one of the carers who will doubtless be in the audience watching her every move (fortunately not the 'odd' man from Thursday. I'm reliably informed he no longer works in the caring professions. I'm actually very glad. It saves me a lot of soul searching and wondering what is the ethical thing to do.)

And in case people are losing the flow, Elsie/Pauline keeps us all on track, as is her job and says, 'Aiken is about to leave, but the Sunshine Sisters stop him by calling out.' Annie needs no more cue, she's really nailed her lines this time. She's practiced every night with her CD for over a month. She tells me she's learned the script. I know that not to be true, but I take my hat off to her for the amount of work she has to put in to hide the fact she can't read. It's a real tribute to her. Though I can't help but thinking that if someone put enough time in with Annie she *would* be able to read. If they could keep her motivated.

'Don't go. You look tired,' she says to Aiken/Kelly.

'And hungry,' Meryl/Deirdre adds. She's always better with a follow on line but I never thought Annie would be the one to feed it to her. After all, Deirdre *can* read. But she can't remember her lines for toffee (if you don't mind my saying so.)

'Please come home with us,' Beryl/Annie says, grabbing Aiken/Kelly in the same armlock I've seen her use at traffic lights in real life when she's trying to catch a new friend. Art reflecting life?

'I have some food. If you have a fire, we can cook together. I'm happy to share what I have with you,' says Aiken/Kelly. Nice. Polite. Don't judge a book by its cover eh? She may look like a demented overgrown green budgie, but she's nothing to be afraid of, see.

'That's very kind. But don't let the Trades see,' Beryl/Annie says, casting an overt glance at the Trade Triplets who are busy with their hats in their ledgers.

'Why not?' Aiken/Kelly asks.

Ah, this is Annie's big expositionary moment. She's learned that she can act with the lines as well as through improvisation. She knows how to suck the marrow out of each line.

'Everything has to go through his books,' she says. I'm not sure she really knows what it's all about, but then, remember, she is the one who runs her own black market parallel economy and so maybe I shouldn't be so quick to dismiss her level of understanding.

'Come on back with us,' says Meryl/Deirdre.

And they all go back to the Sunshine sister's house (stage left) for dinner.

Now we are at scene three and the lights go up for night time at the Sunshine Sisters House. Aiken and the Sisters are having a nice wee chat (unscripted and too low to hear) over dinner and then, as I crank up the intro music they deliver their lines.

'So, tell us a bit about yourself,' Beryl/Annie says.

'Who are you, and where do you come from?' Meryl/Deirdre asks. (I'm waiting for her to say, if you don't mind my saying so, but she manages to stay in character and resist.)

'I'll tell you,' says Aiken/Kelly, standing up and positioning herself in the spotlight, (if we had one) centre stage.

This is the cue for another Bilbo/Kate version of a familiar tune. I have a dream. Penned originally by Abba but I'm sure they'd approve of our version. It's Kelly's first solo and she is giving it her all.

'*I have a dream, a song to sing, To help me cope with anything , If you see the wonder of a fairy tale, You can face the future even if you fail*, (so far so familiar?) *People call me Aiken I see good in everything I see, You can call me Aiken, I don't work for money, that's not me. I work for free and that's my dream.*

Led by the Sunshine sisters, the rest of the cast join in singing,

*'He has a dream, a fantasy, To help him through reality. And his destination makes it worth the while, Pushing through the darkness still another mile. We can call him Aiken*

*He sees good in everything he sees. We believe in Aiken, He won't work for money, he works free. And that's his dream, yes that's his dream.*

And yes, thanks, the audience really liked that number. Big applause. When it dies down, Elsie/Pauline keeps us moving along.

'That's all very well, but Beryl and Meryl need money to survive don't they?' She says.

'You can't survive here without money, can you Meryl?' Beryl/Annie states.

'No, you need money,' Meryl/Deirdre agrees.

'And do you have enough money Beryl?' Elsie/Pauline asks. A question and a surreptitious cue line. The beauty of theatre.

'There's never enough money here. The Trades seem to be well off but the rest of us are struggling to get by,' says Beryl/Annie.

'There are more important things than money you know,' says Aiken/Kelly.

And yes thanks, I did steal that from Annie's 'nothing's more important than being a princess line on Tuesday. Nothing is wasted with us. We can recycle any old line.

'I don't know what, do you Meryl?' Beryl/Annie says. Professional. She doesn't go with her nature – there's nothing more important...

'No, I don't know what either,' Meryl/Deirdre says.

Lest we go back into land of echolalia/repetition, Kelly holds focus and keeps us on track with *this* play. I sometimes wish I had Kelly's sense of focus.

'Let me help you,' she says, 'I'll help you with your work – for no pay.'

This is clearly an astonishing concept and Annie reacts with all the emotion she can muster.

'For no pay?' she says.

'I think you're crazy, but we're desperate. We don't have a choice,' Meryl/Deirdre says. Remember folks, the Sunshine Sisters are in a bad, bad way thanks to the evil Trade Triplets. And no National Health service to fall back on. Or benefits of any kind. No social policy, good, bad or indifferent to save them. They are victims of the Trades. That's unfettered free market capitalism folks!

'You'll see. Working together, everything will come out right,' Aiken/Kelly says (presaging the creation of the Co-operative movement, I'll be bound.)

'Okay. But it's time to sleep now. I'm tired,' Beryl/Annie gives a loud yawn and rubs her eyes theatrically.

'Me too,' says Meryl/Deirdre, rather less theatrically. But then diva twins would be just that bit *too* much don't you think? Someone needs to do understated sometimes. And Deirdre is the queen of understated acting.

'You can sleep over there by the fire if you like,' Beryl/Annie says – another set of lines remembered and delivered with feeling. Well done Annie.

'Thank you,' Aiken/Kelly says, because, as we all know, good manners cost nothing.

They settle down to sleep as the lights fade.

And rise again to the next morning. Elsie/Pauline sets the scene.

'Next morning, when Beryl and Meryl woke up, they found that Aiken had been hard at work for some time. He had made lots of beautiful things. He showed some of them to Beryl and Meryl. He was singing as he worked,' she says.

If you are familiar with Sam Cooke's 'Wonderful World' (which Kelly is) you'll get this instantly. We have, of course changed the words but the tune stands and she sings it, perfectly in tune.

*Don't know much about industry, Don't know much about commodities, Don't know much about stocks and shares, Don't know much about market forces. But I do know that the world is free, And I know that if you work with me, What a wonderful world this would be.*

How's that for political musical theatre. Kicks the ass of Les Miserables doesn't it?

Aiken/Kelly moves onto the next verse, *'Don't know why you want to work for money, I don't think consumerism's funny, Don't know why people need more and more, I don't know what trade rules are for. But I know that one and one is two, And if you can learn to work with me, What a wonderful world this would be.'*

That's one great song, and it gets the applause it deserves. Lucky for me, Elsie/Pauline is right on hand to keep things going. I'm risking getting totally caught up in the moment. But drama requires movement and so we must move on.

'Then Beryl asked Aiken how he made all the lovely things,' Elsie/Pauline says.

'But how did you make all these things?' Beryl/Annie asks.

'These lovely thing,' Meryl/Deirdre repeats. No hint of a laugh.

'I found things, lying around. Not being used. I can show you how if you like,' explains Aiken/Kelly.

'So Aiken Drum and the Sunshine Sisters sat down together to make things. They made lots of beautiful things. They sang as they worked. When they were finished they gathered all the beautiful things together and took them to the market place,' Elsie/Pauline says, taking us to the next scene where, as the lights come up, we discover the rest of the cast, milling around.

It's Trade Town Market. Everyone is queuing up behind Ethel Parker, selling their goods, trying to get the best price from the Traders. Trying to make enough money to survive another day.

Elsie comments on what we see, 'Here in Trade Town, it's a buyer's market and it's the Trades who decide if you will have steak or sausages for dinner.'

There's a little comedy moment while Terence/Duncan and Timothy/Bilbo wrestle with some cardboard sausages with Stevie. Then the scene is broken as the Sunshine Sisters make their way towards the table. They are laden down with the fine recycled and very very shiny things that Aiken has made. The Trades cannot fail but be amazed. And they are. To a man. They hold up the goods. Look at them. Take off their hats. Scratch their heads. Do all manner of things and finally, pay top dollar for the goods.

Amazement acting prevails all round. And the Sunshine Sisters rush excitedly back to Aiken, waiting stage left at the Sunshine Sisters house, to tell him their good news.

They are followed by the whole cast, clamouring to find out how they managed to do this. It's a bit of an unholy crush, chaotic as only we can do, but Aiken/Kelly is up to the task of explaining his philosophy to the people of Trade Town in yet another song. First brought to you by Lennon/McCartney and called 'We can Work it out.' Look out for our own special words!

Aiken sings, 'Try to see it my way, Do I have to keep on talking till I can't go on? While you see it your way, Run the risk of knowing that our world may soon be gone. Let's all work for free, Let's all work for free.'

The rest of the cast pick up the song, 'Think of what he's saying. He'll undermine our way of life if we work for *free. Think of what he's saying He'll change our world and we'll have no economy, We can't work for free We can't work for free.'*

Yeah, they're not going to be that easily convinced. We're not even half way through the show remember. There's still a long way to go.

Aiken resumes with the chorus, *'Life is very short, and there's no time, For fussing and fighting, my friends, I have always thought that it's a crime, To ask for money for my work. Try to see it my way, Only time will tell if I am right or I am wrong. While you see it your way, There's a chance that things might fall apart before too long. Can't we work it out? Can't we work it out?*

The Sunshine sisters are converts and they take up the song, *'Life is very short, and there's no time, For fussing and fighting, my friends.*

Aiken joins in, *'I have always thought that it's a crime, So I will ask you once again.'*

But the crowd are still unconvinced and reply in song, *'We can't see it your way, We can only say that we are right and you are wrong. We can't do it your way, Let us know how much we have to pay you for this song? We can't work it out, We can't work it out.'*

A new economic system doesn't get set up that quickly now, does it? They are still stuck in their ways. Elsie/Pauline confirms this much as she brings the scene to a close, 'Everyone went back to their own houses for another cup of tea. Meryl and Beryl Sunshine and Aiken Drum sat in the Sunshine's workshop and started to make more pretty things.'

Lights down. Lights up. Later that day.

'And after their tea Ethel Parker and Annie and Fanny Favour, and just about everyone in the town, came along to the workshop to see what was going on. They could hear Aiken singing and they weren't used to work being such fun. They gathered round watching and listening.

Then someone, I think it was Ethel Parker, asked Aiken "Can you show us how to make the pretty things?"

This is Mandy's cue to deliver her line. She does it, hooray! 'Can you show us how to make the pretty things?' she says.

'Of course,' says Aiken/Kelly. 'The secret is to create from the heart.'

And this leads us to another song. I have to confess I don't like this song. But the group do and they demanded that we have it in the musical. So I had to go along with it. It is our version of 'I believe I can fly.' I think it's tuneless at the best of times and I'm not convinced we rise above the basic nature of the tune. You're lucky you can't hear this one. Just read the words and if you know the tune, la it in your head, please. And pretend it's good.

'*I used to think that I could not go on,*' Aiken/Kelly sings.

'*And life was nothing but an awful song,*' Meryl/Deirdre joins in

(Yes, I think to myself. Never a truer word!)

'*But now we work together we are free,*' Beryl/Annie sings.

And the group joins in, '*Don't need more money, we are all we need, If I can see it, then I can do it, If I just believe it, there's nothing to it, We will win if we try, I believe I can make things right, I think about it every night and day, Work together and we're on our way  We will win if we try, Working together and we'll all survive, It will work if we try, We'll find love if we try, Yes we believe so we try.*'

Well, they all believe in the song. They all sing with gusto. I try to appreciate it but I can't. I just find it sad that they are so keen to 'win' in a life which has sidelined them. I suppose I should just appreciate their optimism in the face of adversity, but I'm afraid this song just always reminds me of the labels we are trying to lose. I think this is my problem, not theirs so I should shut up and let you get on with the show.

Except that this is the interval of the play. During which time, when on tour (which we aren't today, but usually we are) the group runs a 'making things' workshop with the audience – because this show has got funding to tour to care homes, activity centres and the like and we wanted to share skills as well as do a play. And to be honest, in order to get the cast to stay focussed through a whole musical which lasts the best part of an hour, we really do need a decent break half way through. Biscuits. Drinks. Recharge batteries.

Stamina regained we open for the second act. We are back at the Trade Town Market. The gang's all here. We open with a song. You need to know that Aiken taught the people this song and they sing along because he's shown them (in the interval) how to make the pretty things that will attract top dollar from the Trade triplets.

It's a familiar song – Accentuate the Positive. The group love this. Even Lauren joins in with gusto and Stevie leads the movement.

*'You've got to accentuate the positive, Eliminate the negative, And latch on to the affirmative, Don't mess with Mister In-Between, You've got to spread joy up to the maximum Bring gloom down to the minimum, Have faith or pandemonium's liable to walk upon the scene.*

It's a spirited rendition. But, as Elsie/Pauline points out, 'The Trades were not amused.'

And they sing (to the tune of You cannae shove yer granny off the bus)

*'Well you cannae work for nothing not for us, No you cannae work for nothing not for us No you cannae work for nothing ,Cannae work for nothing, Cannae work for nothing not for us.*

And what follows is a raucous, and only barely in control, singing competition. Once again I recycled this idea from Godspell where there are two singers/two tunes going on at the same time. What made me think I could have one group sing 'accentuate the positive' while the other group sings 'you cannae work for nothing,' I do not know. But we practiced it long and hard and it's actually very funny, especially when it's speeded up. But exhausting all the same.

So Elsie/Pauline gives us all a breather and says, 'Then everyone went home for yet another cup of tea.'

And the cast file out to sit down. Leaving the Trades and Aiken in charge of the stage.

It's clear the Trades are not happy. They confer amongst themselves and decide that something must be done.

Aiken is called up in front of them. Time for a showdown.

'I suspect,' Thomas/Barry says, 'that some of the people are trading amongst themselves, swapping one thing for another, without including us.' (Sound familiar Annie?)

'What's that? What's that? They're cutting us out of the market?' Timothy/Bilbo says.

'Cutting us out of the market,' Terence/Duncan says. Big game player. He delivers lines when he has to. As long as they are good enough lines. This one obviously passes muster with Duncan. Thanks Duncan.

'I won't stand for it,' says Thomas/Barry, pulling himself up to his full height again.

'Where is your insurance number?' Timothy/Bilbo asks Aiken.

'I don't have one,' Aiken/Kelly replies.

'Then you are not really contributing to our society are you?' Thomas/Barry says.

(Anyone seeing any disability subtext here yet?)

'How do I get an insurance number?' asks Aiken/Kelly.

'You have to earn money,' Timothy/Bilbo says, officiously.

'But I don't work for money,' Aiken/Kelly points out.

'Then you can't have insurance. Can he Terence?' Timothy/Bilbo appeals to Terence/Duncan .

'No,' comes the reply.

'No money, no insurance. That's right isn't it Timothy?' says Thomas/Barry, conferring with his ledger/clipboard to make sure he's got the line right. He knows this is the important part of the play now and he doesn't want to mess it up. Yes, by Friday, even Barry has learned that there is a place for flexible improvisation and this isn't it. It did take him a while to get there, but hey, he made it in the end.

'Yes,' Timothy/Bilbo replies.

'Without an insurance number you are a drain on our resources. We don't want you here,' Thomas/Barry says.

'So fall in line, or ship out,' Timothy/Bilbo says.

'Ship out,' echoes Terence/Duncan.

That's him told then.

Now of course, we're not going to let the baddies win the day are we? So the cast come back on, shocked by the awful treatment Aiken has just received. They understand, as I'm sure we all do, that Aiken was contributing more to society than the Trades ever would. After all, they only do things that are in their own best interest. Aiken works for the community. For free. He is the good guy here. We want him to win through.

So the cast come back from their tea break and a confrontation between good and evil is about to be worked out, in song of course since this is a musical. The tune this time is Only You. Made famous by Yazoo and later, by the Flying Pickets. Appropriate no?

The Trades start the song, '*Looking at the things that he's made, What he's done to our trade, Do we need him?*'

The rest of the cast join in to offer their opposing point of view, *'Look how much he makes in one day, We should ask him to stay, Don't we need him?'*

Beryl/Annie gets a solo now (she's earned it don't you think?) *'All he wants is to be one of us, Live together without a fuss, He's happy with no pay, Let him stay.*

Aiken/Kelly enters the song, *'They don't like the look of my face, And this isn't my place.'*

*'We all need you,'* sing the cast. *'Aiken we all want you to stay, Won't you please take some pay, Just this one day.'*

Aiken sadly shakes his head. They are missing the point. *'All I needed was the love you gave, All I needed for another day, I don't want any pay Let me stay.'*

The Trades have been silent too long. They have to have another go, *'We can't let him go on like this, He's too hard to resist,'*

But they are losing the group, who sing, *'But we like him. From rubbish he can make pretty things, And when he works he sings,'*

The Trades sense they are losing so they give it one last effort, *'It undermines us.'*

Aiken is a man/creature, he is also known as the Brownie of Bodsbeck, so the jury's out on whether he actually is a human or something supernatural. It doesn't matter. It's just a label. But during this line Beryl comes up with the brilliant but flawed idea of pressing a couple of notes into Aiken's hand to entice him to stay. It's as if the money burns him. He drops the notes and sings, sadly, *'All I needed was the love you gave, All I needed for another day, And all I ever do, It's for you.'*

And reluctantly, Aiken leaves the stage. You remember the basic story – that Aiken Drum can't work for money/pay and that Beryl has offered him money so that's curtains for him.

And for those who might have dose off, Elsie/Pauline informs us that, 'Trade Town went back to the boring, terrible, sad place it always had been before he arrived.'

And in case you'd forgotten that, the cast do a reprise of the song Nothing Ever Happens and this time there is added poignancy to it. Now that we know the story behind it.

The song over, Elsie continues, 'Even the Sunshine Sisters had lost their smiles. The Trades, well, they were happy because they were back in charge' which leads us into a reprise of Money Makes the World Go Round (you might call it a medley reprise. I think we call it recycling within recycling. Anyway, it gives the audience another chance to hear the songs we worked so long and hard on.)

After this song no one is any the more cheered as Elsie points out, 'mainly, people were just miserable. They went to sleep miserable, they got up miserable and they all missed Aiken.'

Lights down. But that's not the end. Far from it. This one isn't a tragedy. It's not really a comedy either is it? It's a social drama musical. A musical with a message. So read on.

The lights come back up and we are trying to get used to life without Aiken. You don't miss what you've got till it's gone, right?

'Time passed but the people didn't forget Aiken,' Elsie/Pauline says, 'They used to talk about him, and the strange clothes he wore and the strange ways he had. And a funny thing happened. After a while, they missed his songs and so they made up a song of their own, to sing to while they worked...'

Cue the actual title song. Aiken Drum. I hope you know this one. Everyone should know this song. The group added bits to the verses themselves of the things that he made, but here's the basic idea, *'There was a man came to our town, To our town to our town, There was a man came to our town, And his name was Aiken Drum, And he played upon a ladle, A ladle, a ladle, He played upon a ladle, And his name was Aiken Drum.'*

Even Stevie joins in with the word 'ladle' and waves his own cardboard ladle aloft to show that he's part of the gang.

We then progress to each cast member having a line. These sometimes differ depending on the prevailing mood, but I'll give you an example.

Annie sings, '*He made pretty things from rubbish, rubbish, rubbish, he made pretty things from rubbish, and his name was Aiken Drum.'*

Mandy sings, '*he made hats and caps from tin foil,'* and yes, believe it or not she wears a tin foil hat to sing this. She may not like hats but she likes hats made of tin foil. So it's like with dogs, (see earlier in the week) her likes aren't always as fixed as *they'd* have you believe.

Deirdre sings, '*He made belts and scarves from ribbons,'* and, you've got the idea by now, the rest of the cast pick up on the line and repeat it to the tune until the inevitable end line, 'And his name was Aiken Drum.'

The song raises the spirits of the townsfolk and it also gives some handy tips on things you can do with recycled 'rubbish,' to make treasures. Not bad eh? Inform, educate and entertain. Checks all the boxes.

But the song can't go on forever (though sometimes it does feel like it, believe me) and Elsie/Pauline has the discipline to bring it to a close and deliver the next scripted line, 'They really just made up the song to make them feel happier, but they had no idea what the result would be. Because one day, when they were singing and working, Meryl Sunshine was sure she saw... and she nudged Ethel Parker, who was sure she saw... and Manny and Fanny Favour were sure they saw... And they all told Beryl...'

This is winding the cast up to their next line and they all jostle around and shout out enthusiastically, 'It's Aiken,' as Aiken/Kelly returns to the stage to great acclaim both on the stage and from the audience.

'And sure enough, it was Aiken. He'd heard the song and he came back to be with the people who had been his friends. Everyone gathered round Aiken and made a fuss of him... except the Trades,' says Elsie/Pauline.

The Trades stand behind their bench, looking on, trying not to get caught up in the excitement. It's not time quite yet.

' They kept in the background,' Elsie/Pauline reminds them, 'but you know, a funny thing was happening to Thomas and Timothy and Terence Trade too... they found that they missed Aiken and the lovely things he made... so they didn't go too far away, and they thought about changing their ways...'

Cue Trades.

'There could be a place for a man like him. I think we might be able to accommodate differences, what do you say Terence?' asks Timothy/Bilbo, desperate to join in the fun.

'Yes,' Terence/Duncan responds.

'And you Thomas?' Timothy/Bilbo asks Barry. He who must be obeyed after all.

'Yes,' Thomas/Barry says, reluctantly. You can't fight City Hall after all.

'If we're agreed then,' Timothy/Bilbo chirps.

'But before the Trades even had the chance to invite Aiken to stay he had started to teach the people of Trade Town another song. A spirited song of Unity.

This is the moment Bilbo has been waiting for. Because it's our chance to sing his own musical creation. To the tune of Ghostbusters everyone – and please, feel free to join in and sing your heart out -

*If there's something bad, in your neighbourhood, who're you gonna call –call Aiken.*

*If there's someone bad, you can make them good, who're you gonna call – call Aiken.*

Repeated a few times for good measure till Elsie/Pauline steps in with the final line of the show, 'And I can't guarantee it, because it was a long time ago, and you might think it's just a story. But as I heard the story, Aiken Drum and the people of Trade Town all lived happily ever after.'

The curtain is coming down to wild applause (as we are getting used to by now) and Bilbo decides it's not enough to big up Aiken. The audience need the chance to join with the drama group itself. Beyond the stage. Bringing everyone together. So he leads the assembled crowd to his original version of the Ghostbusters/No Labels musical logo –

*If there's something bad, in your neighbourhood, who're you gonna call, NO LABELS. If there's something bad, we can make it good, who're you gonna call, NO LABELS.*

And with this the curtain falls and everyone goes home for the weekend but I bet they can't get that theme tune out of their head for days. Way to go Bilbo. Congratulations to the whole fictional crew and the real people they have been representing throughout this week.

# SATURDAY

## *Something for the weekend?*

It's the weekend. The end of the working week. That thing that 'normal' people hang out for, for five long days at a time. The time when you can be free to do the things you want to do. Be your own person. Live life. Except. Except that's not the way it is if you are an adult labelled with learning disabilities. Think about it. I mean really think. Like I admit I never did until we got the invitation to go away for a weekend as a group. I assumed it would be difficult to arrange. Everything is difficult to arrange when you're dealing with one adult labelled with a learning disability, never mind a group of them. Because their lives are regimented. Ordered. Subject to restrictions and care plans and all sorts from morning to night. We used to joke in No Labels (or I did, I'm not sure the others saw it as a joke and on reflection I think they may be right!) that they all had a much better time of it than I did. A better social life. Activities right, left and centre. Never a dull moment. If I ever tried to organise something for us on a different day of the week than our usual day, I'd discover that Annie was having her feet seen to, that Bilbo was down for carpet bowls and a tea dance, that Deirdre was doing her voluntary day at the local CVS, that Duncan was off to an art gallery, that Lauren was being taken shopping before a session at the ice rink (yes, the ice rink, let's not even go there. I went there once and I can tell you Lauren on ice-skates is a formidable sight!). Kelly would be detailed out at the college doing a horticulture class which she hoped, always in vain, might lead to a proper job, Mandy was

183

also down for carpet bowls and a tea dance (even though she doesn't like either bowling or tea very much) and Stevie, well Stevie was just hanging out at the resource centre wandering around checking out brown – oh, no, what's that Stevie, you're making cakes? Chocolate cake. Way to go. So you see, I could be forgiven (so I thought) for thinking that their lives were actually pretty busy and fulfilled and therefore trying to organise an out of the way 'activity' for No Labels wasn't usually worth the effort. Unless there was a performance. Sometimes we are paid for performances and in that instance (especially if there's food involved) the group will break any and all engagements to take part. Though Barry, Pauline and I still all have to put in a lot of phone calls and negotiations to 'spring' everyone from the important not to be missed carpet bowls and shopping regime. The regular 'routine' which must be imposed on those with care packages. And yes, that's the thing. It's more a regime to pass the time, to keep people busy than anything else. Routine for routine's sake. It's not that they have a lovely time all week when you are slogging your guts out in an office or on a building site or factory. So please don't worry, they are not abusing your taxes. They are not getting some great deal. Any one of them would swap your job with you in a heartbeat. And not just for the money. For being a valued (even though I know you think you are an undervalued) member of any workforce. Think on that next time you whine on a Monday morning. There's a load of people out there who would happily swap. Would you?

And then we come to the weekend. I assumed (wrongly as it turns out of course) that with this busy lifestyle during the week, doing something as a group at weekends would be an absolute impossibility. Until I asked. This is the lesson. Don't assume. Question. So I questioned.

And it turns out that no one does *anything* fun on a weekend. Here's a typical example. Annie goes to her mum. She does the shopping for her mum, who is housebound, but mostly she just gets bullied by 'the ugly sisters'. I'll admit, I've never met her sisters but their personalities as described by Annie and various others are certainly ugly enough to give them that soubriquet (or label). You'll remember that she's not the only one with such siblings. Having a sister labelled with a learning disability doesn't always bring out the best in people it seems!

Bilbo sits at home watching the TV. If he's lucky there's golf unless it's the football season. If not, horse racing. He doesn't have Sky TV. He's stuck with whatever Freeview has to offer. It's a long weekend. Deirdre isn't doing anything much either. She's got a house 'meeting' to organise and then she'll type up the minutes afterwards. That's all I can get out of her. For a whole weekend? I know she has to type with only one arm, but even so... Duncan is hoping he may get out to the cinema. If his 'friend' Archie is on duty. Yes, Archie may be Duncan's friend in Duncan's mind – and he's a nice guy, don't get me wrong, very friendly and nice. But he's a paid carer. So he's not in any *real* sense Duncan's friend. He is paid to spend time with Duncan and if he's pulled a weekend shift and there's something Duncan wants to see at the cinema, Archie will take him. Which is being a friend, because I know plenty of 'carers' who decide what the film will be and the 'client' just has to go along with whatever the carer wants to see (while paying for tickets for themselves and the carer out of their 'personal allowance' mind you). Archie lets Duncan choose. He's a pal. But if they went on holiday Duncan would still have to foot the bill for them both!

Lauren is lucky. She goes home to her parents at the weekend and has a great time. She wishes she could live there all the time and it's only recently that she's moved out into a group independent living arrangement. It's not her parents being mean. It's just that now they have both retired, they have come to terms with their mortality and there's no one to look after Lauren when they pop their clogs, so they have bitten the bullet and are getting her adjusted well in advance of that unhappy but inevitable day. It's not a situation any of them likes, but Lauren doesn't have sisters, ugly or otherwise, and so at weekends she goes home and gets pampered. Kelly does nothing. Absolutely nothing. She might go to the shops (without any money) and if she has a carer 'rostered' on then she might get to go to the garden centre where they have budgies in a cage and she can have a cup of coffee and listen to the budgies sing. Other than that? Watch TV. Soaps not sport. Mandy cannot be drawn on her weekend activity further than she 'cuddles her toys.'

'All weekend?' I ask, perplexed and not a bit disturbed.

She nods. She's not always the most reliable of witnesses, our Mandy, but having just heard what everyone else gets up to (or doesn't) over the weekend the penny begins to drop with me that carers, like you and me, have weekends off and therefore the 'caring' is more sporadic. I try not to get annoyed that this means that people I have come to call friends are basically chucked in a corner and left to 'get on with it' until Monday comes round and the 'duty of care' is re-established. It seems that for most of the group a care package doesn't include activities on weekends. I never find out what Stevie doesn't do on weekends because by the time I've got past Mandy I'm so incensed that it's all I can do to keep my ire to myself. If I let out that they are being badly short-changed on a weekend, how's that going to help? I can't change things, can I?

As it turns out, fate intervenes and means that we have an 'opportunity' to do something as a group. On a weekend. And I don't care how hard it's going to be to organise. We're going to do it. We're going to have a weekend break. No Labels. Together.

Here's how it happens. If you were paying attention on Monday you'll remember that someone once called Mandy a vegetable. And it was pointed out that indeed Mandy had 'been' a vegetable in a play. Well, it wasn't really a play at that point, more of a sort of, well, something between an improvisation and a project I suppose. But here's the thing. We had spent a lot of time (and some funded money) working on healthy eating. And someone had heard of it, and us (Barry has his ways of spreading the word) and I got this letter and this is what it said and what I read out to the group:

*Dear No Labels, (the joy of a group identity)*

*We run a training hotel for adults with learning difficulties and we have heard that you do plays. We would like to offer you the chance to come to visit and stay with us for the weekend in exchange for you putting on a performance of a play. We have heard that you do things about healthy eating and we think that would be a great idea. We can put the play on in the ballroom. There's no money involved but you can stay in the hotel on Saturday night for free. Please get in touch and let us know of a suitable weekend.*

*Yours sincerely,*

*Marge and Kim*

*Proprietors Otterbank Hotel.*

What do you think? I ask the group. Bilbo whistles and Annie whoops.

'Wowee,' Bilbo says, 'A holiday.'

'Do we have to pay?' Annie asks.

'No Annie, it's all free,' I say.

'A free holiday,' Bilbo is up and dancing.

'When did you last have a holiday?' I ask him.

He thinks. Long and hard.

'Never.' He says. 'Not since I was a wee boy.'

'We went to Englandshire on the bus once,' Kelly reminds him. 'With the school. Remember?'

She is about to go off into what everyone was wearing that day and where she sat on the bus, engrained as it is in her memory even forty odd years on, but Bilbo stops her.

'Adrian's Wall,' he says. 'That was it. Adrian's Wall.'

'Not really a holiday though,' I say. 'A school trip.'

'It felt like a holiday,' Bilbo says.

'Duncan was sick on the bus,' Kelly adds.

'Not much of a holiday for you then Duncan?' I say, eager to draw him into the conversation.

'Otterbank,' he says. He *was* paying attention.

'Yes, Otterbank,' I say, 'do you know it?'

Stevie is running round shouting 'o..er..annkkk,' which doesn't mean that he knows the place of course, just that he likes the word. Or maybe he knows that Otters are generally brown.

'Yuss,' Duncan says, and smiles. An enigmatic smile.

'Have you been there before?' I ask, ignoring the fact that I know Duncan doesn't like being asked questions.

'Yuss,' he replies.

'He went there for his fortieth birthday if you don't mind my saying,' Deirdre announces and no, for once, I don't mind her saying so!

'So,' I say, winding up for the big finale. 'What do we think? Do we want to go to Otterbank for the weekend?'

'Can't go,' Mandy says, 'Dad's coming circus.'

'No, not this weekend,' I hastily add, 'We'll have to arrange a weekend, that suits us all (my heart sinks thinking of the organisation, then boosts again as I remember my mental promise to make the weekend something to remember) and we'll have to get a play prepared. It'll mean a lot of rehearing.'

'Commitment,' Barry says. 'It will mean commitment.'

'Yes Barry,' they chorus. 'Commitment.'

'So,' I say, remaining democratically hopeful. 'Hands up if you want to go to Otterbank for a weekend some time and put on a play about healthy eating.'

Hands go up. It's a stupid way of coming to a decision though. There are no shortcuts. Some people aren't necessarily listening. Some people put their hands up not to be left out and some people (Lauren) put both hands up and start wiggling around as if they are on a gameshow. And Duncan doesn't put any hands up at all. Which might mean he's not listening or that he doesn't really want to go back there again, or... well, you get my drift. We need to find a better way of getting assent. I've got broad agreement, now I need to deal with each person as an individual. Hmm... maybe that's not such a bad thing anyway?

'Annie,' I say. 'Do you want to come to Otterbank?' Before I give her a chance to respond I can't help but add, 'because if we agree to go, we'll have to stick to the agreement and we'll have to rehearse...' I peter out because I see her sitting there, not altogether patiently, waiting to reply. 'Sorry,' I say.

'I was waiting,' she says pointedly, 'for you to finish talking. So I didn't butt in. It's rude.'

'I'm sorry,' I repeat.

She's happy with that. Me put in my place at last.

'So, do you want to go to Otterbank one weekend and do a play?'

'Yes,' she replies. 'As long as my mum says it's okay.'

What happened to 'I'm a forty six year old woman?' I wonder and then feel mean. Annie has a housebound mother, she 'looks' after her at the weekend. She becomes a carer, fulfils (not only in her mind) a valuable service. Who am I to denigrate that role?

'I'm sure we can organise for someone else to look after her. Do the shopping. One of your sisters maybe?' I suggest.

Annie snorts. 'Them,' she says. 'They don't know what to buy.'

'Well,' I say, feeling my excitement dissipating big time, 'in principle, are you happy?'

'Yes,' she says.

I move on.

'Bilbo, what about you?' I ask. He looks at me a bit blankly. I need to repeat the offer. Clearly.

'Do you want to go to Otterbank Hotel one weekend with No Labels and put on a play?' I ask.

For just a moment he looks at me as if I must be completely barking, and I can't work out what he's thinking. Then he breaks into the biggest smile, gets up and starts to boogie and says

'Oh, yes, oh yes, oh yes,' doing that odd sort of windmill hand movements that people do when they do this chant.

'Even if it's during the football season?' Barry asks. I could slap him. Why make problems, I think, then realise that actually, he's right. We can't do this under false pretences. It has to be an informed choice and Bilbo, if we're to be sure of getting him to come, needs to know that he may have to miss the odd football match.

'Football's for girls,' Bilbo says, somewhat inaccurately, but rather carried away with the excitement of a prospect of a holiday. 'I want a holiday.' He goes into a version of Madonna's old party classic 'Holiday' and everyone laughs fit to bust.

'You're a tonic,' Annie says to Bilbo. 'A tonic.'

Deirdre is a bit more non-committal about the whole holiday thing. At times she can be a bit of a spoil sport. But maybe that's me being unkind. Because even though she says something I don't want to hear, she makes a good, realistic point.

'Will there be carers?' she asks. 'Not for me of course,' she points out, 'but for, you know, Mandy and Stevie?'

She fixes me with a steely stare that tells me she knows I've never even thought of this. I've got no more sense of reality about it all than Bilbo. I'm just excited by 'the plan.'

'Uh, I don't know,' I say. 'We'll have to work it out.'

'Because I don't want to go if there's carers,' Deirdre says. End of.

Oh. Okay. That's a new one. Now I have to stop and ask the group what they feel about carers coming. It's pretty much a resounding no. Which may, or may not present a problem. There are members of the group, Mandy and Stevie as Deirdre points out, who are generally accompanied by 'carers' if we leave the base. Neither of them seem bothered. Neither of them has ever seemed to 'need' a carer's intervention.

'It's the weekend,' points out Pauline, 'you'll never get a carer to come along. No one will pay the extra.'

Thanks Pauline. Cold water poured firmly on, I think, and then realise that no, this problem could in fact contain the seeds of its own resolution. Barry is there one step ahead of me,

'There are no problems, only solutions,' he states.

'No carers available then we 'care' for ourselves. And anyway, it's a hotel with staff on site. Carers for the trainees. Trained people. So...'

It just might work.

'Brilliant, Barry,' I say. And feel rescued.

As I work my way through the rest of the group we are now all aware that it's a weekend away, without carers, but with the responsibility of putting on a play about healthy eating. And Duncan, Lauren, Kelly, Mandy and Stevie all seem reasonably keen on this idea. Enough for me Pauline and Barry to start the wheels in motion.

I check with Otterbank (which Barry has laughingly christened 'cockroaches' Hotel, a joke which may yet come back to haunt us as Stevie and Bilbo have both picked up on this and think it a massive joke) that they do indeed have 'trained staff' on site at all times and so can confirm to our group's 'care providers' that each member will be 'safe' at all times.

In fact it turns out not to be nearly as much of a hassle as getting folk 'sprung' during the week and nothing like as difficult as trying to organise an evening activity. As I pointed out before, the rules all change at the weekend, and when push comes to shove it seems that the combined and general attitude is that if I'm foolhardy enough to want to spend my weekend with these people then as long as they are all back in their places by Sunday night, checked in, ready to be 'cared' for again Monday to Friday, I'm at liberty to do more or less what I will. It's all too frighteningly easy. All too like that opera where the toys go on the rampage. Or is that a cartoon? Whatever. It's not a nice image.

And Annie's mum, and Lauren's parents are more than happy for them to go away for a weekend. Like 'normal' people do. And Mandy's care home are ecstatic. I sense that 'cuddling toys' is not all Mandy does on a weekend and that whatever else she does might be described by her care staff as 'challenging' behaviour. But then I'm not surprised. I mean, what alternatives are available? Wall to wall TV? Stuck in your bedroom with your soft toys. If you can't read and write and you don't have access to money then what the hell are you going to do with your time? It's a long forty eight hours. Mandy's weekend sounds a lot more like prison than anything else, to me.

Of course in the three months it takes for us to organise and rehearse for this weekend, Mandy's staff are driven up the wall by her constantly asking or telling them that 'I'm going to a hotel', 'Is it this weekend?' and the like. I am therefore mentally prepared for the minibus drive to Otterbank, fully expecting Mandy to start with 'are we there yet?' five minutes after we leave base.

We are working through detail. I'm trying to get us rehearsed on the funny, interactive play that will become 'Meat Your Greens' and others have other concerns. Which must be addressed.

'Will there be otters?' Kelly asks.

I'm not sure where this might lead, and indeed not at all sure of the answer, or what the consequences of any answer I might give might be, so I just tell the truth,

'I don't know,' I say. 'Is it important?'

'Otters are brown,' she says. 'Stevie likes brown.'

I'm not sure if this is just a statement of fact, or an example of empathy, or a veiled suggestion that if there are otters gambolling in the water by the hotel we'd better watch out and at the very least take enough spare clothes for Stevie.

'Can you swim Stevie?' I ask.

He nods and does the doggy paddle.

'I don't like swimming,' Mandy says.

'No, don't worry, there isn't swimming,' I say. 'I just wondered.'

Kelly smiles at me. She's made her point. There's a lot more about this trip that I need to know and work out before we go. A lot more than simply getting the play right.

But the play is the thing as we all know, so we do need to 'get it right.' And here's what we end up agreeing on. We're going to do a sort of play come workshop which will be both funny and educational. And like a cabaret, with magic (Barry is very keen to show off his magic skills.) Sounds incredible, doesn't it. Believe me. It will be.

If we pull this off we'll have more than paid for a weekend break. We set to rehearsing with a vengeance. But because the performance isn't till Sunday afternoon, we'll keep the details, like the rabbit, under our hats for now, if you don't mind.

Saturday morning finally dawns. It's sunny. Which is nice. Everyone is there on time. Which is remarkable. And Eddie the driver is there with his mini bus and his open, stout heart. The trip is a good hour and a half, and fortunately Eddie is used to travelling with No Labels. It is an acquired taste you might say. But Eddie is always 'up for it.' And often joins in on things when we get there. He doesn't just lurk in the bus waiting for us to come home, no, he joins in. He becomes a 'No Labels' member for the duration of the trip. Not this time though. This time he'll drop us off at Otterbank in time for lunch on Saturday and pick us up after tea on Sunday.

'Not coming with us?' Mandy asks him. Mandy loves Eddie. I'm sure it's reciprocated but Eddie doesn't love any of us enough to want to spend the weekend with us. Even when Mandy tempts him with the offer,

'You could share with Barry.'

Barry laughs. Eddie laughs. Mandy laughs, though it's clear she doesn't know what she's said that's funny.

'No can do, love,' Eddie says. 'The wife would miss me. And I've got a wedding to get back for this afternoon.'

'Getting married, darling?' Lauren asks. Eddie brings out the best in many of the group and they seem to both listen and chat to him in a way they don't with most other people. Maybe it's because Eddie is literally their bus pass to freedom. When they get on Eddie's minibus they are No Labels. The labels drop off and they are free. So we all love Eddie.

'No, love,' he says cheerily, 'I've been married for near fifty years. It's a customer.'

Hard to compute. Some of the group have never considered that Eddie's minibus is his 'job' or that they may be hiring his services. He's just Eddie. Our pal Eddie. Always there to take us where we want to go.

'You're abandoning us,' Kelly says. Her delivery is so dead pan, I'm expecting trouble.

'You're abandoning me,' he says. 'You're the ones going on your holidays. Now, where's your bag?'

Crisis averted. Everyone gets their bags onto the minibus and they follow. We do a quick headcount, though really, you'd notice if any one member of the group wasn't there. We are packed in like sardines, buckled up for safety and it's all systems go.

'Are we there yet,' Bilbo shouts as the bus pulls away.

'Very funny,' Barry replies.

I just hope that's not going to set Mandy off, but as it turns out there are other distractions. First we have the town to negotiate. Now, some members of the group have unhappy associations with buses. The BLUE BUS is a hated thing. It's the bus that the council provides for adults (and children) labelled with a learning disability to get to and from their 'activities' and most if not all of the group will do anything to avoid travelling on it. But many of the group are not 'risk assessed' to travel on service buses. So a taxi is a status symbol and a bus is a mark of shame. Not Eddie's bus though. Eddie's bus is No Labels on wheels and we travel the mile or so through town with much regal waving and pointing at people out on the street. You'd think we've won the world cup from the behaviour! On the BLUE BUS people hide in their seats because it's the folk on the street who point and shout things. On Eddie's bus, it's the other way round. We are royalty. We are King of the road. As Bilbo reminds us by singing it at the top of his voice for a good ten minutes.

Soon enough though, we're on the open road and there are other things to see. We have a cow counting competition. It doesn't go very well. They move. We aren't that interested in numbers. Pauline attempts I spy with a couple of the group but it turns completely anarchic very quickly due to 'something beginning with a letter' being a bit difficult for some to deal with. The highlight is when it's Mandy's turn and she shouts out,

'Eye pie tiddly eye, something beginning with SHEEP.'

Hmm, would that be a sheep then Mandy?

'No,' she says.

'What then?' I ask, confused.

'A COW,' she says. Without a hint of humour.

You wouldn't play charades with Mandy, that's all I'll say.

But it raises a laugh. Again, Mandy isn't sure why people are laughing and so the moment happens, barely twenty minutes into our journey when she says the immortal words,

'Are we there yet?'

'Time for a communal singsong,' Eddie says, and I remember why it is that everyone loves Eddie. Because Eddie will let them SING on the bus. To their hearts content. Despite the fact that with the singing tends to come rocking and it becomes more like a journey on a rollercoaster than a bus. How Eddie keeps it on the road I don't know. How he manages to concentrate on the road I don't know. Eddie. You're one in a million. We love you. And you deserve a week away all expenses paid after this journey!

Eddie and Bilbo lead us on a medley of the finest songs of the fifties and sixties. Duncan knows all the words. The girls are more keen on more current pop music with Boyzone and Daniel O'Donnell being a particular favourite. But it's the boys who are leading the singing on this trip.

Fortunately, despite all the excitement, no one is sick and we only have to stop once for the toilet and, despite

Barry being quite keen for us to break the journey with a cup of tea at a nice little roadside café, I point out that a) Eddie's on a time frame and b) breaking for tea will mean another 'wee' break and we'll never get to Otterbank before lunchtime. Reason prevails.

At precisely eleven fifty five we pull up on the gravel outside the imposing Victorian building, set in beautiful grounds, that is Otterbank Hotel, and, wired to the moon we unbuckle and pour out. We're on holiday. The only thing missing is buckets and spades. Cliff and the boys never had it so good.

Right enough, Mandy's not quite sure that she wants to get off the bus and thinks maybe she'll just go home with Eddie, but we manage to persuade her that she wants to join in with everyone else, and what fun it's going to be for her to share a room with Deirdre (this is quite a job in and of itself) and mostly that LUNCH will be served very soon.

'And you might see an otter,' is Bilbo's best shot. 'Otters are fluffy.'

That seals it. Mandy has brought a couple of soft toys with her (in her bag) and the thought of them and a real live fluffy otter means that we coax her out of the bus. But possibly condemn ourselves to a weekend of 'when can I see the otter?' which will become fairly tedious fairly soon I'm guessing!

We are met at the door by a smiling Marge and Kim. Marge and Kim are legends. They are like Pauline with infinite energy. They are like everyones favourite grannies. With just a wee touch of the headmistress thrown in for when things threaten to get out of control. Otterbank is their dream. Their own personal way to 'give something back' and to redress the balance against the labelling system. On sight I like them immensely. They have a no nonsense attitude like I've never met before and it's clear we're going to have a ball. We will be welcomed with open arms and treated with respect like paying customers.

They usher us into reception where we all sit in plush chairs as they 'register' us in and explain the 'philosophy' of Otterbank, which culminates with Marge stating,

'There are no labels at Otterbank.'

'Yes there are,' Bilbo shouts out, pointing to us. 'We're here.'

Marge laughs. 'Yes, you're right,' she says. 'This weekend we have No Labels as our honoured guests.'

'Who're you gonna call,' Bilbo sings and everyone joins in 'No Labels.'

It's going to be a blast. Marge and Kim are well up for it.

It turns out that we are the only guests for the weekend, the season not having taken off really yet as Kim explains. But our performance tomorrow has been advertised far and wide and it will be an 'event' in their calendar which they expect a lot of people to attend. The trainees will have to 'cater' the event and they've been practising this nearly as long as we've been rehearsing.

'And of course our trainees will serve you lunch at twelve thirty,' Marge says. 'We hope you'll enjoy the service.'

I should try to explain the Otterbank set up I suppose. The hotel has fourteen double bedrooms so its occupancy is just short of thirty I suppose. Marge and Kim head a staff of eight with a further twelve trainees, who live in another building in the grounds, a sort of bunkhouse really, for the duration of their training which can be anything from six months to three years. They are accredited to turn out qualified hospitality industry people. In you go as a young adult labelled with a learning disability and you can come out with an NVQ or an HNC if you apply yourself. They can't possibly make any money.

'It's not a sausage factory,' Marky tells us. He's our assigned waiter at lunch. We don't fill the dining room by any means, we take up three tables in total, two of four and one of three. And Marky is waiting on our table. He's a star. A younger version of Bilbo is how I see him and feel a pang of sorrow that Bilbo never got the opportunities Marky is having now.

'This is a place you learn something. A lot of something's,' he tells us as he waits for us to pick from the menu. Confusingly for Mandy, who is on my table along with Lauren and Bilbo, there are no sausages on the menu. There is fish and chips or macaroni cheese or cottage pie. With apple pie and ice cream or sponge pudding and custard for afters.

'Cooked in the kitchen,' Marky tells us proudly. 'By my girlfriend.'

We make suitable noises in response.

'She's very clean,' he says.

'Cleanliness is next to godliness,' says Bilbo, happy to engage Marky in conversation. He's on holiday after all, It's only polite.

'Wash hands,' I hear Lauren squeak and she makes hand washing gestures as she wriggles in a seat which is just a little bit too high for her.

'Always washing her hands,' Marky says. He sighs. 'Part of the job.'

'Do you like washing your hands?' Bilbo asks him.

Marky sighs. 'Not really,' he replies.

'Me either,' Bilbo says. 'Life's too short.'

And I sense a friendship is forming.

Marge and Kim are really great at giving the staff their head, but making sure they are kept on task when necessary and Paul, the waiter trainer (a man without a label) gently suggests to Marky that he actually take our order so that Clare (his girlfriend) can get on with her cooking job, and we order as follows: Bilbo has fish and chips. Mandy has fish and chips. Lauren has cottage pie, once we've established it's not made from cottages, and I have fish and chips.

Marky shows us (he tells us from behind his hand he shouldn't really show us this but since we're friends) how he notes the order down. He's using a sort of hieroglyphic rather than words. Three little fish and three pictures of what could be sticks but are obviously chips, and a little house (fortunately he doesn't show this to Lauren who might change her mind thinking she *is* about to be forced to eat a building.

'Good, innit,' he says. 'I don't write so good,' he points out, 'but Marge showed me how I can take the orders this way.'

'Excellent,' I say. We order three ice cream and apple pie – depicted by three ice cream cones – and one sponge pudding and custard. I actually only want the custard but I'm not sure Marky will be able to work that into his 'system' and I'm sure Bilbo will eat both apple pie and sponge pudding if I offer him mine!

Which indeed he does and forty minutes later, when we're all ready to move on, I think it's possible Bilbo may indeed physically explode and provide us with our first casualty of the holiday. But he looks supremely happy.

I suggest that he might like a nap when he goes up to his room to unpack.

'A nap?' he says. 'I'm on holiday. I want FUN.'

Of course. Fun. That's what we'll be having. Wall to wall, side splitting fun. And why not?

'Don't forget commitment,' Barry points out.

There is a communal sigh.

'We have to rehearse,' Barry says. 'In the *space*,' he adds grandly. He wants everyone to remember we are here as actors. To work.

He starts on in, 'Marky and Clare and all the others, they are here working, but we are working too.' I sense he's almost about to say that it's not a holiday and then realises the riot that might ensue. But he's saved because out of nowhere Stevie shouts out, 'Pigs in space' (or iii---ggs in--- aaaa---ccceee) but Bilbo swiftly translates and joins in 'Pigs in Space...' and Duncan and Lauren also join in. We all like *Pigs in Space* it seems!

'Okay,' I say, keen to keep the peace without breaking the soundbarrier and outstaying our welcome before tea time. Which will be at four pm sharp.

'Let's get into our rooms and get our stuff sorted out. Then we'll meet down in the ballroom at two o'clock for a rehearsal. Okay?'

Everyone agrees and heads off to their rooms Their bags have been lugged up there before them by some hapless trainee and, unlike many a fine establishment, all the luggage ends up in the right room first time. And no one is hanging around for a tip.

The arrangements are as follows: Annie is sharing with Kelly, Mandy is sharing with Deirdre, and Pauline is sharing with Lauren. Bilbo is sharing with Duncan and Barry is sharing with Stevie which leaves me in a room on my own. I feel a bit guilty about this, but it seems I am a focus of sympathy as more than one person asks me if I'll be 'lonely' on my own. Part of the fun of a holiday it seems *is* sharing a room. I guess that while we all value privacy, you can have too much of it and Annie in particular suggests that while it's nice to have a room to go into when you want to 'sulk' or 'cry', the rest of the time she's lonely in her own little isolated accommodation. And she would be most happy to share with me 'to stop me being lonely.'

'But what about Kelly?' I ask.

And Annie agrees it would be mean to leave Kelly on her own. Kelly is, after all, at this moment in time Annie's *best* friend. So I get a room to myself and am happy that Annie and Kelly are going to have a great time sharing a room. Best of friends. Unless someone else takes Annie's eye.

I'm not sure how Barry will cope with Stevie, but he's a man with a strong and very very kind heart and he's determined for the weekend to be 'a success' for all of us. We just need to make sure that we give Stevie his medication at the right time or we've been warned 'there'll be trouble.'

At two o'clock, on the button, much to my amazement (because remember most of the group not only can't tell the time but have little concept of time) everyone is there in the ballroom, ready to rehearse. I think Barry's lunchtime speech may have had something to do with it.

'We are not sheep,' he says. 'We don't have a sheepdog. We don't need rounding up. Everyone has to be responsible to turn up on time. And to help each other.'

It's clear. Those who can deal with time, Kelly, Bilbo and Deirdre will help those for whom it's a more nebulous concept. We keep each other right. We are 'professional'. Even on holiday.

The next couple of hours are spent in rehearsals – but that's still under wraps remember, we don't want to spoil it for you – and then we are ready for tea. Which is served in the 'garden room.' This is a huge conservatory looking out on the grounds. We like it. We like tea. It's sandwiches and cakes (including fairy cakes) and every plate that is brought by Marky and several other waiters and waitresses we have still to get to know, is polished off quickly and efficiently by the No Labels locusts.

We now have 'free time,' until dinner which will be served at six thirty. In the dining room. I can't imagine being able to eat again at all today, never mind in little over two hours, but I suspect most of my companions will not have that problem. So maybe it's important for us all that we get some physical exercise.

'Anyone want to come and explore the grounds?' I ask.

My suggestion meets with rapturous applause.

'Exactly what I want to do,' says Deirdre.

'Me too,' says Mandy.

'An otter hunt,' Bilbo says with a wicked glint in his eye. 'Let's go down to the river. You can swim can't you Stevie?' he asks.

'There's no swimming,' I say, turning for a moment into something between a mum and a carer. It doesn't go unnoticed.

'Party pooper,' laughs Bilbo.

He's got a point. But I feel a sense of 'responsibility.' I share my fear with Barry and Pauline. They both suggest, in their own ways, that I lighten up and realise that everyone here is an adult and can take a certain amount of responsibility for themselves. After all, we're on holiday.

'Stop thinking about what can go wrong, start enjoying life,' Barry says.

And he should know. He's been on a week long holiday with Bilbo before. And Annie.

I know that Bilbo's just taking the rise of me. I think I know that even Stevie is not going to rush headlong into the water in pursuit of an otter just because it's brown. And Mandy doesn't like water so she's not going in just to stroke one.

As we walk towards the river which runs through the grounds of Otterbank, I reflect that the person who's most likely to end up in the water is me, pushed in by Bilbo if I don't stop being such a killjoy. And I'll deserve it! So I resolve to enjoy myself.

'You're on holiday too,' Annie points out to me as I'm fussing (again) over whether Duncan is keeping up and whether Stevie will ever stop hugging that tree.

And I realise that I should give them that respect. Of letting go a bit. Of letting people just *be* on holiday.

Barry puts his arm on my shoulder, 'Take the weekend off,' he says.

So I take his advice. And things start being much more fun and much less worrying.

As it turns out, we all have a really nice little tour of the gardens. The pace of No Labels is never fast. Only Duncan and Stevie really have it in them to move fast and both of them seem to be pretty weighed down either by the food or the freedom. We all stick together as a straggly, but identifiable group. And there are benches by the water's edge which everyone is more than ready for. The grass is short and the distance can't be more than about a quarter of a mile, but we haven't gone in the straightest of lines, more a meander, and we are all happy to sit down side by side and reflect on 'our holiday' and what fun it is.

When Pauline announces to everyone, in response to a request from Annie about what is happening that evening, that we are going to have a disco after dinner, the benches erupt. Now that's something everyone wants to be a part of. As one who has to be more than a little drunk to contemplate dancing in public, I am not in tune with the rest of the group, but then I've never really 'partied' with No Labels. A major omission I realise, but one that is going to be remedied this very evening, whether I'm ready for it (which I'm not sure I am) or not.

Annie and Kelly start debating what they will wear. Lauren keeps saying 'party, party, party,' excitedly and even Deirdre looks like she'll find it easier to let her hair down than I will. That'll be the 'learning disability' then eh? *They are so much more uninhibited, aren't they* I remember someone saying to me after one of our performances. I found it patronising then and I stop and realise that maybe in one sense (a good sense) it's true. There is no artifice with any of my No Labels friends. They may see life in a unique and sometimes a seemingly

204

off balance way, but they meet it on its own terms. They don't let themselves get weighed down by the trivia of trying to 'be' something. They just 'are.' If that's uninhibited, you know, I think it's probably a lesson they are teaching me and one I'm long overdue in the learning. So then and there I resolve that I'm going to 'join the party' in the fullest sense of the word. Little do I know what I'm letting myself in for.

The excitement of the disco sends us back to the hotel, all talk of what to wear, who will be there (Bilbo and Annie both have an interest in Marky as a new friend... for Annie maybe a new *best* friend) and Kelly is always up for meeting new people. And the trainees (relieved from their work burden after dinner service) and the permanent staff will all be there. It's going to be a great party, for people without labels.

Annie, Lauren and Mandy all turn up for dinner at six thirty dressed to the nines. However much I suggest that maybe they don't need to be quite this glam till after we've eaten, imagining the debris that will coat their clothes after the meal, they refuse to go and change. They agree to use the wonderful cloth napkins provided though.

I'm on a table for dinner with Annie and Lauren and Mandy – all girls together. Pauline is with Kelly and Deirdre and Barry is sharing with Duncan, Bilbo and Stevie. It's a boy/girl split. In anticipation of all good dances the sexes are parted? And when I turn round to see 'the boys' they are all dressed up in ties. Duncan and Bilbo have suit jackets on. Barry has a cardigan and even Stevie, who I've never seen in anything other than jeans (blue) and a t shirt (of varying colours) is wearing a tie. And guess what. It's brown! So it gets more attention than a tie strictly should do. He's got a brown tie and a sort of blue check gingham short sleeved shirt on. Barry bought him the tie specially. It's a clip on one. This level of detail may be important later on, so keep paying attention.

I realise that everyone has made considerably more of an effort than I have. Mandy is even wearing a skirt. Deirdre and Kelly have dresses on for goodness sake. I think to myself it's maybe something of an overkill situation but then pull myself up again and realise that while to me this is just a weekend, to them this is a 'holiday.' And an 'event' in their lives the likes of which they don't often have and may indeed never have had before or again. The enormity of what we've achieved here hits me. And I wonder whether we'd have nearly such a good time if we were at a 'posh' hotel which didn't cater for 'labels'. And I am grateful and thankful and somewhat in awe of the vision and generosity of Marge and Kim.

I go upstairs to change after dinner. I don't have a skirt or dress but I make sure I'm dressed as smartly as I can achieve out of the clothing I've brought with me. I understand the importance of 'making the effort' finally. Once again, No Labels have jointly and individually taught me something very important about how one relates to other people with respect.

When I come down, the party is already underway. It's barely eight o'clock but everyone is up and dancing. And what dancing. Bilbo and Stevie I expect to be up there strutting their stuff. But Duncan is an absolute revelation. As is Lauren. And Barry and Deirdre are cutting quite a dash dancing something resembling a waltz even though I'm sure the tune is *'hippy hippy shake.'* Pauline is the only one still sitting, and that's only because her legs are not as well functioning as she'd like and she *has* to sit down. I sidle along to sit beside her.

'They look to be having great fun,' I say, hoping to hide my nervousness. *They.* I shouldn't have said that should I? It's *we* isn't it? It's about to be.

Duncan and Bilbo come over and drag me onto the floor to dance. This is what I would consider my room 101 moment, I think. Until it happens. Then, something really strange occurs. I let go. I abandon myself to the experience. For possibly the first time in my life I don't consider 'what people think' about my movements and I just dance. And you know what, it's great. I'm here, with my friends, doing some crazy kind of twist routine with Duncan to the Dire Straits classic 'Twisting by the pool' and I'm having a ball. I feel free. I feel part of the group. I have finally shaken off my own label.

The next few hours just fly by. We have so much fun I can't even begin to describe it. We own the dance floor. Barry gets us up doing a conga at one point for goodness sakes and normally I would DIE rather than do one. It's the only thing worse than 'you put one hand in, one hand out' that I can imagine. But you know what, here, with the combined forces of No Labels, the trainees and the staff, it's just the best fun you can have without alcohol. Suddenly I realise that Agadoo and its like have some purpose. Everyone here loves Agadoo!

Okay I'm not strictly speaking the truth about the booze, because there is a bit of alcohol on the go. Not enough to get anyone drunk though. There's a free drink for everyone but after that you have to pay at the bar and most people haven't brought a lot of money with them. For obvious reasons. They don't handle money without carers around. Annie is piling her way into the rum and cokes, but everyone else has a couple of alcoholic drinks and then resorts to soft fizzy stuff. Duncan drinks orange juice all night. Stevie drinks coke. But it's brown so it lingers in the glass a long time. At one point I swear I see him having some kind of discussion with himself around the notion that he's got brown in his hands in the glass and then he'll have brown INSIDE himself as well. And I smile. It's great to see him so happy.

And then, while I'm watching him, the funniest thing in the world happens. Now you might just find this slightly (or even grossly) disgusting, and I am prepared to accept that you probably had to be there, but seriously, just believe me, I was there and it WAS funny. Really funny.

Stevie has swallowed his coke (fortunately) and finished his private debate over how he was now part of the brown, and he sneezed. Not a little sneeze. A full blown snot all over his face sneeze. Snot dribbling down his face sneeze. Should this have been my call to go and wipe it off for him? Come on now, he's a man in his twenties. On his holidays. How insulting would it be for him to have me wiping his snot? If you are thinking – less embarrassing than letting him sit there with snot all over his face – I can only tell you that you still have a few levels of enlightenment to go. Stevie works out his own solution. He doesn't have a hanky. Why would he? Normally his care staff would wipe up his snot. He looks at his sleeves. I can see the thought process as if it is a slow motion car crash scenario. He has short sleeves on remember. And even Stevie's not going to wipe his snot on his arm now is he? He's not an idiot. He's a resourceful chap. He comes up with a solution. By some dexterity I never imagined he had (and if you try this yourself you'll see how impossibly hard it is) he manages to raise his leg and wipe his nose on his jeans.

Okay, I know it's gross. But believe me, I hadn't had more than one drink and at that point in time it was just impossibly funny. It's still the funniest thing I think I can remember ever seeing.

And then he just carries on. Problem solved Stevie style. And no one says a word. Okay, I do snort some of my Irn Bru (I don't drink Coke on principle) down my nose (a motion perhaps more disgusting and certainly

208

less funny than Stevie's) but that is it. No one else bats an eyelid. The dancing continues.

By ten o'clock people are beginning to tire. Lauren has made new friends with Robbie who turns out to be Marky's brother. Marky might have a 'label' in the 'outside' world but Robbie is just your average, everyday kind of guy in his early twenties. Stop. No. Not true. Because Robbie, perhaps because he'd grown up with with Marky, is an absolute gem of a guy. No Labels with Robbie. No ugly siblings here. He's quite good looking actually and from the way he and Lauren are dancing I can see that while it's not a romance in the conventional sense, they are both really into each other and enjoying each other's company in a way that I've never seen from Lauren and never seen from any 'normal' person in interaction with a 'labelled' person. Otterbank Hotel is a place of surprises and hope and I am so glad we were invited to go there. Not so much a holiday, more a life changing experience. For all of us.

Annie is dancing with Marky and Bilbo is dancing with a somewhat more reluctant Clare – maybe she's worried that she should be washing her hands, or maybe she's a bit bothered by Annie potentially 'making a move' on her boyfriend, but it's all fairly well intentioned as far as I can see. It's so nice to see my No Labels pals making new friends, and everyone feeling comfortable and having a good time.

And then it's karaoke. Well, the dancing has to stop sometime, right. Everyone is exhausted, even the fittest. I don't think even the Japanese love karaoke as much as Barry does. He's died and gone to heaven. And everyone has a turn. More than one turn. Many turns. More and more and more until we are hoarse and it's turned midnight and Marge and Kim suggest (politely) that breakfast is usually between eight and nine but since we are the only guests and the staff are having a ball along with us, perhaps we could put it back to between nine and ten, but either way, it might be a good idea to call it a day.

And we have one last song before we go to bed. It's a duet delivered by Barry and Pauline and it would break your heart. What it lacks in tunefulness it more than makes up for in feeling. It's a version of the James Taylor classic 'You've got a friend,' and as I slow dance with Duncan amidst the couples on the floor, I realise that yes, for the first time in my life I can confidently feel that I do have a friend, many friends. That I am among friends. And there's even this tiny part of me that wonders if I should take Annie up on her offer to 'share' a room with me in case I'm lonely. For the first time I'm not sure I will enjoy being alone as much as being with someone else.

We all manage to wend our way to bed, tired but happy in the extreme. This has truly been 'a perfect day' in my books. And I only hope that everyone else is feeling half as happy as I am as I go to sleep. I no longer feel I have to 'care for' or take 'responsibility' for this group of people. I realise that I just care for them. As friends. And that's the way it should be.

# SUNDAY

*The final curtain.*

I wake up on Sunday morning, having slept really well, wondering exactly what happened last night. And looking forward to the day ahead. I'm an early riser even when it's been a late night and I'm out for a walk well before the 9am breakfast time. I meet Barry and Stevie going for a walk.

'Great night,' Barry opines.

'Yes, wasn't it,' I reply.

Stevie smiles. He's got a brown jumper on. He's happy.

'This is an amazing place, isn't it?' I say, wondering what Barry's opinion of Marge and Kim is. They are so like him in many ways. Except that they have business brains where he is, by his own admission, more of an 'ideas man.' And most of Barry's ideas are great, but they need someone with a business brain holding his hand.

'Yes,' he says. 'We could do great things together,' and he's not going to be drawn further than that, but I can see the wheels in motion in his mind and I'm sure that one day soon I'm going to discover Barry's latest scheme to remove labels from the world.

'Stevie and me were going through some magic tricks, weren't we Stevie,' Barry says, steering Stevie away from a tree.

Stevie smiles. He's going to make a unique magician's assistant, that's for sure.

We go back inside for breakfast. Everyone is there, spread out across the three tables laid out for us. Mandy and Annie are on one table, Deirdre, Duncan and Bilbo at another and Lauren, Kelly and Pauline at the third. Barry and Stevie go to join Mandy and Annie and for the first time I don't think, I should sit with Deirdre's table because then we've got an 'appropriate adult' at each table to 'help', I just sit there because they are my friends and Bilbo is jumping around saying 'I'll get your chair madam,' so it would be rude to ignore him.

'Fancy a new career in the hospitality business Bilbo?' I ask him.

He shakes his head.

'No money in it,' he says. As if he's seriously considered it. 'And my job's with No Labels anyway, isn't it. Couldn't abandon you.'

'That's very kind of you Bilbo,' I say.

'Wash hands,' Duncan says and I think for a moment he's suggesting I should do this. Before I have the chance to embarrass myself, Bilbo interprets.

'Yes, Duncan, you're right, there's too much hand washing as well,' he laughs.

'We were talking about it this morning,' he says.

I love the casual way he says 'we were talking about it,' as if Duncan conversed in the standard way, freely. And then I realise, that at these tables, in this context, there *is* much more of what to the outside observer would be described as 'normal' conversation. I realise that if I was recording this for my module on conversational analysis (I never dreamed of doing such at thing, but perhaps I should have done) and you read back the transcribed tape, you'd be hard pressed to realise that this was a group of adults labelled with learning disabilities. They can talk perfectly well about things that interest them, when not being pressed by the likes of me into the question answer games that they find annoying and perhaps intrusive. Here, on holiday, Duncan and Bilbo are getting on like a house on fire, forging a friendship that sharing a twin room without 'intervention' has allowed to blossom. This truly is an amazing place. These truly are amazing people.

'I want to come here again,' Duncan says. This is the kind of full sentence you get once in a blue moon from Duncan. The kind of sentence some people who have done assessments suggest he's incapable of making. I realise that when it's important enough, Duncan can talk. It's all a matter of choice. His choice. I must try not to blow it by asking him questions.

'It would be great, wouldn't it?' I say (rhetorical question, hopefully okay but I need something more) I want to say *are you enjoying it?* or *what's the best thing about it?* but I'm saved by Bilbo who is much more adept at 'real' conversation with Duncan.

'We'll come together,' he says. 'In the summer. We can save our money and tell them we're just damned well coming when they say we can't. Just you and me. Mates.'

I have no idea if this would be possible but Duncan likes the idea.

'Yuss,' he says, 'You and me Bilbo. On holiday.'

And at that moment something tells me I will do anything to make sure this pair get their wish. It's such a small thing isn't it? A couple of days away with a mate at a hotel less than two hours drive away from home. Without supervision. Is this too much to achieve for a couple of men one in his forties and one in his fifties. If so, there is something very wrong with the 'system' and something that needs to be changed.

'It's a great place for a holiday,' I say, hoping I'm joining in without becoming the dampener on their 'real' conversation.

'But we're here to work,' Bilbo adds, grinning. 'We know that. Holidays are over for now. We've got to rehearse. We've got to put on the play. We've got to wow the crowds and show them what we're made of.

'You've got it Bilbo,' I say. 'But let's eat our breakfast first eh?'

'Slow down, eat your breakfast,' Bilbo chimes back, chiding me gently.

'Wash your hands,' Duncan says and we all roar with laughter. Even Deirdre who has been uncharacteristically quiet. Maybe she's just not a morning person. Maybe she feels out of place, redundant as Duncan's personal 'keeper' now that he's got Bilbo as his 'friend.'

We manage to stick away a full Scottish breakfast, complete with sausages, which Bilbo reminds us that Marky said don't come from a 'factory.' We laugh a bit more.

'Marky and Robbie are brothers,' Annie confides in me as we leave the table. 'That's nice isn't it?'

'Yes,' I say, wondering where this is going. It's going nowhere. She just thinks it's nice. Maybe she's wishing her relationship with her ugly sisters was as good at that between labelled Marky and non labelled Robbie. I wish so too, for her sake. Robbie shows that there's no reason to be mean to your sibling just because they've been landed with a label.

'We're all equal in the sight of the lord,' Kelly states. She's obviously been thinking much the same thing.

'That's right Kelly,' Pauline says. I don't feel qualified to talk about the lord and his vision so I keep quiet. Sometimes its best. I'm learning. Sometimes I don't have to do all the talking or lead things. Sometimes I can just listen and learn. Just be one of the gang.

I'm going to pass over the morning rehearsal and the coffee break and even the most wonderful carvery lunch which the No Labels locusts dispose of in double quick time. Because we want to move onto the performance and time is limited. The day will be over before we know it and Eddie will be there, ready to take us home. We'll be glad to see Eddie I'm sure but I think more than me will be sad that we're having to leave this magical place without labels and go back to the 'real' world.

So. It's two thirty. The performance is about to begin. Take your seats. Believe me, you're so stuffed with food you don't even want to think about rustling your popcorn. The ballroom is laid out just how we wanted it, with a stage area to the front and the rows of chairs facing are filled with happy, expectant faces. Some we recognise as staff and now new found friends from Otterbank (all trainees have been given the afternoon off to watch the performance) and there are a good thirty other assorted folk, who have come from goodness knows where. A good audience. We're about to earn our keep.

'Welcome to Otterbank Hotel,' Barry says.

Thank goodness he didn't say 'cockroaches' I think. I know he was just joking but every time he asked Lauren 'have you seen a cockroach' during our stay I've been terrified that at this, the most important of moments, he's going to blow it all by welcoming the guests to Cockroaches Hotel. I need to learn to trust him, I know. Sometimes I just get scared by the randomness. Sometimes I'm more like Deirdre than I'd ever care to admit.

'Did you all have a lovely lunch?' Barry asks. He's the master of ceremonies for the day. He has his clipboard and all's right with the word. He's also wearing the hat from which he promises he'll pull something better than rabbits later on.

'Yes,' everyone choruses back, enthusiastically.

I'll admit, the food at Otterbank is good. I'm not sure it's as nutritionally balanced as one would ideally like, but then hotels are for holidays and who wants to stick to a rigid healthy diet on a holiday eh?

'We're about to present our Healthy Eating show,' Barry continues.

'Meat your greens,' the group chorus and all enter, wearing t shirts specially made for the events. Each of them has their photo superimposed onto a specific vegetable. We open with a musical number. It's called *The Allotment Song* and goes to the tune of *If you go down to the woods today.* Feel free to sing along.

*If you go down the allotment today*
*You're sure of a big surprise*
*If you go down the allotment today*
*You'll never believe your eyes*
*Cause every veg that ever there was*
*Is gathered there together because*
*Today's the day the vegetables go to market*

*See those little cabbages, the beans and peas and spuds*
*All polishing up their skins*
*See them wash their dirt right off*
*They shine so you want to dig your teeth right in*
*See them smile and preen and primp*
*They are so very cute we know you just can't resist*
*At six o clock the market shuts because they have all*
*been sold, They'll be your dinner when all is told.*

We already have the audience on side, clapping in time, before we even begin. This is one performance I think I'm going to enjoy. It's my line.

'We'd like to introduce ourselves to you,' I say and each cast member steps forward in turn to take a bow. Taking a bow at the beginning as well as the end was a very popular move choreographically and does at least mean that for one part of the drama everyone bows while facing the front.

Barry, or as we should now refer to him Colonel Caulie winds things up to feverpitch. Think Jimmy Saville meets 'The Herbs' and you're getting something of a picture.

'Okay Pop Pickers, he says, 'Today's your lucky day. Today we give you the No labels Top 10 Vegetables. In reverse order at NUMBER 10' we all break into song(you can guess the tune I'm sure)

*It's that red devil called Tom again.*

'That's right, Barry/Caulie says, 'Teresa Tomato. Strictly speaking a fruit not a vegetable but with flavour like that she's welcome to join the party.'

Lauren, who is Teresa Tomato, takes a bow.

Barry/Caulie continues, 'At NUMBER 9.' We all sing:

*Don't cry for me leek and garlic, we like your taste and you know your onions.*

'Yes,' he continues, this is role he was born for, 'Onions, or more specifically SALLY SHALLOT.'

Step forward and take a bow, Deirdre.

'At NUMBER 8,' Barry/Caulie says and we sing:

*It's beginning to look a lot like Christmas*

'It's BELINDA BRUSSELS SPROUTS,' Barry/Caulie says giving it big for Kelly who takes a huge bow and goes back to the vegetable lineup.

Barry/Cauli is working his way up the charts and down his list.

'At NUMBER 7,' he says but gets no further because we all break into song instantly,

*'Celery, you're so crunchy and low calorie, I could eat you just indefinitely, for all the good you do for me.'*

That's me. I'm celery so I take my bow as Barry/Cauli says, 'A big hello for CHANTELLE CELERY.'

I don't know how I got selected as celery. I don't even like celery. I think it was one of Bilbo's little jokes. Or maybe just that everyone else got to choose what they liked and I drew the short straw. Maybe nobody likes celery. Ah well, we can't have everything can we. And it's only a play after all. I've just got to be the best stick of celery I can be.

While my mind wanders Barry/Cauli has reached number six.

'At NUMBER 6. Who's the Daddy?.' He says.

He marshalls everyone around chanting: *Cauliflower, cauliflower, cauliflower, cauliflower, cauliflower, cauliflower, cauliflower, cauliflower, cauliflower, cauliflower... CAULIFLOWER.*

Inevitably there is applause to which he responds with his carefully prepared ad lib, 'That's a bit cheesy for me.'

More applause.

He takes off his hat and pulls out a baby cauliflower, (the magic has started early I note and I didn't know he was going to do this. Come to think of it I don't know *how* he does this)

'Yes, I'm COLONEL CAULIFLOWER,' he says. 'I'm in charge of the allotment mob.'

He pauses for people to take this in and Duncan and Bilbo shout out, 'Boss of the allotment.' I don't remember writing this line but it's too funny for a complete spur of the moment and I wonder just how much unscheduled magic Barry has been working when my back's been turned!

There's no time to think because the play must and will go on and Barry/Cauli has reached the top five.

'And we're into the top 5,' he says, giving all those Top of the Pops DJ's a lesson in winning over the audience, ' At NUMBER 5,' He's barely got the number out and the whole group are up and boogying

*ba da ba da ba la bamba, get up and just shake those beans around..*

'It's FENELLA THE FRENCH BEAN,' Barry/Cauli shouts above the rumpus. And Mandy takes a bow. She is a vegetable today, and proud!

The steady climb up the charts is relentless and Barry is not a man to let the audience go once he has them eating out of the palm of his hand, so each announcement is given with more panache and verve were that possible. And the whole group are working together seamlessly, fully focussed (despite being stuffed with Sunday dinner) and the phrase *sing for your supper* has never been more appropriately displayed.

'At NUMBER 4,' Barry/Cauli announces and we sing

*It's not that easy being green* (you must know the old Kermit Classic?)

'Yes, it's BILLY BROCCOLI,' Barry/Cauli says and Bilbo takes a bow and can't resist his own ad lib (sanctioned by me this time)

' Packed with goodness,' he says and flexes what might be his biceps as if he's a strongman.

The audience laugh uproariously. It is funny. Now we all love broccoli.

Barry/Cauli continues, 'AT NUMBER 3,' and we sing (to the tune of the Flintsones) *Carrots, crunchy carrots we can help you to see in the dark...*

'It's CHARLIE CARROT,' says Barry/Cauli giving Annie her moment of glory. She milks the audience as Barry/Cauli states, 'no dinner plate should be without one.'

At this point (well probably earlier) I should point out that we did a group survey to decide which were the top ten vegetables. We didn't just pick them at random. We voted for our favourites (which makes me wonder how celery ended up at number seven because I don't remember anyone liking it that much and certainly no one wanted to 'be' celery. Maybe this is another example of the vagaries of statistics) Anyway, we voted for the top ten favourites and then, as far as possible, everyone got to pick their own favourite. Which is why Stevie has made it to number two in the charts. He likes purple and he likes beetroot and he likes the way you can smear beetroot over any and everything and turn your world purple. And why not?

Barry/Cauli announces him, 'At NUMBER 2,' and we all sing (to the tune of you ar my sunshine) *We are the beetroots, we are the beetroots, we make* you *happy, when skies are grey, We'll turn you purple, we're tasty pickled And our colour just won't go away.*

Barry/Cauli waves Stevie (whose face has gone the colour of his vegetable as he stands in the metaphorical spotlight, a thing I've never managed to get him to do before. Barry really is a magician!) into place and shouts out, 'A warm welcome to BERTIE BEETROOT.'

'Bertie's got a beamer,' Marky shouts out from the crowd but even this isn't enough to stop Stevie from standing and taking his bow. There's obviously some secret deal going on between Barry and Stevie that I've not been party to.

No time to think about that now though, as we are hitting the heights. Stevie goes back to his place and Barry/Caulie announces, with a crescendo of excitement in his voice,

'AND THE WINNER IS... THE VEGETABLE EVERYONE LOVES.... At NUMBER 1 for the nine hundred and twenty second consecutive month....'

This is the moment we've all been waiting for. The moment Queen wrote their song *Flash Gordon* for I'm sure, and we freely adapt: *Spud, aaaah, saviour of the universe. Spud aaaah... he'll save everyone of us.*

The crowd go wild. Duncan is pushed to the front by an adoring allotment of vegetables, because yes, everyone loves potatoes and everyone loves Duncan. Perfect casting.

Barry/Caulie shouts out above the applause, 'THE SUPER SPUD..... Yes that's right, the most versatile vegetable in the world, I give to you PADDY POTATO.'

And we all sing as Duncan stands firm after his bow. He sings too, at the top of his lungs. He loves the Beatles. He loves Potatoes. He loves drama. This must be a great moment for him.

*Spuds, spuds, spuds. Spuds Spuds Spuds.*
*All you need is spuds (da da da da da)*
*All you need is spuds*
*All you need is spuds, spuds,*
*Spuds are all you need.*

And then, like all good drama, there is a change of pace. Jeopardy. The legs cut from under them.

Pauline stands up. She is not wearing a vegetable t shirt. She's wearing a purple cape which is shiny foil in the inside. She is the evil chocolate bar.

'What about me?' she says, swishing her cape in best Dick Dastardly fashion.

'What about you?' Barry/Caulie says. He's the boss of the allotment remember, he's not going to take a challenge lying down.

'I'm more popular than all your vegetables put together,' Choco-Pauline says.

'Who are you?' the rest of the vegetables chorus.

And Pauline sings. She's been terrified of this moment ever since it was first suggested. But she's prepared to put her fear to one side and sacrifice her body for the team and you know what, she does the most marvellous job of it. She sings (think Shirley Bassey in brown not gold – I know, that's Stevie in heaven!)

*I'm Chocolate. Da na na na*
*I'm the one, the one that you love to eat*
*I'm Chocolate da na na na*
*And you know I taste better than greens or meat*
*I am a treat.*

It's my turn to shine. I stand in front of her. We do look a little like Laurel and Hardy. I'm not thin, by no means, but it's true to say that next to Pauline I may look like celery to her chocolate bar. I suppose it *is* funny. If we are laughing at ourselves.

'This is a show about VEGETABLES!' I say. ' Not Chocolate.'

There is a moment's standoff. Then Barry remembers it's his line,

'Yes, quite enough of that, moving right along... enough heckling. On with the show.'

And on with the show it is.

Remember I told you that this was a more interactive sort of production than a strict play, more a sort of music hall meets magic meets sketch kind of thing. Well, we now have a sort of front of the curtain interlude, read out by Deirdre (that's Sally Shallot to you) She doesn't read with great feeling, but she *can* read and that's how she got the gig. No one would have been able to commit the whole of this story to heart. So here goes.

'Please settle down everyone,' she says. 'I want to tell you a story.'

See Max Bygraves had something going for him. He could provide us with our own moment of comedy!

'This is a story about our favourite vegetable,' Deirdre continues, a bit confused as to why everyone laughed when she said 'I want to tell you a story.' Bilbo doing his Max Bygraves impersonation behind her might be the answer. She carries on regardless. Even when Marky shouts out from the audience,

'Wash your hands Bilbo,' and the audience erupts again.

Back to Deirdre. Consummate professional. She carries on.

'It's the story of SuperSpud. You may have noticed that Super Spud doesn't talk very much. There's a reason for

222

this, and I'm ashamed to tell you that it might be because he was bullied when he was a new potato. Vegetables can be cruel. I myself heard him being called "Potato head" and "couch potato" just because he didn't run as fast as other vegetables. Of course, it might not be because of this at all. Have you noticed that often the most interesting and cleverest people are the ones with the least to say! People with nothing to say, well, you can never stop them. They are full of empty calories. But Super spud, he likes to save his energy. He's too cool for school.'

She pauses for a moment, not just to let the audience take in the enormity of her story, but mostly because she's struggling to turn the page. I have laid this story out in more pages than was strictly necessary, specifically to achieve this goal, slowing Deirdre down. Like many people reading out in public, she does tend to rush things when nervous. So even though she curses me for all the pages, I'm really doing her a favour.

She carries on, page resolutely turned, 'You might have heard him called "the humble potato" but don't think that means he should be overlooked or ignored. Paddy Potato is perhaps the most versatile vegetable there is...'

This is the cue for Duncan to do a twirl, which he does but sadly Deirdre ignores it and ploughs on so the full comic effect is lost, 'and that's why he can become SUPERSPUD. He can be just plain boiled, baked or mashed, or he can be all kinds of fancy french names, but he can also be everyone's friend, the chip. And more than that.. The crisp. Oh yes, in one guise or another everyone loves superspud, even chocolate and she HATES vegetables.'

Deirdre pauses again, to turn the page, and to glower at Pauline because she knows that for the purposes of this story Choco-Pauline is *the enemy.*

'Of course when he gets up close and personal with too much fat,' she continues, 'he's not quite as good an influence on your body as he might be. But naturally, he's packed with carbohydrates. Even his skin is good to eat.'

That draws a laugh from the crowd. You can never tell what will get them.

' So don't judge by appearances,' Deirdre is winding up for the big finale, 'Chocolate might come in flashy wrappers and the potato... well, naturally he's a bit plain. But when it comes to doing you good, Paddy Potato is the friend to choose every time.'

She is finished. Leaving the final glory to Barry/Cauli who doffs his hat (taking out a bag of crisps – *how?* - and calls out, 'Let's have a round of applause for Paddy Potato.'

Which we duly get. And Duncan plays his part admirably, taking curtain call after curtain call and a good two minute standing ovation. This is an easy audience you have to agree. Never were vegetables so appreciated!

Now it's time to move on.

We need a seat. Everyone positions themselves in a semi circle, facing the audience and Barry/Cauli explains that we are in the allotment. He puts on his best David Attenbourgh impersonation (which is actually rather good) and continues:

'You probably only see vegetables when they are on your plate. Or maybe in the supermarket. But we want to show you the life vegetables have before they come to the table. Where do vegetables live? In the allotment. So let's go to the allotment and see our vegetables in their natural habitat.'

It's time to play a game we have called 'I went to the allotment.' It goes something like this.

Annie/Carrot is at the end of the circle (if such a thing is possible) and begins,

'I went to the allotment and I picked up a trowel,' she says.

Next to her sits Bilbo. It's his turn now.

'I went to the allotment and I picked up a trowel and stepped on a rake, ow,' he says, miming the sore face he got from the rake. The audience laugh.

Next up is Stevie. He's going to need a bit of help. I help him.

'Hey, Beetroot,' I say, 'you went to the celery and what did you find?'

'Dirt.' He says. 'Brown.' (its more like irrr and oww, but we know what he means)

'Yes,' I say, but first. I hold his hand and we walk down the line. We stand in front of Annie. 'What did Carrot do?' He looks at me. 'She picked up a trowel, didn't she?' I say, 'to dig dirt,'

'iiirr...' he says, concurring.

We move on to Bilbo Broccoli. 'And what did Broccoli do,' I ask. Bilbo mimes stepping on the rake.

'ooowww,' Stevie says, laughing.

'That's right,' I say, 'he stepped on a rake. So Carrot picked up a trowel and Broccoli stepped on a rake and you, Beetroot, you found dirt?'

He nods.

We go to sit down in our respective seats. On with the game. It's Mandy, French Bean next. She's rehearsed her spontaneous response, never feeling comfortable with having to think something up on the spot. But she has to face the hurdle of remembering the others first. She puffs her cheeks out and tries hard to concentrate.

'I went to the allotment,' I prompt her, and she's off,

'Carrot found trowel, Broccoli hurt rake, Beetroot ate dirt,' she says proudly and stops.

'And you?' I prompt.

'Me?' she looks confused.

'What did you do at the allotment,' I ask.

'Climbed a pole,' she says, smiling. She remembered.

'Good, I whisper at her as we continue along the line. It's Barry/Cauli next.

'I went to the allotment,' he says, 'and I found a trowel for Carrot, a tidied away the rake Broccoli stood on, I dusted the dirt off Beetroot, I tied French Bean to a pole and I sat down on a bench.'

Applause. Barry/Cauli is in his element. He doesn't like this game. His memory isn't that good.

Next it's Duncan. Again I step in to 'help.'

'So, Superspud,' I say, 'we're at the allotment and what did we do?'

'Trowel, rake,dirt, pole, bench,' he rattles off, amazing me.

'yes,' I say. 'That's right, and what about you?'

'Picnic,' he says.

'You deserve one after that,' I say. 'Fanstastic.' As I'd discovered before, Duncan is a big game player. Never to be under-estimated.

Next up is Deirdre. She prides herself on this game. She preens, sure she's going to get them all right.

'I went to the allotment,' she says, 'and I found carrot's trowel, broccoli's rake, Beetroot's dirt, French bean's pole, Cauliflowers bench and...'

She can't remember. It happens like that with this game. You are concentrating so hard on what you're going to add that you forget the one you just heard. It's natural. It happens all the time, but Deirdre is clearly devastated.

'Picnic,' Duncan says to help her.

'Oh yes, a picnic,' she says but she's flustered now and can't remember her own choice.

'And you?' I ask.

'Oh,'

'Sausages,' Marky shouts out from the audience with somewhat inappropriate comic timing.

'Don't be silly,' Deirdre says tersely, 'there's no sausages in an allotment.'

'It's not a sausage factory,' Marky shouts out. I wonder if there's any way we could get Marky to come regularly to No Labels. He definitely has what it takes!

'Wash your hands, Marky,' Bilbo shouts out and the game threatens to descend into anarcy.

'Okay,' I say, trying to pull us back on focus, ' What did you do at the allotment Sally Shallot?'

'I cried,' Deirdre says, with genuine heartfelt pity.

Unfortunately, it is so funny being said at that time, especially when Marky shouts out,

'Cry baby onion,'

That we have to pause for the laugher to die down.

I give Deirdre a squeeze on the shoulder to try and convince her that this is not a total disaster, that she hasn't let the side down,

'I don't understand why they are laughing?' she whispers quietly to me amidst the furore.

'Don't worry, Deirdre,' I say, 'it's funny, that's all. They think you are really funny. They're not laughing at you.'

As someone who has lived with the uncomfortable feeling that your sense of humour is few degrees off all my life, I feel her pain. I hope she believes me when I say,

'You've been really funny Deirdre. It's good.'

'Am I funny?' she asks, tears subsiding behind her bottle bottom glasses.

'Yes, Deirdre, you are,' I say. 'And I think Marky really likes you.'

'I'm not sure I like him,' she says. Then pauses, 'but I like being funny.'

I give her the thumbs up and we try to get thing back under control. It's Pauline next.

'I went to the allotment,' she starts.

'Not welcome here,' Mandy says. 'Go away chocolate,'

Pauline looks a bit surprised. This has never happened before.

I improvise. 'Ah, but maybe she's going with Teresa Tomato,' I say.

'Tomato flavoured chocolate, bleeugggh,' Bilbo shouts out. He's on fire today!

Mandy knows that Lauren needs help with this game so the appeal to her reason is enough to shut her up and by the time Marky and the rest of the audience have stopped laughing at the thought of tomato flavoured chocolate we are ready to continue.

Pauline leads Lauren down the line, prompting her every time.

'We went to the allotment together,' she says.

'Hand in hand,' Lauren/Tomato says looking up cheerily at Pauline, oblivious to the audience entirely it seems.

'Yes, hand in hand, Pauline confirms. 'And what did we find. Look there's Carrot's trowel,'

'Trowel,' says Lauren/Tomato, employing her echolalic tendencies to good effect.

'And Broccoli's rake,' says Pauline.

'Rake, oowww,' Lauren/Tomato says, showing that she has been paying attention all along.

'And Beetroot's dirt,' Pauline says,

'Dirt. Dirty. Wash hands,' Lauren says and gets a round of applause which she studiously ignores.

'And a beanpole,' Pauline continues,

'Beanpole,' Lauren echoes.

'And Colonel Cauliflowers bench,' Pauline says, relieved that she's still on track.

'Bench. Sit down,' chirps Lauren.

'And Duncan's picnic,' says Pauline,

'Picnic. Like it,' says Lauren.

'And Sally shallots tears,' says Pauline, not quite knowing what to say about that.

'Don't cry, darling,' Lauren says and breaks free from Pauline's hand to give Deirdre a big hug which makes her very very happy. Now she's funny and loved. It doesn't get much better than that does it?

'And what about us?' Pauline asks. 'What shall we find at the allotment?'

'Sunshine,' Lauren says.

What a great idea!

'Yes, sunshine,' Pauline says. 'Everyone loves sunshine.'

They go and sit down. It's my turn to follow that.

I pull myself up to full height. I'm ready to go. I know how to play this game. Despite all the distractions. You just link the thing with the person and in this instance the person with the vegetable and you're good to go. But I find that the whole event has distracted me more than I think and I'm stumbling through the list, raising laughs and jeers from the group and the audience every time I make a mistake. Which is fine, because it's all part of the game but I'm relieved when my turn is over and it's my choice to make.

'A wheelbarrow,' I say. And breath a sigh of relief. There's only Kelly to go and she always remembers everything. Every time. It's a gift. So here goes.

'I went to the allotment,' she proudly states, 'and I saw Carrot with her trowel, Broccoli stepped on his rake, (there's no time for people to interject with 'owww' before she continues, woman on a mission) Beetroot ate dirt, French Bean climbed a pole, Colonel Cauliflower sat on a bench, Superspud had a picnic, Sally Shallot cried and Chocolate Tomato made the sunshine. Celery sat in a wheelbarrow and I... and I.. I locked the gate on the way out so no one could steal the vegetables. That's what I did.'

And that's it. She stands to take the applause which is totally spontaneous.

'I can do it backwards if you like,' she offers.

Normally I'd let her, but I look at my watch and see we are already well behind time, thanks to Marky and his interjections and the other varied distractions.

'I'm afraid we don't have time today but that was excellent,' I say and Kelly takes her second round of applause and sits down. Then stands up again, because she's remembered she's next up. With another story. She probably knows most of it by hand but I give her a sheet of paper to read from anyway.

'This is my story,' she says. 'It's called Counting Calories.' She takes a deep breath and then begins.

'There are a lot of strange things in the world, don't you think? For example Calories. What's a calorie I hear you ask? (she doesn't pause for Marky to intervene, she knows we're on a deadline here) 'Well, let me tell you a story about calories...' (again only the faintest of pauses. 'What are calories? Calories are the mathematicians of the food world. And it's a world where less is more. The less you eat the better off you are. Why do we count calories? Because calories tell you how much ENERGY you are taking in and in what form. We measure this in percentages. This is basically a way of saying if you had a 100 of something, how much of that 100 would be each part. 10 parts would be called 10 per cent. That means that there are 10 in every 100.'

She has to draw breath here, but the audience are either so wrapped up in the story or so confused that they are stunned into silence. Even Marky.

'Everything you eat has calories,' Kelly tells us, 'and the calories are made up of different things called CARBOHYDRATES, FATS and PROTEINS. We need the right balance of these to stay healthy. And counting calories is a good place to start.  There are loads of vitamins and minerals as well... too many to mention but each one does something to help you stay happy and healthy.'

You'll see this is the guts of the show so to speak. The roots. Where we really teach people about healthy eating. In bite sixed chunks. Large chunks, I grant you, but the audience are all laughed out and ready to sit and listen.

Kelly continues, 'Everyone needs a certain amount of calories every day to be able to have the energy they need to do the things they want to do. As a general rule men need 2500 and women need 2000. But too many calories will make you unhealthy and overweight.' She pauses for the fullness of her statement to sink in. Then continues, 'How do we know how many calories there are in things? We read the labels. Remember labels are for calories not for people. Today there are lots of labels and they can be confusing, but if you look at the traffic light system and go for the GREEN things you won't go far wrong.'

And that's the end of the story. We know that there's only so long people can sit and listen and so Barry/Caulie steps in to save the day (scripted of course).

He says, 'I can see some of you nodding off there... you didn't come here for a maths lesson after all... so how about we play a game?'

There is a murmur of general assent from the assembled audience and he continues, 'The game we're going to play will show you something more about calories. It's like that tv show THE PRICE IS RIGHT. Join in if you want.'

He starts the game by calling out, best game show host voice on, ' Which is higher in calories - A cooked carrot or a cooked tomato?'

There are various shouts from all over – tomato, carrot, don't know etc.

Barry/Cauli expected this and he responds, in character, 'Let's have some order here. We have to play the game properly. Do we have anyone in the audience who would like to join in the game? Okay. Let's have two teams. And I'll ask each team in turn. We'll have 10 questions, turn about. The team with the most correct answers wins.

At this point the room is split into two teams. Each team has some 'vegetables' and some audience members. Barry is the question master and he begins. Question one. To team one.

'How many calories do you think cooked French Beans are?' he asks.

Team one answer, 'Fifty calories.'

It's a good enough guess.

He asks team two, 'Do you think it is HIGHER or LOWER than this?'

They can't agree, some say higher, some say lower. He gives them the answer, 'The correct answer is 228 calories.'

He moves on to question two. To team two.

'How many calories do you think there are in a BIG MAC?' he asks.

'Too many,' shouts Marky. He's in team two. 'Eight hundred,' Pauline says. She's fond of a big mac now and again.

'Team one,' Barry asks. 'Higher or lower than this?'

They think about it for a time. No one wants to believe anything has that many calories in it, even if they can't work out how high a proportion of their daily allowance it might be.

They settle on lower.

'You're right team one,' Barry says, 'The correct answer is 492 calories.'

You get the picture? This game goes on for a good fifteen minutes and so that you aren't wriggling around in your seat desperate for a cup of tea and a sandwich or cake, which is what's on offer when the performance is over, I'll abridge things for you and tell you the all important answers which are that cooked celery has twenty seven calories, whereas a small bar of Dairy Milk Chocolate has 255 calories (but is considerably more tasty and thus worth it, in my opinion,) that cauliflower cheese weighs in at 318 calories (bear in mind these are standard portion sizes and the likes of you and me are probably stacking away twice that if we make it at home!) And brace yourself. There's no easy way of telling you. A 9 inch cheese and tomato pizza racks in at a massive 750 calories. I don't even want to tell you how much that increases if you add pepperoni to it! Cooked broccoli may not be to everyone's taste, I'm sure but our quiz reveals that at 98 calories per serving it just might be offering something that that tasty pizza isn't! Value for calories. But lest you have become upset by all this, I can remind you that it's not the food itself that's bad, you just have to box and cox how you consume it, keeping an eye on the calorific value, and we discover, to our great joy, that a small beefburger (not a giant quarter pounder mind you) without the bun, chips or cheese and relish stuff, is a reasonable 120 calories. I'd like to add a personal aside here that a quarter pounder venison burger is about the same so if you want to 'supersize' I recommend venison. It's leaner meat and so better for your heart – and just as tasty too! On a conservative estimate a fish supper comes in at 420 calories, which is not too shabby as long as you're not going to go to town on a high stodge pudding afterwards. At this point in our 'game' I can report that team two are beating team one by 5-4 and so it's all down to the final question. Either team two will get it right and there'll be a runaway victory, or they'll get it wrong and the game is tied. High drama no?

So. The final question. Barry pulls himself up to his full height and delivers it to team two.

'Do you think a baked potato is HIGHER or LOWER in calories than a portion of chips?'

This is a facer. It seems to be obvious. Maybe it's a trick question. Team two answer with the obvious – lower. Bilbo, in Team one, punches the air. He knows the answer to this question. He's been doing his homework. He understands that everything isn't as clear cut in the world of food calories as you'd think.

'Higher,' he shouts out, unable to contain his glee.'

Barry concurs. 'You're right,' he says.

The teams and the audience are shocked. Can it be true? How can it be that a baked potato has more calories than chips. I mean, chips are next to chocolate in the denizen of don't eat foods aren't they?

Barry declares the quiz a tie and suggests a tie breaker to establish the winners. He'll take the answer that's closest.

'How many calories in a standard sized baked potato?' he asks.

Team one (who remember have the 'insider' knowledge of Bilbo to go on, offer their answer as three hundred calories. Team Two, still unable to compute that a baked potato could count for more than a poke of chips, but realising they've been duped, offer four hundred calories, but you can see they don't believe it.

'The correct answer is 278 calories,' Barry declares proudly. 'Which makes Team One the winners. Congratulations.'

As the applause dies down there is still one burning question. If a baked potato is 278 calories and it's higher than a portion of chips, how much is a portion of chips? The answer may at least make losing easier to take.

Bilbo has the answer, it's his moment of glory. He also has the crib sheet. He tells everyone, 'A standard portion of chips contains 143 calories.' Stunned silence. 'That's a portion half what you usually eat though Marky,' Robbie calls out.

Bilbo hushes everyone. 'Yes,' he says. 'You have to understand, it seems that there are more calories in baked potato than chips... but that doesn't mean that chips are better for you?'

There are groans from the crowd.

Deirdre picks up the cue line.

'No,' she says firmly. 'Because we have to look at other things as well as calories. We have to consider the FAT in the food. And a baked potato has only 3 per cent fat whereas chips have 37 per cent fat.'

'That's more than ten times the amount,' Kelly remembers her line.

'Too much,' shouts out Lauren, well into the spirit of things.

'Indeed,' says Barry. 'So you see, calories don't give you all the answers, but they are a good place to start. And because of that, we've got a song to teach you..... it's called the calorie song. Maybe you know the tune...'

And we prepare ourselves for the final song which is sung to the tune of *The Bear Necessities* from the Jungle Book. Join in or just hum along, whichever you feel more comfortable with.

*That's why we're counting calories, we're always counting calories*
*We do it every single time we eat*
*And if we're counting calories you know that we can rest at ease*
*And live a happy, healthy sort of life.*

*When I eat a pizza or burger and chips*
*It might make me happy but it sits on my hips*
*But if I eat my greens each day*
*I know I'm eating the right way*
*Five portions of the healthy stuff*

*You know that you can't get enough*
*Of calories like these*
*They'll keep you healthy and your life will be a breeze.*
*That's why we're counting calories, we're always counting calories*
*We do it every single time we eat*
*And if we're counting calories you know that we can rest at ease*
*And live a happy, healthy sort of life.*

The audience love it and demand that we do an encore right then, right there. So we do. At this point we are scheduled to perform a short improvised piece called 'who stole the nettle juice' but I can see that time is running on and Barry hasn't had the chance to do half his magic tricks so we'll cut that and just move on to the magic which was the finale of it. You have to be flexible and pragmatic in live dramatic situations. And we can't deny Barry (ably assisted by Stevie) his moment of glory. After all you can't be too po-faced about food now can you. Healthy eating can be fun. That's our overall message. So bring on the magic.

Barry does a number of tricks pulling things out of his hat and generally diverting people's attention so that he can remove French beans from their ears and baby carrots from down their noses and a whole range of other amazing things that are never going to stand up to the seeing through the translation of words. And for his finale, he does a trick which I haven't seen since I was four years old. I was convinced then that it was real magic, and I'm convinced now, because Barry does it just as well and I still have no idea how it's done.

Basically he has this sort of metal cake tin and he puts into it all kinds of revolting things (not revolting in their own right you understand, just all mixed up together as a cake.) Things like toothpaste and shoe polish. And Stevie is by his side the whole time, handing him things, helping him out. Yes, maybe distracting attention. And then, with a sweep of his magic wand (of course Barry has a magic wand for this, do you need to ask?) and a tap on the enclosed cake tin, Barry lifts the lid and out pops what seems to be a perfectly cooked chocolate cake. It's brown so Stevie is happy. I'm convinced that even to keep Barry's trick alive, and even given his predeliction for brown things, Stevie is not going to tuck into something made of toothpaste and shoe polish. And Barry wouldn't let him, because surely, shoe polish would be poisonous to eat, right? But Stevie takes a slice of that brown cake and he loves it. Lauren demands to have a piece and I'm afraid I can't resist, because I'm starting to believe in magic all over again and you know what, I eat a piece and it *is* delicious and I have no idea how he did it. Sometimes you just have to give in to the magic. I give in.

But there isn't enough cake for everyone of course and the audience are getting restless so that's the end of the magic show and we decide that we should give the quiz we've written onto a sheet out during tea time so that people can fill it out themselves in their own time, because soon enough Eddie will be there to take us home. Since the quiz gives everyone a chance to learn more interesting things about food and since we feel you've shared our journey all week and so deserve not to be left out of anything, here's the answers to the quiz questions. Knowing all these answers you'd be up for a prize if there was one to give you. There isn't of course. Sometimes knowledge is its own reward, right? Okay, here goes: Breakfast is the most important meal of the day, half your dinner plate should be made up of vegetables, you should eat five portions of fruit and veg every day. Carrots grow underground (we had to put in some easy questions right – and some people do believe that they grow on trees Mandy, don't they? Well, not any more but they did). You should eat between 2 and 3 portions of dairy products each day, cauliflowers are a member of the brassica family, a tomato is strictly speaking a fruit not a vegetable, celery is member of the onion family, a woman should eat 2000 calories a day and a man can have 500 more. It's better to get your energy from pasta than sugary drinks or chocolate (yes, I know, not as tasty but...) vegetables tend to have more calories when they are cooked than raw, you can grow vegetables all year round in a polytunnel but not in a shop. (Contrary to what Lauren would tell you, you don't *grow* vegetables in a shop you just buy them there. If you don't grow your own.) And the main reason we should always look at food labels is because they tell us about the nutritional values, of which calories are one part. So now you know. And even if you're smug and knew all those answers already, I can take you down a peg or two by suggesting that you may know it all, but do you always choose the healthy options? If you know and you don't, what are your excuses?

Which brings me, while the gang are all having tea and before we have to deal with the sad fact of collecting bags and leaving new found friends and piling back onto Eddie's bus, which I've just seen pull up outside, with an unpalatable truth. One as unpalatable as Barry's cake would have been if the magic hadn't worked. Generally speaking, you and I, the people without labels, have a lot of freedom of choice when it comes to healthy eating. Generally speaking people with labels don't. Very few of my No Labels friends are 'allowed' to go shopping for themselves and even if they do go to the supermarket as part of their 'care package,' they are encouraged to buy ready meals or things that can be easily heated up in the microwave. No one takes the time to ask them what they really want to eat, or to go through the labels in the shops or to make a weekly meal plan for or with them. It's all about 'convenience' though I wonder exactly whose convenience it is? Even though every single member of No Labels has a food hygiene certificate (it was one of the 'options' against carpet bowls at the resource centre one year) and even though many of them do 'cooking' as an option there on a Tuesday afternoon (or have done in the past) the opportunity to actually do any cooking of their own is strictly limited.

Those who live in a group home like Duncan and Mandy and Lauren and Bilbo have most meals prepared for them as a group with few options for 'choice' It's the dish of the day or nothing. No wonder they eat like locusts when let off the leash. And those in more independent circumstances like Annie and Kelly are generally not 'risk assessed' for cooking. They get to use a microwave but not a cooker. Now both Annie and Kelly would be more than willing and able to cook their own food either alone, or with assistance as part of their 'care' package, but this would mean people coming in at dinner time every day and there's no way the money stretches that far. I think Annie kicked up a fuss one time and for a few weeks she had people coming in to 'cook' with her but it meant she either had to eat her dinner at four thirty in the afternoon, or let it go cold and heat it up again in the microwave later on. It's not really a wonder that Annie gorges herself on sweets and junk food whenever she gets the chance is it? It's not any wonder that fresh vegetables were a strange concept to most of the group when we first started on the project. And sadly, once we go home from Otterbank, freshly cooked, nutritious vegetables will once more be a thing of the past. It's iniquitous. How would you like to be condemned to eating school dinners or an approximation of hospital food (no slur intended on either institution) every day. Hospital food is probably a better example, because there you can often have to eat the choice of the person who was in the bed the day before you – and that's why food is like for most of No Labels in their everyday lives. If they have any choice at all it's very little choice. And it all comes down to money. It's not because they are too stupid or incapable to engage with choosing food, buying it, working out a weekly food plan or cooking on their own or with some assistance. It's because our creaking social care system just doesn't factor this into their lives. Perhaps you'll understand why I get hot under the collar when I think of MP's or the G20 or anyone like that having a nice 'dinner' or a 'working brunch'. That's the equivalent of No Labels eating at Otterbank I know and one shouldn't begrudge anyone a decent feed out once in a while, but *They* (surely you hadn't forgotten about *them?*) can afford to eat good quality food. If they don't have time or inclination to buy food and cook it for themselves they have wives or cooks or housekeepers who do it for them. So they are not living in the same world as No Labels folk. And before Health Secretaries pontificate about what people should do to eat healthily I suggest they look and see what they could do to help people. Real help, how they need to be helped. Time spent. Resources allocated. Education given but most of all an ongoing commitment to the view that everyone is entitled to have choices about the most basic things in their lives like eating. And that informed choices are not the norm for people with learning disabilities, not because of their own intellectual failings but because of the system. And that there's no point giving someone an informed choice if it doesn't translate into 'real' choices. These people are my friends. Why don't they have the freedoms I have? It's not fair and it's not right. And I am stepping off my soapbox only for long enough to pick up my bags and hug Marky and Robbie and Marge and Kim and all the others at Otterbank who are doing more than government agencies and council service providers and the rest of *them* to read the important nutritional labels on the food and to recognise that these are the important labels, not the ones placed on the people we term Learning Disabled.

So. Eddie is greeted as a conquering hero, even though he's taking us away from the freedom and magic of our holiday without labels at Otterbank, and everyone kisses and hugs everyone else and many tears are shed because we have all had such a great time, and we are on the bus ready to return home like the toys to our boxes so that the care system can take us out and 'play' with us again Monday to Friday.

*No Labels will be back soon with many other adventures. In the meantime we hope you've enjoyed your time spent with us. We'd like to think of all our readers as friends we've yet to meet. Please tell our story to other people and encourage them to buy the book either as paperback or an ebook and become our friends.*

*And we hope more than anything, that when you are next presented with the opportunity to interact with someone who is 'labelled' in some way, you are big enough and wise enough to throw off the label and just make a new friend. People are all different. They all have the right to individuality and respect and no one should be stuck with a label. And No Labels advice to anyone who has ever been burdened down with a label is:*

*Throw it away, you are so much more. Labels are for tins, not for people.*

# ABOUT THE AUTHOR

Cally Phillips has had a 20 year career writing for screen and stage and latterly novels and short stories. In 2003 when she set a small ad looking for people to engage with drama from the 'disability fraternity' as part of a European Year of Disabled People funded project, she had no idea how that small action would change the course of her life (for the better!) and how many challenges and good, true friends she would find as a result.

She has a Diploma in Health and Social care, and an MSc in Applied Psychology of Intellectual Disabilities to show for her time working with 'real' groups who share the 'learning disability' label, but more than this she has developed deep and lasting friendships and a more enlightened view of the world. .

This novel is a tribute to the many people she has worked with It is, hopefully a piece of advocacy but it's also a personal tribute and an expression of deep gratitude to all those who changed her life.

Cally lives in the rural North East of Scotland with her husband and two dogs. You can find out more about her work from her website www.callyphillips.co.uk

Made in the USA
Charleston, SC
18 December 2012